An American in Scotland

An American in Scotland

A SCOTTISH ISLE MYSTERY

Lucy Connelly

CROOKED
LANE

NEW YORK

Copyright © 2023 by Candace Havens

Published in the United States by Crooked Lane Books, an imprint of The Quick Brown Fox & Company LLC.

Crooked Lane Books and its logo are trademarks of The Quick Brown Fox & Company LLC.

Library of Congress Catalog-in-Publication data available upon request.

ISBN (hardcover): 978-1-63910-350-8
ISBN (ebook): 978-1-63910-351-5

Cover design by Jim Griffin

Printed in the United States.

www.crookedlanebooks.com

Crooked Lane Books
34 West 27th St., 10th Floor
New York, NY 10001

First Edition: April 2023

10 9 8 7 6 5 4 3 2 1

To my mom and dad, and the rest of my family village, for assuming I can do anything.

Chapter One

Scotland was gorgeous—even more so than I'd imagined. Any last-minute doubts I'd had about moving across the pond, leaving everything and everyone behind at home in Seattle, were gone.

To the left was the sea and jagged cliffs; and the mountains, with their snow-capped peaks, loomed like stately soldiers to the right. The village ahead was a mix of pastel buildings that belonged on a postcard.

"I can't believe I'm going to live here," I said.

"And we are so happy to have you, Dr. Emilia McRoy," Mr. Wilson said. The cheerful man had been my point of contact and helped me with the paperwork necessary for the move.

"You can call me Em."

"It'll be good to have a doctor in town again, especially with winter coming on. Would you like to stop at the pub for a bite to eat, or head on to your new home?"

I was starving, but the excitement about seeing where I'd be living outweighed the grumbling in my belly. "Home, please, Mr. Wilson." I hadn't been this excited about anything since graduating medical school a hundred years ago.

Okay, it hadn't been quite that long, but it felt like it.

My family came from here. I'd known nothing about my heritage until a DNA test showed that I had roots in this area. It still boggled my mind.

When a recruiter called about a job in this part of Scotland, it was like the universe was shoving me out of my comfort zone and into the unknown. After fifteen years of being inside the stressful hamster wheel that was emergency medicine, I was ready for something new.

"Welcome to Sea Isle, lass," Mr. Wilson said as we drove through the picturesque village. There were antique stores, tea shops, and a couple of boutiques. I couldn't wait to explore everything the town had to offer.

"We're coming up on your new home, just around the corner. But we'll have to walk up the hill a bit. The streets are too narrow for the lorry."

He turned the corner and then parked in a small gravel lot behind a row of stores and pubs. At least I'd be close to everything.

Mr. Wilson had to be pushing seventy, but he jumped out of the big truck like a young man ready for adventure. I, on the other hand, couldn't figure out how the handle on the door worked.

There was a clicking sound, and it opened. Mr. Wilson offered a hand to help me down. Then he pulled my two large suitcases from the back.

The cobblestone path was lined with a mix of colorfully painted buildings and older stone ones. This street was just as quaint as the main one.

My cases weren't light, and I ran to catch up with him. "Let me help you," I said, breathless. In my defense, the hill was steep. Well, not that steep.

"Nae bother," he said. "We're here."

Here was a stone church with a gated entry. There was an English garden in front, full of roses and small trees, and it was incredibly quaint. But I was confused.

From the emails, I'd thought I'd be living in a home above my office. "It's a church," I said.

"'Twas," he said as he pulled a massive key out of his pocket and put it in the keyhole of the ancient arched door. "For the last twenty or so years, it's been the doctor's office and his home. Now, it's yours."

"Oh." I wasn't sure what to say. I'd made myself a promise not to stress about the little things. If there was a bed and the heat worked, I'd live. I'd been traveling the last twenty-two hours, and I was sure I'd be able to sort it all out, no matter how rustic it might be.

He had to shove a bit on the door, but then it opened with a loud creak. He held it for me to enter. The large vestibule had been turned into a quirky reception office, with a desk and file cabinets on one side and a row of leather chairs on the other.

After I went through, he rolled in the cases. "Your living quarters are in the back. Down the hallway, here are the exam rooms."

"It's very efficient," I said, which was another way of saying I had no idea how I felt about working in an old church.

The previous doctor had died a few years ago. The place probably hadn't been used since then, but at least it was clean.

Don't be a snob. You wanted adventure.

It was the main reason I'd moved. My life for so long had been nothing but work, punctuated by personal tragedy. No one here knew what had happened with my husband, or even cared.

I'd wanted away from all of that, and here I was.

Being in Scotland, I'd be able to travel around Europe at the drop of a hat. I smiled again. I'd been doing that a lot the last hour or so, from the airport in Edinburgh.

The long hallway opened to a beautiful space. A large living and dining area replaced the altar and pews. The gothic stain-glassed windows only added to the charm. An eclectic mix of furniture blended so well; it was as if a designer had done it.

There were beautiful tapestries on the wall, and the fireplace was so big, I could have walked into it.

I let out the breath I hadn't realized I'd been holding. "It's lovely." I meant those words. "So charming."

He grinned. "Would you like me to take your cases to your bedroom?"

I shook my head. "I've got it from here but thank you." Again, all of this was so much more than I'd imagined.

It was quiet here on the hill, and that's what I'd needed. After working the last few years in a busy ER, I'd craved the life of a small-town country doctor and a peaceful place to live.

What's more peaceful than a church?

"You'll be hungry after your travels. Once you settle, come down to our pub around the corner. My missus is looking forward to meeting you, and our granddaughter has been talking about you for weeks."

"I can't wait to meet them. I'll be down in just a bit."

I followed him to the front door. "You'll be needing this." He pulled a large brass key from his pocket. "Works on the inside and the outside. The laird has a copy, but best not to lose this one. He's busy, and we don't like to bother him."

The laird. The guy was probably a grumpy old Scotsman who hated Americans.

After Mr. Wilson left, I couldn't resist checking out the whole place. The exam rooms were more extensive than I'd expected, and each one had a stained-glass window. Everything I might need was already there, and much of it looked new. The scent of disinfectant was everywhere. Someone had cleaned everything to the corners.

Thank you, whoever you are. That saves me loads of time.

Hmm. In my new living space, the leather couch was soft and worthy of naps. I'd need a few throws and some pillows, and it'd be perfect. A large-screen television was on the wall, and a vast iron and glass dining table sat near a large opening to another room.

"I wonder where the kitchen is?" I said aloud.

There was a door on the far left wall on the other side of the fireplace, but I turned right and found the kitchen. Instead of the wall-to-wall cabinets we were used to in America, there were individual furniture pieces. A few of the cupboards had tiny brass plates on them.

It was a deVOL kitchen. I'd watched the series more than once on television, to help me wind down after a tough shift. But I'd never thought I'd have one of their kitchens. The painted blue furniture was gorgeous, and there was an Aga stove worthy of a chef.

Maybe, I should learn how to cook?

Heating soup and making coffee were the only kitchen skills I had.

My face hurt from smiling so much. Over the charming farmhouse sink, I glanced out the window.

"No." I gasped. Then I closed my eyes and opened them again. Yep. Still there.

"What am I going to do?"

Chapter Two

There is a cemetery in my backyard.

The headstones—I should say, statues—were beautiful, but still. I'd come to Scotland to get away from dead people. After working with trauma patients for so long, I'd come here to live a more peaceful life.

I'd never been the sort of doctor who could let go of death quickly. My psychiatrist, Dr. Hartford, used to tell me: *"Put them in a bubble on a shelf, and don't think of them. Eventually, they'll float away."*

Dr. Hartford had never been in the trenches like I had.

It's an old Scottish cemetery. Get over it. I didn't believe in ghosts, and I'd just look at it as unusual European art. Yes. That was the plan.

Double doors with stained-glass panels led out to a side yard, where the stone hedge surrounded the graveyard.

I'll explore that another day. I wonder where the bedroom is.

A figure ran past the window.

"Ack!" I yelped.

An older man sneered at me through the window.

"Yikes." My hand flew hard into my chest, and then I laughed. I glanced out again. No one was there. "Enough. I'm exhausted from traveling. And now I'm talking out loud to myself."

Creepy as it was, I ran out to the graveyard.

No one was there.

Maybe, I'm more tired than I thought?

My stomach growled.

As I passed through the kitchen, I explored it. There was a small fridge in the bottom of one of the cupboards and then another metal door at the far end of the kitchen. I opened it and found a giant walk-in freezer. I'd read winters were brutal in Scotland, so they probably had to stock up on food and staples to last through spring.

After checking around the sanctuary, I found a door, off the living area, that opened to a narrow—as in I had to turn sideways to get up it—stairway. But the second floor was worth it.

It was loft-like, with worn wooden floors and an enormous stained-glass window filled with sunlight. The dark four-poster bed was huge, with plush linens. My predecessor, it seemed, had had exquisite taste.

My stomach growled again. As much as I wanted to unpack and sleep, it had been hours since my last meal.

The unpacking could wait.

* * *

I left the church—well, my new home—and went in search of food.

As I reached the end of the cobblestone road, to turn the corner, several routes shot off to the left. There were rows of houses through the trees, some of them with thatched roofs and everything painted with the same pastels as the seafront businesses.

The salty air filled my lungs, and I smiled.

I loved it already.

The Pig & Whistle was painted seafoam green, with a charming sign of a pig blowing a whistle over the door.

Once I went inside, I blinked a few times as my eyes adjusted to the dark interior. The scent of stew and beer felt like a warm hug. My shoulders dropped a good inch.

The rich scent of the food made me want to eat the air.

The walls were a moody green and mixed with the dark wood of the tables. I'd never been to a Scottish pub, but this should have been the model for all of them.

It was probably close to happy hour, though my jet-lagged brain was confused about that.

The place was packed and silent.

Everyone stared at me.

Awkward.

A gray-haired woman in a dark green apron came toward me with her arms out. "Blessed soul. Dr. McRoy, we're so glad you've arrived."

At least, I think that's what she said. Her charming Scottish accent, mixed with the incredible speed with which she spoke, made it difficult to understand.

She squeezed me tightly to her. I wasn't against hugging. It created serotonin in the brain and made people feel better. But doing it with strangers added an extra layer of anxiety for me.

"Hi." I found it hard to breathe.

"Let her go, Gran. The poor woman needs oxygen." A slim woman with a towel over her shoulder gently pried her grandmother away from me. Then, she stuck out her hand. "I'm Mara," she said. "This is Gran, also known as Mary Wilson. You met my granddad earlier."

"Oh." I smiled. "It's nice to meet you. And Mara, you're the granddaughter Mr. Wilson told me about, right?" With oxygen back in my lungs, my brain was able to make the connections.

"I am."

I shook hands with her. She looked to be about my age, maybe a little younger. Her auburn hair was piled on top of her head in a riot of curls that made me jealous.

My dirty-blonde locks, which were beginning to turn white, were straight and couldn't be coerced into any other style.

"Let's get you fed," Mary said. "You must be starving."

"I can't believe Granddad didn't stop on the way to get you something," Mara added.

"It's not his fault." They guided me to the bar at the back of the pub. "I was in a rush to see my new home."

"Take a seat, luv. I made you a meat pie," Mary said.

"That sounds delicious." I sat down on the smooth wooden stool. The bar had a brass kick plate, and the beautiful wood was worn and highly polished.

I glanced around. There were hints of a green plaid on the seat covers and curtains.

I love this place.

"We have stew, if you'd prefer," Mara said. "Or a salad. You're from the West Coast. Maybe you don't eat meat?"

As a doctor, I probably should have watched my diet a bit more, but I was always on my feet. By the time I reached home, I either ordered out or popped something in the microwave. "I'll have a chance to try the whole menu at some point, but for now, the meat pie sounds great."

"What can I get you to drink?" Mara asked.

"A black and tan and some water."

"A woman who knows her ales." Mara filled a massive glass mug with light and dark beer. "You'll be popular around here. The men like a woman who knows how to order."

I laughed aloud. Part of it might have been exhaustion, and the other part nerves.

She stared at me with a strange look on her face.

"I think I'll be busy with my medical practice," I said. "I won't have time for that sort of thing."

"What sort of thing?" Mary asked as she sat a steaming pie in front of me. The whole meal was in a large bowl, and the crust on top was a golden brown. My mouth watered.

"Men," Mara answered for me. She handed me the beer. I took a sip and sighed. My friends back home had been right about the beer here. It was warm, but it was also good. I wasn't much of a drinker, but my husband had taught me the love of good ale.

"I don't know, Doc—it's cold in the winter. You might want someone to help keep you warm." Mara winked and then laughed.

I poked a few holes in the pie, to let it cool a bit. The scent was so rich. It was as if I was already eating it.

"She's only just arrived," Mary scolded. "Let her get settled." Then she grinned. "But my granddaughter's not wrong."

We all laughed.

"How do you like the church?" Mara asked.

"It's gorgeous. Truly. I couldn't have imagined anywhere more beautiful."

They smiled. "You're going to fit right in," Mara said. "Is there anything you need to know?"

"I saw a man in the graveyard at the church."

Mara shook her head. "Aye. That might take some getting used to."

"What?"

"Strangers in your backyard. Many of our ancestors are buried there, and it's considered community property. We use the back entrance, though, so no one should disturb you."

The pub door opened, and I turned to see the man with the white beard enter. Like me, he blinked a few times and then sneered when he focused in on me.

"Who are you?" he growled.

The pub went silent again. Pointing a finger at me, he shuffled forward.

I held out my hand. "Dr. Emilia McRoy," I said.

He glanced down at my hand, and then took a step back. "McRoy, you say?"

"Yes," I replied calmly. I was used to dealing with sick, grumpy patients.

He spit on the floor. "Bunch o' lying, cheating, thieves, the lot of you." He spat the words like a curse.

"I'm the new doctor in town," I said.

"You won't be here for long," he threatened.

"Smithy. If you want your whiskey, you'll apologize to the doctor now," Mary said. "She's only just arrived, and she's perfectly lovely."

"I'll not drink in a pub that serves a McRoy," he grumbled. Then he left.

"Grumpy old fool." Mary laughed and then headed back to the kitchen.

Everyone stared at me again, and I focused on my food.

"I'm sorry about him," Mara whispered.

"He seemed to take offense when I mentioned my name."

She rolled her eyes. "Smithy doesn't like anyone. I promise."

Mary came back out of the kitchen with a tray of food and handed it to her granddaughter.

"Gran, Smithy didn't seem to like her name. Do you know why?"

Mrs. Wilson shook her head. "I'm sorry he bothered you," she said. "Pay him no mind. Truly."

"I'm used to grumpy patients, but now I wonder what one of the McRoys did to him."

She smiled. "Luv, it was nearly fifty years ago. I think the story was that Smithy lost the pub to my beloved in a card game. And in that same game, lost his cottage and fishing boat to the last McRoy, who lived in town. I believe he was a vicar or a priest."

"Really?" There hadn't been a great deal of time to research my family's background before I arrived.

"Aye. He died mysteriously not long after that. I think the police thought Smithy might have had something to do with it, but there was no proof."

Wait. That man had possibly murdered my great- . . . whatever he was?

"Smithy got his cottage and boat back. But he's still mad about the pub. He comes here to give us a hard time. My husband is the only one who can stand to be around him for more than five minutes," Mary said, and then continued, "Pay him no mind, luv. You'll find our people are kind and very excited you're here.

"Isn't that, right?" she said to the group.

The pub patrons raised their glasses. "Aye," they said in unison.

I smiled—a bit embarrassed that they'd been listening in.

"Let her eat, and then introduce yourselves. We don't want her judging us because of old Smithy," Mara said.

The meat pie was delicious.

"I've got to head out on some errands, but come back tomorrow morning for breakfast, and let's chat," Mara said.

I smiled. "I'll do that."

The talking had started again in the pub, and I honestly only understood a few words. I hadn't thought about there being any language barrier here. Maybe I needed a dictionary and to rewatch some of my favorite Scottish detective shows.

After the meal, my eyelids were heavy, but my internal clock would never be sorted if I went to bed so early.

My departure was delayed as, one by one, the pub patrons came up to say hello. The first was a pregnant young woman with strawberry-blonde hair.

"I'm Caitlin," she said. "I'm so happy you're here. The idea of possibly having this baby in the lorry because we couldn't get to the hospital in time has scared me to death."

"How far along are you?"

"Seven months, but feels like one hundred," she said. She rubbed her belly.

I would have guessed closer to nine. "Did they do a sonogram at your doctor's appointment?"

"Nae," she said.

"I'm opening the office. Why don't you come by, and let's chat? I just want to make sure I'm familiar with your medical history."

"Thank you."

Several more people came up, and all of them had various ailments. I'd be busy, but I looked forward to it. These people were so grateful and kind. It was going to be a joy to serve them.

After speaking to the last customer in the pub, I said my goodbyes and headed back up the hill.

My mind danced over everything I'd learned in such a short time.

Had Smithy killed one of my ancestors? I shivered, and it wasn't from the cold. That man had been menacing.

I continued up the cobblestone path and stopped to study the church.

Curious when it had been built, I circled around the side. There was a path leading up a hill. I needed a walk to clear my head, and I was grateful to find it was dirt, and not cobblestones like the streets in town.

I wonder how many twisted ankles come in a week? I smiled. It was August, but the air was brisk. I shivered a bit.

I'll just go a little farther up the mountain.

Everything from the past few months rolled around in my brain. A hint of anxiety slithered across my skin. My husband's face flashed through my head.

I forced myself to walk faster.

Don't think.

I was out of breath when the first raindrop plopped hard on my face.

I glanced up at the sky that had been filled with sunshine just a short bit ago. There were angry black clouds and rain so heavy I could barely see in front of me. I took a few steps to go back down the hill, but I slipped. I'd end up breaking an arm—or worse, a leg— if I tried to go down to the church.

Ahead of me, I could barely see the outline of a house. Moving off the slippery dirt, I stepped onto the grass, where I had a bit more traction.

I finally made it to the doorway.

No time like the present to meet the neighbors.

I hoped they were nice. I already felt like the dumb American who hadn't been paying attention to the weather.

I knocked hard on the rickety door. No one answered. Maybe nobody was home. The stinging rain hurt, and the temperature had dropped at least twenty degrees.

I tried the door, and it opened.

"Hello? I'm Emilia. Is anyone here?"

Silence.

I tried to find a light switch, but there wasn't one. I fumbled to get my cell out of the pocket of my sweater, but it slipped and clattered to the stone floor.

"Darn. Don't be broken."

My hands were so wet and slippery, and wiping them on my soaked clothes was no help.

The coppery scent of blood filled my nose.

It's a deserted house—probably a dead animal or something.

I rubbed my hands together, and the friction helped dry them. I bent down and picked up my phone.

It still took a few tries to get the flashlight app to work. The room was so dark, the light didn't help much, but at least I could see a few feet around me. The windows were as dirty as the stone walls. Dust flew up under my feet with each step.

A couple of wooden rocking chairs sat in front of an old fireplace that had seen better days.

From the enormous spiderwebs on the walls and chairs, the person who lived here hadn't been around much.

Good.

I flashed the light through the doorway of a side room. A figure sat on the bed.

"Ack." I dropped my phone again. "I'm sorry to intrude," I said. "I'm new here, and I was trying to find a place to get out of the rain."

The figure didn't move.

"Are you okay?

I stepped inside.

"Excuse me?" I said.

A low, menacing growl sent a shiver down my spine.

A piece of fur jumped out and nipped at me.

"Ahh!"

After screaming for a good minute, I forced myself to calm down.

Breathe.

My hands shook, and my body trembled, but I moved forward.

The growling mutt started again. It was soaking wet and couldn't have been more than eight pounds if that.

"Okay. Look. I need to check on your owner. Just so you know, you're doing a great job protecting him, but I think he might be hurt." I tried to keep my voice calm, like I was talking a junkie off a ledge. I'd done it more than once when they'd escaped their restraints at the hospital.

While I couldn't see its eyes through its fur, the dog's sharp teeth were prominent.

"So. I'm just going to step close enough to feel for a pulse. I'd appreciate it if you didn't bite me."

The ball of fur didn't back down, but it didn't lunge for me as I placed two fingers on the man's neck. Nothing. I tried to lift the arm a bit, but rigor mortis had set in. He was dead. His legs were straight out in front of him on the bed. He appeared as if he'd just gone to sleep sitting up against the wall.

I moved the light around to the front.

Smithy. The man who'd been so mean and had possibly killed one of my few remaining family members.

My stomach roiled. I glanced to see what time it was on my phone. He'd been in the pub not three hours ago.

"What happened to you?"

I shifted around to the back of him. His head was misshapen, and blood left a trail down the wall. Had he been murdered here in the house?

I'm in the middle of a nightmare.

I flashed my phone around. There wasn't much on the floor, though it was hard to see in the dusty, dark room. The only blood was on his head and where his head had touched the wall.

The dog growled when I moved. "I need to find help," I said. I was near the front door when it flew open and clattered against the stone wall. A large figure loomed before me.

The killer is back.

15

Chapter Three

The figure in the door was huge, and I had nothing to protect myself. Using my phone, I flashed the light in the man's face, praying he'd turn away and I could run past.

"Bloody hell, what are you playing at?" The man's voice boomed. Instead of turning away, he grabbed my phone. "What's wrong with you? Why were you screaming?"

Did I scream? Everything had happened so fast, I couldn't remember.

"I've already called the police," I warned as I took a step back. Maybe there was a poker by the fireplace.

"Not bloody likely," he said. And then he pulled out a giant flashlight. "Who the hell are you? And why are you in my bothy? It's marked on the map that it's closed for renovation."

"If you've come back to hide your victim, it's too late. As I said, I've already called the police." With the light shining brightly in my eyes, it was hard to see.

"I *am* the deputy chief constable. And I'll ask you again: Why are you in my bothy?"

Wait. The police? I tried to breathe, but it was more like a wheezy gasp.

"Are you hurt?" His tone changed to that of someone worried, and he probably thought I was insane.

"No. Can you get that light out of my face?"

"Give me a moment," he said roughly. The flashlight went away, and then the soft glow of a lantern came to life, brightening the room enough that I could see his face.

Oh. My. The man was huge and dressed in a cable-knit sweater and jeans. And he had a pleasant face. And by pleasant, I mean handsome.

Everyone looks good in lantern light.

"Thanks," I said. "There's a dead man in the bedroom. We need to call your medical examiner or coroner. I'm not sure what you call them here. I mean, I read it when I applied here for my working visa, but you frightened me, and now my brain is—anyway, I found a dead body."

There was enough light to see his eyebrows go up. We never called our patients crazy, but we thought it sometimes. He was giving me *that* look.

"Maybe you should sit down," he said softly.

I snorted. "I'm not crazy. I'm a doctor. I was trying to get out of the rain—"

He continued to stare at me.

"Fine. Just go look in the bedroom."

I sat down in the dusty rocker more because I was tired than anything. It had been a day. The adrenaline from being scared to death more than once in the last ten minutes wore off.

He stared at me for a few seconds and then walked to the bedroom. I'm guessing more to appease the mentally ill woman in his— what had he called it? A bothy?—than anything.

"Bloody hell."

I snorted. It was everything I could do not to say, "Told you so," like some petulant child.

"We need to call the coroner or whoever attends to your dead," I said again.

His boots were loud on the stone floors. "Did you say you're the new doctor?"

I nodded but didn't bother looking up at him.

"That would make you the coroner, then."

I stood so fast, I nearly tripped on my own feet. "No. I'm afraid you're misinformed. Wait. Are you joking? It's hard to tell. Did I mention I just flew in today? My jet lag has jet lag. I'm not in the mood for jokes."

"I'm quite serious, Doctor. I think you'll find in your contract that you must attend to the living as well as do examinations of the dead for death certificates."

I remembered that bit. "I thought that meant, like, elderly care patients in a nursing home or something."

"We don't have one of those," he said. "We care for our elderly *personally*."

His comment sounded like a judgment.

"Okay. Well, in case you didn't notice, there's a fierce animal in there protecting the victim. I can't do much of an examination until it's removed. And I'll need some decent light to examine him, and this house doesn't seem to have any."

"Bothy," he corrected. "And do you mean Fred?" He opened his jacket. The tiny furball nestled against him. "He's harmless. His owner, Margie, will be looking for him. He has a habit of running away. Probably followed Smithy, looking for treats."

"Whatever you say. Somebody bashed in the dead man's head. Time of death had to be a little less than two hours ago."

"If you couldn't see him well, how do you know that?"

"I spoke to him in the pub two hours ago. Then I took a walk, so I think around two hours. Rigor mortis is just setting in, and that's about how long it takes."

"Were you the last one to see him, then?"

I sighed. "No. There was a room full of people who could have conked him on the head. I'll need him moved to the morgue. Since you're the constable, can you arrange for transportation? I'm not sure this place is the crime scene, but I'll need it to be protected until I can get back here in the daylight tomorrow."

Thank goodness for my training—and by that, I mean watching at least two hundred hours of British, Irish, and Scottish detective shows. Those and home and garden shows were all I watched on television. I vaguely sounded like someone who knew what she was doing.

Coroner? Really? How had I not seen that in the fine print?

I'd been excited to get started on a new life.

"I'll call my men, and we'll have him to the church within the hour."

"The church? That's where I live. I need him to go to the morgue."

"Right, which is at the church." He sounded as if he were talking to a child.

I was about to unload my stress from the last few months of getting ready to come here when it hit me. "The big walk-in freezer off the kitchen. It's not for storing vegetables," I said as if that explained everything.

"No, lass. It's where Doc stored the dead."

Lovely. Just lovely. At least, I'd never have to travel far to work.

"Okay. I'll meet you at the church." I needed a warm shower, a cup of coffee, and some dry clothes. Maybe not in that order.

I opened the door and stepped out. It was still raining, but in a soft mist.

"I could get you some wellies," he said in that deep voice of his. "You're going to fall down the hill in those." I glanced back to find him pointing down at my slide-on Keds, covered in mud and dirt.

"I'm fine," I said, but I slipped a little. I righted myself and walked with purpose. Once I was out of his sight, I didn't care if I slid down the hill on my butt. I would not be asking that man for help again.

* * *

By the time I made it down to the church, my clothes were covered in mud, twigs, and something foresty that I couldn't quite identify.

Moss, maybe?

I stripped down to my sports bra and Batman boy shorts in the vestibule, then carried my probably ruined belongings to the laundry room, which was also off the kitchen.

I left the clothes on top of the washer. I had no idea where the detergent might be, or even if there was any. I'd have to go to the shops and buy necessities.

In the kitchen, I tried to get some coffee started, but there wasn't any. It was just as well. It was a fancy machine, and I had no idea how to use it.

I did find some old whiskey. I took two swigs from the bottle and then coughed most of it out in the sink. The rest of the drink burned a fiery trail down to my liver.

"You should sip whiskey," a voice said from behind me.

I jumped, but I didn't scream.

I'm making progress.

"Do you know how to knock?"

"I did, on the back door, but you were probably coughing so loud you didn't hear me. I came ahead to let you know the boys are on the way."

"Great."

"They'll be here soon," he said urgently.

"I heard you the first time."

"You are *very* American." It was more than clear his tone was insulting. "Maybe you're used to that sort of thing, but the boys, well . . ."

I turned on him then. "What are you talking about?" My hands fisted. Yes, he might be handsome, but he was also an infuriating jerk of a man.

"Aren't you cold?" he asked, and then waved toward me.

I was. I glanced down and realized what I was wearing.

Damn him.

"I'll be right back. Make yourself useful and figure out some coffee or tea, or whatever you people drink. I don't care, as long as it's hot enough to scald my tongue."

He chuckled as I left the room.

There was no way to get my giant suitcases upstairs, so I opened one of them up on the floor and grabbed the first sweater and pair of jeans I could find. And a dry bra and boy shorts.

Using the downstairs toilet, which was the size of a confessional—as in, while sitting on the toilet, you could wash your hands—I dressed. Then I found a clean pair of sneakers and some bootie covers. If I had to do an autopsy, I wasn't going to ruin another pair of shoes.

I found a box of rubber gloves in my other case.

By the time I made it back to the kitchen, the scent of coffee had never smelled so good.

He sat at the table, reading something on his phone and drinking the fragrant brew.

He'd left out a cup for me.

"There's no sugar or milk," he said.

"I don't need it."

He nodded without looking away. I'd probably embarrassed the hell out of him by running around half naked. But it wasn't my fault. He was the one who'd entered my home without being invited.

I was about to say something but stopped myself. I was tired and grumpy—and definitely out of sorts.

If I was the coroner—and I'd be checking my contract soon—I'd have to work with the police. I was a practical woman except for that one time when I quit a promising career to move to the other side of the world.

"Hi, I'm Dr. Emilia McRoy. My friends call me Em." I held out my hand.

He put his phone down and then pushed his chair back to stand.

"Doctor, it's nice to meet you." He smiled as he played along. "I'm Ewan Campbell, constable, mayor, and laird of Sea Isle."

Mayor and laird. Was there anything this guy didn't do? And wasn't a laird like royalty? In addition to "bothies," I'd be doing some other internet searches soon.

"I'm jet lagged and not quite myself," I said.

"It's understandable. I'm sorry you must work on the day of your arrival."

"Nothing like just jumping into the deep end of the pool."

There was something in his eyes. I'd taken him at his word as to who he was. But I hadn't asked for proof.

Am I so tired that I let a killer in my house?

I eyed him suspiciously. There were plenty of handsome serial killers.

"I do have a question for you, though. I know how I ended up at the bothy. I'm curious: Did you kill Smithy?"

Chapter Four

I'd never been in a grownup version of a staring contest. Ewan's eyebrow was up again, and he smiled, but he didn't say a word. His cell rang, and I was proud of myself for not jumping when the shrill tone broke the silence.

"Aye," he said. Then he hung up.

"Boys are here." Then he headed to the back door.

What was with him?

He didn't answer my question.

I chugged my remaining coffee and put the mug in the sink. Their voices echoed, but they didn't come through the kitchen.

Where are they?

I moved toward the back door, only to find no one there, but their voices were on the other side of the laundry room wall. That's when I saw it—a small seam on the back wall, near the dryer.

I pushed it, and the panel opened to another freezer door. I hadn't noticed it before, but at least the dead wouldn't be rolling through my kitchen.

An image of zombies dancing flitted through my brain, and I laughed, perhaps a little too hard.

When I stepped into the freezer, five men stared at me, including the laird.

"I didn't know about the secret door," I said, as if it were perfectly normal that I was laughing so hard I couldn't breathe.

The freezer light was bright, and they had put the dead man on a gurney.

"I don't suppose there's a secret door to an autopsy room.

"Autopsy? Why would you need that?" Ewan asked. "This is Smithy. He's a drunk. It's obvious he slipped, hit his head on something, and then stumbled into the bothy and died."

"Bless him," the men said in unison, and made the sign of the cross. They took their hats off and bowed their heads.

I'd stepped into an alternative world.

"Well, you've got it all figured out, why do you need me?" I put my hands on my hips and eyed him suspiciously.

"To sign the death certificate," Ewan said.

"Sorry—I won't be doing that until I've performed at least a cursory autopsy."

"Are ya daft? I told you what happened," he said. Ewan wasn't happy.

Maybe he's the killer and doesn't want anyone to find out.

"And you're wrong."

The other men's eyes grew wide, and they turned to Ewan.

"What?" He growled the word.

"I'm guessing not many people around here tell you when you've made a mistake, but Smithy was murdered."

The men took a step back from the body.

"The skull has been bludgeoned on the top right. And there was very little blood at the scene. It was dark, but it was only on the floor. He was probably murdered somewhere and brought to the bothy. Though, after the rain, the evidence may have washed away."

They all stared at me as if I'd come from another planet. Well, maybe I had.

"You mentioned the house had been closed for renovations. The killer probably thought no one would go in the bothy until the renovations began. Or perhaps he or she planned to store the body until the rain stopped. But just my luck, I accidentally wandered in there. So, I'll ask again. Is there a secret autopsy room?"

Ewan didn't say anything. He went to the back of the freezer and pushed a button. A steel panel that looked like part of the wall slid open, revealing a large room with lab equipment.

"It's like something out of *Star Trek*, with the sliding doors."

"Doc was a fan of secret rooms and doors," Ewan said. "It was his hobby putting them around the church. There wasn't much cause for him to do autopsies, but he ran his labs here. He didn't trust the one in Edinburgh."

"What do you mean he didn't have much cause for autopsies?"

He shrugged. "People around here tend to die from drowning, fishing accidents, or old age. Occasionally, there's cancer involved."

I sighed. "Good to know. Unless Smithy grew an extra limb and then hit himself with something so hard it cracked his skull, you need to find his murderer."

I thought for a minute, then asked him: "Will you inform the family? Or is that another one of those things that falls under my contract?"

His eyes narrowed. I'd worked in the field of medicine for years and run into my fair share of arrogant surgeons and doctors who thought they knew everything. This guy didn't scare me.

"I'll let the family know and take care of any expenses and the burial."

And just like that, I was deflated. He was willing to take care of the older man's burial. He couldn't be that bad.

Unless he's the killer and feels guilty. He had shown up rather quickly.

"Are you ready to do it now?" he asked.

"I've been awake for thirty hours straight," I said. "I'd rather get some sleep and start fresh in the morning. I'll let you know what I find."

"What time tomorrow?"

"I don't know—whenever I wake up. Technically, I don't start working here until late next week. If you want someone to do an autopsy at your beck and call, you'll have to take him somewhere else."

"I only asked the time because, as the constable, I have to observe it." His voice was level, with no hint of anger.

I sighed—again. "If you leave your number on the kitchen counter, I'll text you before I begin. Now, if you don't mind, I'd like to get some rest."

A wave of tiredness washed over me. Coffee wouldn't work this time. I headed out and didn't bother to say goodbye. I dug around in my suitcase and found my favorite sloth pajamas.

"I'll just lock up then," he said, a hint of laughter in his voice.

I yawned and nodded. After half crawling up the steep stairs, I stepped into the bedroom. It was dark, and I had no idea where the light switch was. But the outline of the bed was there.

I put the pajamas on the cover, but it seemed like too much work to change. I kicked off my shoes and laid down. As my head hit the pillow, I remembered that serial killer Ewan had never answered my question about how he'd arrived on the scene so quickly.

* * *

The following morning, I woke and sat straight up in bed.

Where am I?

Light filtered through the stained-glass windows.

Scotland.

I smiled. The troubles from the night before had melted away. While I wasn't exactly bright eyed, I felt so much better.

I had an autopsy to do, but first I needed to clean up and find the coffee. My stomach growled.

There was a bathroom suite just off the bedroom. The shower fit under a low eave. I turned on the taps, but only cold water came out. I brushed my teeth and let it run a bit, but it was colder.

Fine. Cold shower it is.

I'm only five foot four, but I had to bend down to get my face under the showerhead.

I lasted for precisely the time it took to soap up and rinse off.

Since I had no idea where Ewan had found the coffee the night before, I headed down to the pub, praying it was open this early.

I shouldn't have worried. The place was bustling with people. The pub had the atmosphere of a warm hug.

It was so comforting—right up until I walked into the main room. Like the night before, everyone stopped talking when I arrived.

"Morning," Mara said cheerfully. She carried a plate in each hand and set them down on a table at the far side of the room. "There's a seat at the bar for you. I'll be right there."

I smiled. "Thank you."

Everyone turned to watch me as I sat down, and no one said a word. None of them smiled this time, and the room felt a bit colder.

She bustled around and sat a cup of coffee and a glass of orange juice in front of me.

"It's not my ego, right? Everyone is staring at me again?"

She laughed hard. "Bunch of nosy buggers, the lot of you," she said as she waved her towel toward them. "Go about your business, and quit your staring. You're giving the good doctor a complex."

"Um . . . thanks?"

"They're just curious what you've found out about poor Smithy," she whispered. "And there's a rumor that maybe you killed him as payback."

I coughed and nearly spat out the orange juice I'd sipped.

The pub was quiet behind me again.

"What?"

"No one would blame ya," Mary said as she came through the door with a large tray. "We're just curious."

"I found him, but I didn't kill him," I said. "Why would people even think that? And how does everyone know?"

"Ah, luv. Something that exciting was around town before you were back down the mountain," Mary said. "You were asking questions yesterday about the McRoys' feud with Smithy, and this town loves to gossip."

Feud? How did losing at a poker game become a feud?

"I only met him once and had no reason to kill the man."

What in the world was wrong with these people? For a quaint little place, they were awfully suspicious.

"So, is there news? Did he fall drunk again? It happens. Or was he really murdered?" She whispered the last word.

"I'll be doing an autopsy later this morning."

"Oh. How exciting. I don't think we've ever had someone autopsied before," Mara said.

"Aye, we have," Mary added. "Tourists, though. Doc didn't like messing about with them. Most of the bodies ended up in Edinburgh or Glasgow, though Doc didn't trust them with our folk." Mary changed the subject. "I've got a full Scottish breakfast coming up for you, lass."

"Oh, she's right about the vacationers," Mara said. "But not anyone who lives here. During the busy season, people get into all sorts of trouble."

Since I had to investigate the murder and hadn't a clue how to begin, this was as good a place as any to ask a few questions.

"Did Smithy come in here much? And do you know his full name?"

Mara shook her head. "He spent most of his time down the way to Harry's Pub. But he came in at least once a month. He and Granddad were old friends.

"As for his name, we all just called him Smithy. In addition to fishing, he did odd jobs around town. I'd say to pay his bar tabs and gambling debts. Granddad hired him occasionally to fix the plumbing at the house or to cut wood for the stove."

"Okay."

"If you know something, you can tell me. I'm good with secrets."

I liked Mara, but I'd known her less than a day. Besides, I seemed to remember from one of my favorite murder mysteries that official investigations were to be kept confidential until they were complete.

"I understand he wasn't exactly well liked, but did he have any enemies?

There was silence behind us. I had a feeling the pub was the source of all the information in town.

Mary came back through the door with my breakfast plate—I mean, platter.

A full Scottish breakfast consisted of eggs, three kinds of sausage, bacon, beans, tomato with cheese, an oatcake, a scone, and another type of bread I'd never seen before.

I must have made a funny face because Mara laughed again.

"That's a lot of food," I said.

"You'll burn it off here." She grinned. "Trust me. It's something about the air."

I didn't want to ruin the moment with science about calories intake and exercise. Besides, I was hungry.

"Gran, do you know if Smithy had any enemies?" Mara asked.

Mary scrunched up her face. "I don't like speaking ill of the dead. Smithy liked his drink and his cards. He's made many enemies through the years."

"Was there anyone who might be mad enough to kill him?" I asked.

"You met him," Mara said. "What do you think?"

I smiled. "Maybe, there might be someone who was offended by him?"

For people who seemed to live for gossip, getting real answers out of them was tough.

"He had a falling out with Harry over his tab the night before last," Mr. Wilson said as he came in. "Bad business. Harry kicked him out—though he's not the sort of fellow to kill someone over a tab. If he were, a lot of his customers would be dead."

"Granddad." Mara shook her head.

"He didn't pay some of the men who worked on his boat," Mary said. "I remember one of them being in here and complaining night before last. Was it Grady or his brother?"

"I dunno," Mara said. "But I can't see them being sober long enough to kill anyone. As soon as they get off the boat, they're in the pub."

I pulled out my phone.

"What are you typing?" Mara asked.

"Names," I said. "Just of people I might want to talk to. Can you think of anyone else?"

By the time I was done, I'd eaten nearly all my food, and I had four people on my list.

"How much do I owe you?" I asked Mara.

"Oh, don't worry about it. Your tab is covered here in town."

"What do you mean?"

"Well, you can eat wherever you like in Sea Isle. We have two pubs, two restaurants, and Fishies, which has the best chips, down on the pier. You just tell them your name."

"That's—uh. I don't understand."

She smiled. "It's one of the benefits of being the doc. Ewan covers your meals out. Didn't he tell you? The old doc was a terrible cook, so it was written in his contract. You also get a clothing allowance and some other stuff. We're remote, right? So, they take care of things like that. I heard him and Granddad when they were writing up your contract."

"Oh." I didn't need someone to pay for my essentials. It was embarrassing.

"Is something wrong?" She frowned.

"No. I prefer to pay my own way," I said.

"Don't worry about it. We have trouble getting doctors and other professional people to stay. They're just trying to keep you happy."

I nodded. It was enough they weren't making me pay for where I lived, and the office space, but all my expenses? That was extreme.

I said my goodbyes and headed up the hill with so much on my mind that I didn't notice the man and the woman standing at the stone gate until I was a few feet away.

"Morning, Dr. McRoy," the woman said in a singsong voice. "I'm Abigail, and this is my brother, Tommy. I'm the cleaner, and Tommy takes care of the garden and fixes things around the church. Ewan said we should introduce ourselves before getting to work."

Great. I had employees I didn't know existed.

"Why don't you come inside," I said.

Her brother stared out into the distance. The way he touched his fingers together gave me a bit of insight into Tommy. I'd seen the behavior many times before.

"He's not daft," Abigail said as she looked from me to her brother. "He doesn't socialize much. He dinna like people touching or yelling at him. He'll do what you want if you ask gently."

"I'm sure he's brilliant." I smiled. "The garden is gorgeous, Tommy. You've both done a wonderful job around here. I was very impressed when I arrived yesterday."

"Roses," Tommy said softly.

"They are beautiful," I said. "The pink ones that look like ladies' dresses are my favorite."

"Butterflies," he said. "Rosa Bella."

"It takes a minute to understand him sometimes," Abigail said, "but you'll catch on."

I smiled. "I understand. He told me the name of the rose and that he planted it because it attracts butterflies and, my guess, other pollinators."

"Yes." Tommy nodded twice, still looking out at the sea.

"Are you paid weekly or every few weeks? I'll carry on the same way as before. You don't need to worry."

She laughed. "Oh no. Doctor, you don't pay us. The town does."

I was about to question her, but there was no point. I'd need to talk to the laird.

"Right. So, I guess I'll let you get to it. Oh, there are two things I need to ask. Where is the coffee kept, and how do I get the hot water to work?"

"Tommy will take care of the water. There's an automatic switch that turns it off if the pilot light goes out. I'll show you the pantry."

She gave her brother instructions, and he nodded twice.

We headed inside to the kitchen.

"Do you clean the office space as well?"

"Yes, and I restock for the next day. You just need to let me know how you like things."

As we passed through the living area, she pointed to some double doors near the fireplace. "This is where the doc keeps his medicines, and there's another door inside the kitchen that leads to the cupboard where the coffee and cans are stored."

The medical storeroom was dark and had no windows. There was a fridge against one wall, but shelves lined the rest of the space. Every kind of medicine I could have imagined was there. Well, not every category, but a wide variety. The fridge held several vials.

"Is there a pharmacy in town?" I hadn't noticed one as we drove in.

"Yes, but our chemist, Mr. Grudy, is getting up there in years and only works a few hours a week. So Doc always kept a good supply for emergencies. I keep the inventory. And I sign everything in, so if you need me to add something to the list, let me know. Depending on the time of year, it can take a month to three to get shipments in. The winters, when the snow covers the pass and the sea freezes, are particularly slow."

"Goodness, you do a lot of work around here."

She smiled. "I'm well paid, and I like keeping busy. It's just Tommy and me now. As you saw, he's not always the most talkative. We spend our days here starting at eight and then finish up around four. Tommy is best when we keep to our schedule."

I followed her out, and she locked the doors. "This key is for you," she said as she handed it to me. "Doc had a problem with some teens breaking in through the window years ago. They put stone over it, and he liked to keep the doors locked unless one of us was in there."

"Oh," I said. "Do you have a lot of that sort of thing in Sea Isle?"

She smiled. "No. Young people do crazy things everywhere, right? But nothing like that has happened while I worked for the doc."

In contrast, the kitchen was lovely and bright, with windows on both sides. "The coffee is in there."

I opened another set of double doors and was surprised. "This is huge." In the walk-in pantry all the staples were labeled in airtight containers. My new home was full of surprises.

"I'm a bit—well, I like everything in its place," she said. "It makes things easier."

I was organized in my work life. I had to be in the ER. At home, I tended to eat out a lot. The only staple in my kitchen was coffee.

There was plenty of that here. From Columbian to Ethiopian, I had a little coffee shop all to myself.

"I always have a coffee going, even at night. Though, I drink decaf after four or so. Where did the doc get all of this?"

She smiled. "Oh no, miss. The doctor only drank tea. I ordered this for you," Abigail said. "You filled out some paperwork about the sort of things you liked. Ewan and I went over the list and tried to make sure you'd have everything you needed. We want you to be happy."

"Oh. Thank you." Dumb of me. The coffee wouldn't be good after years in a pantry. Of course, it was new.

And Ewan helped her? Ugh. I didn't want to think of him as doing anything nice.

Childish? Maybe.

"You are welcome. I usually did Doc's shopping when I did ours. Make me a list if you need anything."

"I can do my shopping," I said. "I feel like you're doing so much already."

"How do you say it in America? No worries. I like taking care of people. And you'll be busy during your days, even on the weekends sometimes. You'll see."

It was a small town. It couldn't be that bad. I sometimes saw fifty patients a day at home.

I grabbed some of the coffee. "I'll make a pot and then get to work," I said. "I need to do an autopsy."

She led me out. "I'll show you how to use the machine. It's fancy and has a mind of its own, but I taught myself how to make it work before you arrived."

I followed her out as she continued talking.

"And I heard about Smithy. He wasn't the nicest man, but I canna believe someone killed him."

"Word does travel fast in this town."

She shook her head. "Sea Isle is full of secrets that everyone knows."

I laughed. "Did you know him?""

"Aye," she said.

"What can you tell me about him?"

She ducked her head and stared at her feet. What was that about?

"It isn't gossip," I said. "As the coroner, I must investigate his death."

"His wife left years ago over his gambling," she said softly. "I was young, so I don't remember much about her. He had a habit of rubbing people the wrong way and wasn't particularly kind."

"From what I heard at the pub—it doesn't sound as if he was popular."

She lifted her face, and her brows drew together. "He was angry for what seemed like no reason. He screamed at Tommy a lot, and I canna forgive him." She seemed to realize what she'd said and held up a hand.

"But not enough to kill him. I think you'll find, though, that most folks will be happy he's gone." Her hand went against her mouth. "I can't believe I said that."

Was she telling the truth about not killing him? And what about her brother? Tommy was tall enough and strong enough to hit someone hard.

Welcome to your new life, Em. You're thinking a poor kid on the spectrum is a murderer.

"Do you know if anyone around town might have been mad enough to kill him?"

"I dinna know," she said. "Ewan might have an idea about his debts," she said. "That might be a good place to start."

She showed me the coffee maker. "I know you said you like to keep a pot going, but this one does it a cup at a time." It was a De'Longhi Dinamica automated coffee and espresso machine. "You need to check this." She pointed to where she put the coffee grounds. "If it's not working, usually that's where it gets clogged up. Just use a wooden spoon to loosen the grounds."

I'd never had such a nice machine.

A short time later, liquid came out, and she filled a cup for me and one for herself.

"Cheers." I clicked my cup against hers.

"Slainte Mhath," she said.

"What does that mean?"

"To your good health." She sipped her coffee.

"You drink it black as well?"

She nodded. "I might be an addict."

"Me too. It's my last vice. Well, and maybe too much wine on occasion."

We laughed.

"Can you translate something else for me?"

"Of course."

"What's a bothy? That's where we found Smithy."

"Oh, that's an easy one. They are rough cottages where hikers and travelers can get out of the rain or weather. It's just a shelter. We have them all over the highlands. The weather changes quickly around here."

"Thanks. I learned that lesson yesterday. I need to buy some of those . . . high boots. I can't remember what you call them."

"Wellies. They have them at most of the shops. You'll see people wearing them all the time. As I said, the weather here changes so quickly. It's best to keep a pair close by."

I took a few more sips of coffee. "I guess I'd better get to work."

"If you need anything, let me know. I'll be cleaning up the exam rooms and restocking today."

"Thanks."

I followed her through the living room to dig out some bootie covers for my shoes. It had been a while since I'd cut into a dead body. Well, I'd done a lot in medical school. But there were simple enough procedures to follow when it came to a chain of evidence.

Even though I didn't want to have him looking over my shoulder, I texted Ewan. I had to follow the local procedures.

I put my rubber gloves on and then opened the freezer door with a towel.

I passed through and pushed the button to open the autopsy room.

"You've got to be kidding me."

"What's wrong?" Ewan said behind me.

I prided myself on not jumping out of my skin. For a big guy, he had the talents of a ninja when it came to sneaking up on someone.

I waved a hand toward the empty room.

"Smithy is missing."

Chapter Five

After years in the ER, I wasn't shocked by much, but there was no way to autopsy a missing body. Ewan stepped past me and looked to the right and left, as if Smithy was hiding in a corner somewhere.

"What did you do with the body?" he asked.

"I didn't do anything. Someone either stole it or moved it."

His eyebrows rose. "Why would anyone do that?"

I sighed. "You're the constable, but I expect it is an effort to hide the fact they'd murdered him."

Ewan grunted. "It was an accident."

"So, you were there? How did he accidentally conk himself on the head at that angle?"

"If he was drunk, he could have tripped. Since you don't have a body, it is no longer your concern."

There was no use arguing with this man. I'd only known him a day and had figured that much out.

"If it's all the same to you, I would like to know, at the very least, how the last hours of his life played out. Please don't tell anyone that he's missing."

He waved a hand and then walked out of the freezer. "Suit yourself, lass. It doesn't make sense for someone to take the body. That sort of thing doesn't happen here. If you didn't move the body, who did?" The words were accusatory, as if I was the one who'd stolen the body.

I frowned. "Well, I'm no detective, but I'd say someone trying to cover his or her tracks."

"Aye. Still, all of this is so strange. You had an altercation with him in the pub. Didn't bother to tell me that last night. Maybe you're the one we need to be looking at. You're the one who *found* him."

"I may be short, but I'm not a weak woman," I said. "Still, Smithy had a good hundred pounds on me. And I certainly wouldn't have had anything to do with that dog. Your line of thinking doesn't make sense."

He kept looking at me,

"Besides, I have no motive to want the man dead."

He clicked his tongue. "He may have killed one of your ancestors."

It took everything in me not to roll my eyes. "First, I have no idea if we were related. There are millions of McRoys, and I'm a doctor. I've taken an oath to save lives. It goes against everything I am to murder someone."

He grunted. "Well, since you aren't doing the autopsy, I've business to attend."

Then he was off.

Infuriating man.

If he decided to make me the fall guy, I didn't have any evidence to prove my innocence.

Great way to start my new life.

* * *

Later that morning, I walked into the pub, and everyone stopped talking—again.

When is that going to stop?

Ignoring the stares, I sat down on a stool at the bar.

As Mara came through from the kitchen, she stopped short. Then she glanced up at the clock.

"I'm not here to eat. I need your help with something," I whispered the last few words.

She motioned her head toward the tray of drinks and food she carried. "Let me drop these off and I'm all yours."

There were whispers all around, and I sensed eyes on me. "And what are you lot staring at?" Mara asked. "The poor woman's going to get a complex. We are a friendly village, and she didn't kill Smithy. It's more likely one of you offed him. Now on with you."

I covered my mouth to hide my laugh. Mara was becoming one of my favorite people.

A few minutes later, she yelled, "Gran, I'm taking my break."

She pointed toward the back of the pub. "We won't have any privacy in here. Come up to the flat."

I followed her to the stairs, which led up to a quaint apartment with a cozy living room and a kitchenette. The floor-to-ceiling windows had amazing views of the sea.

"It's beautiful, like something out of *Cottage* magazine. Is this where your grandparents live?"

She laughed. "No, they have a house up the mountain. This is my place. I don't have to do much more than roll out of bed when I have the breakfast shift."

"I'm not a morning person," I said. "I had no idea I'd be working where I lived, but I like the idea. Did you grow up here?"

Mara motioned to a cushy white couch with beautifully embroidered pillows. "I spent summers and holidays here, but I grew up in Edinburgh. Mom likes the city life, and dad does whatever she wants. They have a law firm. And now you'll be wantin' to know how I ended up here?"

I smiled. "I don't want to pry, but I am curious."

She shrugged. "I had a job at an ad agency making more money than most people should, but I hated it. I woke up at three in the morning with panic attacks for a year.

"Then a week after I turned forty, I had a bad breakup and realized life was too short not to do what makes you happy. My grandparents offered this place to sort myself out, and I started help-ing in the pub. I'm happier than I've ever been.

"But you're not here to talk about me, what do you need to know?"

"Who might want Smithy dead?" I asked. "I don't even know what his real name is, and the constable doesn't seem to be bothered that—"

I'd almost blurted out the victim's body was missing.

"Bothered about what?" she asked.

I cleared my throat. "He thinks it was an accident, but I'm not so sure. Can you keep a secret?"

"Most days."

We laughed.

"Someone carried his body to the bothy. There was evidence that made me think he was killed elsewhere, and I think that's all I should probably say. Do you know if he had family?"

She pursed her lips. "Everyone around here is related in some way. As you know, he wasn't the easiest fellow to get along with, and he didn't have many friends, save my granddad. Abigail and Tommy are his niece and nephew. She might know more about his background."

Hmm. Abigail failed to mention that important fact.

"Where did he work?"

"He owns a fifie down at the harbor. There are two helpers, Sean and Grady. They're a rough bunch, if you know what I mean. Lots of drinking and fighting. One of them is usually locked up on the weekend. We've had to kick them out of the pub a couple of times."

Lovely. And what the heck was a fifie? Since it was at the harbor, I assumed it was a kind of boat. "Is there any reason they might want to hurt Smithy?"

She shrugged. "I've been asking around since you left. The man owed everyone in town money. Granddad had loaned him a lot of money through the years. Smithy had not paid him back. I've never understood their friendship. It always seemed one-sided."

Money was one of the best motivations for murder.

Did wee Mr. Wilson kill Smithy?

"Is your grandfather here?"

She shook her head. "Nae, he went to Edinburgh to talk to my dad about something."

Well, I'd have to wait to question him.

"Tell me how I can find this fifie."

* * *

A short walk later, I found the harbor. Most of the boats were small, so finding the large trawler Smithy had owned wasn't so hard. There was a huge seawall with steps down to the wooden dock. Then, down from the dock, there were steps to a beautiful beach with white sand one way, and the other way was a long strip of moored boats.

Was there any place in Sea Isle that wasn't picturesque?

At the end of all the boats, was a huge antique-looking ship.

Mara had mentioned the fifie was the biggest ship out here.

Is that it?

Figuring out how to get on board was another thing. I found a rickety rope ladder tied on the side of the bow.

"Hello? Is anyone there?" I yelled up.

Nothing happened. I shivered and turned back to the dock to see if someone might be watching me, but no one was there.

Was there some kind of protocol when it came to climbing onto someone's boat? If it belonged to Smithy, and he was dead, I couldn't see a problem. At the very least, maybe I'd be able to find a license or something that told me the man's full name.

I blew out a breath. "Please don't break," I said to the rope ladder as I climbed up. Once I made it over the side, which was no small feat since my upper arm strength was lacking, I stood to get my bearings. The massive sails were tied up, and the whole thing needed a good polish.

I'd looked up "fifies" while I'd been in the pub, and learned they were old-fashioned trawlers used in the late nineteenth and early twentieth centuries. Many sailors in Scotland and Ireland still used them, as they worried that motors from the more modern boats and ships scared the fish and muddied the waters.

Peeled paint and chipped wood took away from what had been beautiful woodwork back in the day.

But I wasn't here to sightsee.

"Hello? I'm looking for Sean and Grady?"

Maybe, they'd gone home for the day. I should at least look for clues to make sure he hadn't been killed on his boat. I moved toward a cabin area. Maps covered the walls, and there was a small area with a hot plate and a couple of bunks.

It felt a bit like breaking in, but police would normally go through someone's belongings if they died suspiciously.

As the coroner, it was my job to settle the case satisfactorily, and I couldn't do that without more information.

One drawer stuck, but I pulled hard. The whole thing came out, and papers flew everywhere. After putting the drawer back, I bent down to gather the material.

There were several unpaid invoices and receipts, along with assorted pens and clips. At the bottom of the pile sat a legal-sized piece of yellowed paper that had been folded in half.

I opened it carefully. A boat title dated more than fifty years ago, and the owner was a Theodore McRoy.

Was I related to him? My heartbeat sped up. I was an orphan now, and as far as I knew, I didn't have any living relatives.

The DNA report had mentioned this part of Scotland for my ancestors.

I forced myself to take a deep breath. I had so many questions. Was this Smithy's real name? Had I been related to him?

Or was this the relative who had taken his boat and cottage? But why hadn't the name been changed?

I had so many questions. I took a few pictures of the document.

If Smithy had this big trawler, he'd need a license. That is, if the laws in Scotland were the same as the States. After searching a bit more, I spotted a cheap gold frame above one of the bunks.

Smithson Brown was the name on the license. I wrote the name down in my notebook and took a picture of it for good measure.

If this was his boat, then why was the title under a different name?

A shiver, which had nothing to do with the damp coolness of the boat, ran down my spine.

Chapter Six

By the time I finished my search, it was near lunchtime. If I were to be the coroner for Sea Isle, I'd have to invest in some forensic equipment I could add to my medical bag—not the least of which was an ultraviolet light to pick up blood traces. Though I hadn't seen any blood on the ship, that didn't mean there weren't traces of some. The place might have been full of chipped paint, and in need of repairs, but there hadn't been a speck of dust in the cabin area.

Someone had cleaned it recently.

I'd also have to view videos on lifting fingerprints and other techniques to help with the job. As frustrating as it might be to have been dumped in the middle of this, I liked the challenge of learning something new.

Since there was very little crime in Sea Isle except for the occasional drunk and disorderly, it was probably up to me to sort out any forensics with crime scenes.

I was halfway down the sketchy rope ladder, wishing I'd brought a heavier coat, when my foot slipped. I caught myself before I fell, but not without a rope burn to my palm.

"Oy!" someone shouted angrily.

I held on tight but glanced behind me and found two large men glaring menacingly at me.

Great.

"What are you doing on our fifie?"

I'd never get used to that name, and it took everything in me not to smile.

"Is it yours? I was under the impression it belonged to the recently deceased Smithson Brown." I climbed the rest of the way down to the dock.

"Who are you, and why are you on our ship?"

They didn't look like the shaking-hands type, so I didn't bother.

"Dr. Emilia McRoy, and I'm guessing you are Sean and Grady— am I correct?"

"Don't see how it's your business, and you're trespassing."

"So, you're saying Smithson doesn't own this boat?"

The guy who'd been doing most of the talking blinked, as if he were confused.

"'Course it's Smithy's," the other guy said.

I pulled out my notebook. "I'm investigating his death."

The two men glanced at one another and then back at me.

"So, the rumor is true?" The taller man asked.

"Yes. I need some information from you. Can you tell me which one of you is Sean and which is Grady? Or would you rather I come back with the constable?"

"No use bothering the constable," the taller one said. "This is my brother, Grady."

"Nice to meet you gentlemen." They wanted to avoid Ewan. We had that in common. "When was the last time you saw Mr. Brown?"

"Nobody calls him that," Gordon said. "He's—I mean, was— just Smithy. And the day before yesterday, right?" He glanced at his brother, who nodded.

"And what was Smithy's mood like that day?"

Sean snorted. "Smithy had one mood: arsehole. Never saw 'im smile, and we been workin' with 'im for five years."

"Okay. And did he mention anything about what might be happening in his life? Was there something or someone who may have upset him more than usual the few days before his death?"

45

I had no idea what I was doing, so I let my natural curiosity take over. That and my training by watching everything BritBox and Acorn TV had to offer by way of murder mysteries.

The men shrugged in sync.

"Like I said, he was a grumpy arsehole. Other than yelling orders, he didn't talk much," Sean said.

"Right. Did you work yesterday?"

"We did," Grady said. "But Smithy didn't show up. He drinks more than most. We had a rule: if he didn't show up by five, we were to be on our way without 'im. We were surprised when he wasn't waitin' for us when we docked."

"And what time was that?"

Gordon frowned. "Wasn't payin' attention but it was in time for tea."

I'd learned that "tea" was a word people used for almost every meal. I assumed, he meant a late lunch or supper. That gave them time to kill him.

Was I staring at two murderers? No one else was around. What if I asked them the wrong thing?

I cleared my throat. "Did he live here on the boat?"

"Nah," Sean said. "Too damn cold for his bones. He had a cabin up near the glen."

I had no idea where that was.

"Any idea if someone might want to hurt him?"

The men shrugged in sync again. It was disconcerting, as if they'd been shrugging off questions together their whole lives.

"Everyone," Grady said.

His brother elbowed him.

"What? It's true. He owed us four weeks' wages. He swore we'd get paid today. If he's dead, that won't be happenin'."

"Why are you here?"

Sean held up some bags with canned goods and potted meat. "We thought we'd take her out for a few days and sell whatever we catch. A man has to make a livin', and rent is due. Any reason we shouldn't?"

There were several that came to mind, not the least of which was the boat needed a forensic search.

But I didn't have the power to say one way or another. That point was moot.

"Since it's Smithy's property, you might want to check with the constable first."

They sneered.

No love lost there.

"Would you mind writing down your address and phone numbers for me? Just in case I need to ask you more questions?" I turned my notebook to a clean page and handed it to them.

They grumbled but wrote it all down.

"Did you kill him?" Grady asked. From the way he asked the question, as if there were no judgment, I had a feeling he didn't care about the answer.

"No. I didn't even know him." I had no idea why I felt the need to defend myself.

"We heard you found him."

I nodded. "Yes, he was dead when I got there. If you'll excuse me, gentleman."

How had these two heard that rumor?

"We heard you tussled in the pub." Grady smiled, and it gave me the shivers again.

"No. That wasn't me," I said quickly. "I'll be on my way."

Halfway down the dock, I made a mistake by looking back. The men were glaring at me menacingly.

I gave them my sweetest smile and then waved.

My knees shook. Had I just put myself in danger? If they were Smithy's killers, they now knew I suspected them. My chest tightened and my hands became fists.

Stop. *You watch too much television.*

That was true.

Think logically.

The men had been waiting to get paid. Why would they kill him before that happened?

Still, they would stay at the top of my suspect list.

There was a bait and tackle shop to the right of the pier. The person who ran it might have seen the brothers go out the day Smithy died. If so, at least then I'd be able to mark them off as suspects.

The white shop had blue trim and a wooden door with a porthole. Every building in this town was so quaint and adorable.

A bell rang over the door as I entered.

"Be there in a wee bit," a heavy brogue sounded from the back of the shop.

The walls were covered in all kinds of poles and reels. Some of the poles were so large, they spanned the roof of the shop.

One of the few memories I had of my dad was standing knee deep in the Pacific Ocean with him. We'd been living in Santa Barbara, and he'd promised to help me catch a shark.

I'd made a pole out of the longest stick I could find and borrowed thread from Grandma's sewing kit. I think I'd been four or five. Maybe even younger.

I just remember my dad being proud of me for making the pole and for my interest in sharks. I'd explained that I didn't want to eat it, that I wanted to touch the skin because it was different.

At the first sign of a fin, I'd screamed and then dropped the pole. Dad scooped me up and ran for the shore. We soon discovered it was a dolphin, but it had been enough excitement for me to decide that I'd rather build sandcastles on the shore.

I had vague memories of so much laughter in our home and of being loved.

A year or so later, he was dead. Mom hadn't dealt with his death very well and had disappeared for several years. I'd lived with Grandma until she had to go into a nursing home.

I'd been left feeling abandoned and so totally alone. All the security of being with loving parents had been yanked away.

For two years after my grandmother went into the nursing home, I'd been shuffled through a variety of foster homes until I'd landed with the Connor family. Friends of my parents, they'd been searching for me.

They were doctors, and I was a sixth-grader with thick glasses and a penchant for reading every book she could find. We'd been a terrific match.

Though—and maybe it had been because I was so young—I never felt quite secure. I worried if I wasn't perfect, I might land in the system again.

I studied hard and made excellent grades. I didn't party like the other kids for fear my new family might abandon me.

It wasn't until the second year of med school that Mom came back into my life. She'd been full of apologies and regrets, but it had taken me years of therapy to come close to forgiveness. She lived long enough for us to build a friendship of sorts.

Now, she was gone, and I had no other family, at least as far as I knew.

"You okay?" A deep voice said from beside me.

I jumped—and maybe squeaked.

What was with my nerves?

I considered myself a calm person, but I'd been jumpy since I'd arrived in Sea Isle.

"I didn't hear you," I said breathlessly. And I should have noticed this guy. He was handsome in an Old Spice kind of way. Did they even make that anymore?

He wore a navy cable-knit sweater and dark jeans. I couldn't look away from his blue-green eyes.

At least a foot taller than me, he was fit. And his hair had a small strip of silver in the front.

"You seemed to be in a daze," he said. Then he smiled, and his teeth were perfectly white.

What is wrong with me?

"The fishing poles sent me back to some happy childhood memories. Sorry about that. I'm Emilia." I held out my hand and he shook it.

"Emilia . . . I just heard that name." He snapped his fingers. "The doctor my aunt and uncle have been talking about."

"You're related to the Wilsons?"

"Aye. Are you looking to start fishing again?"

I laughed, but it came out as more of a wheezy cough. "Uh, I was wondering if you could help me with my case."

"Your case?"

"Yes, I'm investigating the death of Mr. Smithson Brown."

"Poor Smithy." He tsked. After he walked behind the counter, he leaned his elbows on it. "Not sure how I can be of help."

"Were you friends?"

He laughed out loud. "Sorry. No. Acquaintances perhaps. The only friend Smithy ever had was my uncle. At least, as far as I know. He owed a lot of people money, including me. If he saw you coming, he'd cross the street to avoid ya."

"That seems to be a common theme with the deceased."

"Not the friendliest chap. Do you know how he died? I heard a rumor that maybe you were the one who killed him, but I'm having a tough time believing that tale."

I snorted. "No. It wasn't me. Since I'm investigating, I can't say much more than that."

"I see," he said, though, the curiosity in his eyes said otherwise.

"Can you tell me what you did know about him? He had to have passed by here nearly every day."

"That he did. We've played cards. He loses every time, which is why he owes half the town money."

"You gambled with him?"

"You make it sound like we're doing something bad. Just a friendly game now and again."

"I'm not judging, just curious. Any chance you saw his workers take his ship out yesterday?"

He shook his head. "They leave a good hour before I get to the shop. The boat was gone yesterday when I arrived."

"Did you see what time they came back?"

He sucked a breath through his teeth. "Nae. I closed a bit early yesterday. I went into Edinburgh to meet with some friends. I was surprised to see it here this morning. Like I said, they usually leave before I get in. But when I went to grab breakfast at the pub, I heard what happened. Smithy wasn't a good man, but no one wished him dead."

Someone did.

"If you think of anything else, can you give me a call?" I wrote down my number and tore the paper from my notebook. "Do you mind if I get your number? Just in case I think of something else?"

He smiled again. "You can call whenever you like, Emilia, whether it's for the *case* or not."

Heat burned my cheeks.

I'm too old to blush.

I cleared my throat. "Thanks."

"There is one thing," he said. "It probably isn't true."

I'd just turned to go out the door, so I faced him again.

"No detail is too small." I was certain I'd heard that on a television show years ago.

"There's a rumor going around that Smithy liked to blackmail folks. As I said, I don't have any idea if that's true. But there may be something to it. The man blew every cent he made. Yet, he's been able to keep his fishing business going."

Except for the last few weeks, when he hadn't paid his crew members.

"Hmm. I'll check into that. Thank you for helping me, uh . . ." I forgot to ask his name. Great detective work.

"It's Craig."

"Thanks, Craig. See you later."

Money kept coming up in this case.

Okay, Smithy, who were you blackmailing?

51

Chapter Seven

Thoughts rambled through my head as I climbed up the steps to cross over the seawall that protected the main drag. The pastel-colored shops were neatly painted and reminded me of tiny tea cakes. Everything was so neat and fresh here.

The pictures the recruiter sent in the email for the job, coupled with the coincidence of my DNA, had drawn me here. The photos didn't do Sea Isle justice.

My stomach grumbled, and the delicious-looking cakes in the window of the Time for Tea Shoppe drew me in like a bear to honey.

"Afternoon," the lanky man behind the counter said. "Take any table you like, and I'll bring a menu for you."

Intricately designed iron tables and chairs spaced around the front of the shop, and the walls covered in beautiful hand-painted murals, gave the feeling of sitting in a beautiful garden. The flowers were so realistic, one might want to lean over and smell them.

There were a few people at other tables, but as soon as they turned to see who had come in, the chatter stopped.

They can't know who I am. It must be that I'm a stranger.

I tried to ignore the piercing gazes by concentrating on the glass cases full of artful patisserie.

The man delivered some pots of tea, and plates of sandwiches to a few of the patrons and then ambled over to me.

"Hello, luv, you must be the new doctor." He smiled. Tall and slim, his hands moved gracefully when he spoke.

"Does everyone know?"

He pulled the pencil from behind his ear, and then a pad of paper from his pocket. "We're on the tail end of tourist season, so not many new faces, and word gets around. Besides, I'm friends with Mara, who can't stop talking about how kind and beautiful you are."

"That is sweet of her. I feel the same way about her, and at least, someone is saying kind words. The rest of the town seems determined to accuse me of murdering a man I didn't know."

He chuckled. "You are suddenly so much more interesting than I imagined."

I smiled. "In case you're curious, I didn't kill him." I said the last bit a little louder for the rest of the teahouse patrons.

"Good to know. What do you want to drink?"

Espresso straight up, but I was in a teahouse. "What's the strongest brew you have? I'm still suffering a bit from jet lag."

"I have several different kinds of black teas, or I could make you an Americano with a double shot." He whispered the last bit.

"You serve coffee?" I whispered back, since this seemed to be a secret of sorts.

He winked. "Only to friends."

"If you can make that happen, we will be best friends."

He held out his hand. "I'm Jasper."

I shook it. "I'm Emilia."

"I'll get your drink ready while you look at the menu. I do a smashing mozzarella and sun-dried tomato panini if you're needing some lunch—though the chicken salad croissant is popular as well."

He went off to the kitchen, and I glanced down at the thick paper he'd handed me. There was an array of sandwiches, a few salads and soups listed in beautifully done calligraphy, but he had me at the word "mozzarella."

When he returned, I gave him my order. It wasn't long before he came back with two plates. "Do you mind if I join you?"

"Of course not—I'm happy for the company. How long have you owned the tea shop?"

"It was ma and pop's, and I took over a year ago. Mom still does some of the baking, and Pop does the books. But they're off traveling now. What made you decide to land in Sea Isle?" he asked.

I'd just taken a bite of the sandwich, which was delicious. The chatter had quieted down again, as if they were all listening for my answer. In Seattle, no one cared who you were or what you had to say.

I'd been looking for a community where people looked out for one another. Now, I had to learn how to be a part of one that was extremely close-knit.

"Have you ever wanted to run away from home?"

He laughed. "I did. I worked in France as a pastry chef for years before coming back here."

"Oh, that sounds exciting. I love France. Though, I haven't visited in a while."

"And now you're wondering why I would give all of that up to come back here, but you first," he said.

"I'd been working in the ER for years. It's high stress, constant conflict, and incredibly demanding all the time. I loved it.

"That is until the last few years. I had a serious case of burnout. That, coupled with a few tragedies in a row, made it harder to get up and go to work in the morning.

"When the recruiter messaged me about the job here, it seemed like a sign."

"Hmm," he said. He leaned back in his chair and crossed his arms.

"What?" I asked.

"You don't seem the type to chuck it all on a whim."

This time I laughed. "You're right. If anything, I'm quite practical most of the time. It was the pictures they sent of the town. You must admit it's beautiful here. That, and around the same time I'd done one of those DNA tests and discovered I had ancestors here. It is strange to say I was drawn to it, but I was."

"And then you found poor Smithy on your first day. I'm surprised you weren't instantly on a flight back to the States."

I smirked. "It may have crossed my mind, but I promised no matter what, I'd give myself time to settle in and really experience the place. Now, your turn."

He sighed. "My heart had been broken, and it's incredibly difficult to open a shop anywhere in France, especially a patisserie."

I gave him a sad frown, and waited for him to continue.

"Here, it's something special that you can't find just anywhere in Scotland. In Paris, I'd just be another in many great shops.

"And we have being drawn to this place in common. I'd learned through some misadventures that I need grounding and stability. Having my parents around gives me that."

A darkness passed across his eyes. I wouldn't push further on the misadventures.

"Did you by chance know Smithy?"

He smiled again, though not with the same light as before.

"Not well. I saw him in the pubs a few times. He wasn't one to make friends easily, from what I understand. Poor Abigail had her hands full with Smithy and Tommy."

"Abigail?"

"Your housekeeper, luv. Have you not been introduced yet?"

"Oh, right—Abigail. I've met so many people the last twenty-four hours. Did I mention the jet lag?"

"Smithy is—I mean *was*—Abigail and Tommy's uncle. Though, they aren't particularly proud of the fact. Who could blame them? The cruel bastard was mean to poor Tommy from what I understand. Smithy took them in when their parents went missing at sea.

"Abigail had to raise her brother, clean, and cook. She was only twelve at the time. We were in school together. She went from being a chatter box to a mouse." He frowned again.

"What do you mean?"

"She's a good girl, Abigail. She's had to put up with more than most. She used to be the life of the party, as much as you can be when you're a kid. Smithy worked hard to kill the good in people.

"It's terrible, but I don't think there's a soul that lives here who will miss him."

Had Smithy pushed Abigail too far? She was extremely protective of Tommy. I'd seen more than one case of mentally and physically abused patients who struck back at their oppressors.

I stared down at my plate. Abigail was a few inches shorter than me and had a tiny frame. She would have had to be standing on something and to have a great deal of power to do damage like that.

If I had the body to examine, it would be easier to identify the exact type of force needed.

I sighed.

"Everything all right, luv?" he asked.

I didn't mind the endearment. People here used it all the time.

"Yes. Thanks to your sandwich, one of the best I've ever had."

"Bless, you. The secret is I make my own cheese. I picked the art up when I was in France. There's nothing better than fresh cheese."

"I agree. Except for, maybe, cake." I laughed.

He tapped the side of his head. "Now, where might we find some of that? Be right back."

Was it worth upsetting Abigail by asking about her uncle?

Then there was the fact that she and Tommy had keys and access to the body. It didn't look as though the doors had been jimmied, which meant I'd accidentally left it unlocked, or someone had come in with a key.

Was my new housekeeper a killer?

* * *

56

After stopping for a few groceries so I didn't have to eat every meal at the pub, I headed home.

"Abigail, are you here?" I called out as I let myself in but there was no answer. The front area had been cleaned and the chairs spaced out. As I went by the examination rooms, those were ready for patients too.

She's been busy.

I made my way to the kitchen to put my things away, only to find she'd stocked the fridge with fruit, vegetables, and eggs. After adding my bits, I decided to check the walk-in freezer. Maybe someone had put the body back.

No such luck. The room, though, had been cleaned to the corners. The muddy boot prints from the night before were gone, as well as the debris on the table.

I sighed.

No body. No evidence. Maybe Ewan was right—was it worth investigating a murder when there was no body?

Yes.

Smithy deserved justice. There was the small fact that finding the real killer meant people wouldn't think the worst of me.

The espressos finally kicked in. The doctor's old files were in the office. Smithy was bound to have something in there.

I fast-walked to the front of the church. I searched the reception desk for the key to the files but didn't find anything.

After yanking on one of the wooden handles so hard it made my shoulder hurt, I reconsidered. I pulled the keyring with the house key and found the small flat key for the file drawers.

"Genius."

Okay, not so much genius as lucky, but the key worked.

Smithy's file was in the second drawer under "Brown." I opened it. Empty.

"Why would someone steal his medical records?" It didn't make any sense. They could have easily disposed of the file, and I would never have known he was a patient.

Again, there were only a few people who might have needed to get rid of evidence *and* had access to these files. One of them stuck out in my mind.

Abigail.

Back in the kitchen, I started a to-do list.

At the top I wrote:

1. Conversation with my housekeeper.

Chapter Eight

By the time I showered and dressed, Abigail already had coffee brewing downstairs. She was in the room where we kept the medicines, unloading boxes.

"Abigail, I'm making myself a cup of coffee. Would you like some?"

She turned to face me and looked surprised.

"I can get it." She wiped her hands on the apron she wore.

"It's no big deal. You're busy. I'm hoping you and I can go through the inventory together. Do you like cream or sugar?"

She smiled warily. "Both."

"Is something wrong? Did I offend you in some way?" There were so many customs here I'd yet to learn. I needed her to feel comfortable with me.

Waving her hands, she shook her head. "No. No. It's just that I'm used to being the one doing the serving."

I remembered everything Jasper had said about the light going out of her eyes after her parents died.

"No worries. I'll be back in a bit."

It took me a minute to work the coffee maker, but I figured it out. I left mine black, put cream and sugar in hers, and then grabbed a tray. I put the sugar bowl on it, with the cups, in case she needed more.

She'd flipped on several lamps, and it helped illuminate the dark room. Every wall was covered in shelves, and I'd seen many pharmacies that didn't have this kind of inventory.

"You've done a great job keeping this in order," I said.

"Thank you." She sipped her coffee. "We had to send all of what was here before to be destroyed, as it was out of date. Ewan asked me to make a list, so you wouldn't have to worry about it, and we ordered much of the same stock."

"Is it normal in Scotland to keep such a full inventory in the office? Most patients are sent to a pharmacist to fill their prescriptions where I live."

"I don't know about other places, but winters can feel like one long blizzard at times. As I said yesterday, if you feel 'tis too much, or wasteful, we can change it however you like." She didn't say it as a judgment of any sorts. Nor did she seem upset that I'd challenged the way they did things.

She didn't seem like a killer, but I'd read many case studies and had seen my fair share of that sort of thing in the ER. Bad things sometimes happened when people were pushed too far.

"Oh no. I'm grateful we have this available, and you mentioned the pharmacist had odd hours. I imagine it's much more convenient for the patients."

She smiled, and she looked so much younger. "He's a nice man, but he does like to fish and likes his naps. At almost ninety, he takes two a day."

"I'm a big fan of naps as well. I guess I'll have to brush up on my dispensing skills."

She put her cup down. "I can help during office hours since you'll be quite busy. I'm not certified, but the doc found it easier to check my work than to take the time to do it himself."

"Oh, okay. That will be helpful. How good is Tommy with a paintbrush? I'd like to make the waiting area and exam rooms more inviting for patients."

She smiled. "That's a grand idea. If we give Tommy clear instructions, he can do anything. I can order the paint from the hardware store if you give me an idea on color."

I opened my phone to show her the teal-blue I'd been thinking about. It was a calming color.

"Aye, that's beautiful."

"People are always so anxious when they come to the doctor. I always said if I went into private practice, I'd make the place as spa-like as possible."

"It's grand, truly grand," she said.

"I'm glad you like the idea." I cleared my throat. "There's something else I could use your assistance with if you don't mind."

"I'm here to help," she said.

I pursed my lips, and my stomach twisted. "I don't want to pry, but I'm curious about something."

There was a large desk with a chair. She sat down and then tucked her hair behind her ear.

"Is it about Uncle?"

I sat on the edge of the desk. "Yes. I need some background. And since you've cleaned everything, you must know the body is missing."

Her head jerked up, and her eyes were wide. "Missing? I thought you'd sent him to the funeral parlor."

"No. The constable and I are trying to keep it quiet for now."

She'd been as surprised as I was about the body.

Twisting her apron in her hands, she tried to speak, then stopped.

"I won't say a word," she said. "May I ask a favor of you?"

"Yes, anything." I liked Abigail, even more now that I understood her background. Women like her, who had pushed past their circumstances, deserved my respect. It was more than obvious she'd made herself indispensable to the former doctor, and I admired that.

"I haven't told Tommy. He was asleep when Ewan stopped by to explain about Uncle, and death is one of the concepts he has a difficult time understanding. Ewan seemed to think it was an accident, which wouldn't surprise me."

"The constable and I have different opinions. Since he's your uncle, I don't feel right describing the injuries, but they would have been difficult to sustain without some sort of force."

Her hand flew to her mouth. "Are you saying someone murdered him?"

"That's what I'm trying to find out. I'll keep your secret, and I'm begging you to keep mine."

Could Tommy have confronted his uncle alone? Maybe Smithy yelled at him, and Tommy reacted. I didn't want to think such a thing, but I had to investigate all possibilities.

"I'll need to hold a wake. He was the only family Tommy and I have left. I was worried about no one showing up, but I have to do something."

I wrapped her cold hands in mine. "Abigail, I am truly sorry for your loss, and I promise to help you however I can. There are a few more questions if you're up for it."

"Go ahead." She forced a smile.

Here it goes . . . "Was your uncle kind to you?"

She blinked as if she hadn't understood the words.

"Aye, you've been listening to the gossips." She pulled her hands from mine. "No. He wasn't particularly kind, but he gave me and Tommy shelter when we had none. He could be cruel at times, especially when he was frustrated with my brother, but he kept us fed and a roof over our heads. So, I've no complaint with Uncle."

I'd completely offended her. "There is something you should know about me," I said.

Her mouth was a tight line.

"I don't know if you have this phrase here, but I lay my cards on the table, and I tend to go at things directly. I had heard a few stories, but I'm a person who appreciates facts. I feel like your uncle deserves to have this case solved properly."

She was the only one in town who'd had a kind word for Smithy.

"Ewan said he fell down drunk," she said.

I rubbed the bridge of my nose.

"Right. Well, the body was taken before we could establish cause of death, and I wasn't quite as certain as the laird that it was from a fall."

"You're a good doctor, or they'd not have called you here. But it kinna be murder. No one is murdered in Sea Isle. It doesn't happen."

So, I've heard.

"Right. As I said, the body was gone before I could establish exactly what happened to him. Do you know of anyone who might want to take his body?"

"It's evil doings." She made the sign of the cross and then kissed her crucifix.

"Maybe someone close to your family?"

"My auntie and cousins live in London, and they've not wanted anything to do with him since they left twenty years ago."

Abigail twisted her apron again, and it was obvious she needed a moment. Maybe, I could find out more about Smithy's family from Mr. Wilson. Abigail had been through enough.

"There's one last thing I need to know, and I'm sorry to ask."

"'Tis all right, Doctor. You're only doing your job."

I smiled. "Thanks. It's been mentioned once or twice that your uncle may have—there is no easy way to say this—that he might have been blackmailing some people. Do you know anything about that?"

She raised her eyebrows. "No."

It was probably just a rumor.

"But I wouldn't have put it past him. Uncle had a wicked streak and didn't mind taking advantage of people. Tommy and I moved out once I got the job with the doctor."

A shadow passed over her eyes.

"Are you sure he was never cruel to you? Did he hurt you?"

She chewed on her lip. "I know what you're thinkin', but no. He never touched me one way or the other. He did raise his hand to

Tommy a few times, but Ewan helped put a stop to that. Most of the time he just ignored us. He'd stumble in to go to bed and stumble out the next morning. We seldom saw him."

I put a hand on her shoulder and squeezed. "Are you sure you don't want some time off? You've already done so much around here, and you deserve time to mourn."

She sighed and patted my hand. "You're a kind one, and thank you. I prefer to keep busy. Nothing to do at home but be alone with my thoughts. Tommy's been agitated the last few days, and he needs his garden and his chores."

Had Tommy run across Smithy in the woods? He may not have meant to hurt the older man, but if Smithy had been abusive . . .

"Just so I have it for the records. Where were you and Tommy around five or so the day your uncle died?"

"It's starting to feel like I'm on *Vera*," she said, but she smiled. "Do you know that show?"

"One of my favorites," I said.

"Mine too." She closed her eyes. "Let me think. After we finished our chores here, I took Tommy to Fishies," she said. "It's his favorite. We ate down by the pier. We've been doing that almost every day this week."

"Fishies?"

She smiled sweetly. "Yes, the best fish and chips in Scotland, or so the sign says. Though, they are the best I've ever had."

Thank goodness, they had an alibi. I'd just met them, but I had a soft spot for the brother and sister.

"About a month ago Uncle tried to borrow money, but I couldn't help 'im. For once, he was nice about it. We haven't seen 'im since."

She turned around, and a worried look came onto her face. "I need to check on Tommy, and then I can take you through the inventory."

I smiled and nodded. "Take your time. There's no rush."

Abigail had to deal with so much more than a young woman should. And though she might not want to speak ill of Smithy, a life with him as a guardian couldn't have been easy.

I locked the door to the in-house pharmacy.

After grabbing a small notebook from my purse, I sat down at the beautiful kitchen table. I had no idea what kind of wood it was made of, but it appeared ancient. Woodland animals had been carved into the center, but it was in no way kitschy.

Opening my notes app on my phone, I wrote down a list of people I'd talked to so far. Most murders were committed by someone close to the victim. I'd be able to rule out Abigail and Tommy once I visited Fishies to make sure they'd been there.

The brothers, who worked with Smithy, were each other's alibi. So, they moved to the top of the list. There was no love lost there, and I hadn't been able to verify their story.

I forced my brain to slow down. It was a trick I used in the ER because everything happened so fast. I was lucky to have a brain that remembered details even when it was a blur to most people. It made it so much easier to finish reports at the end of a shift.

I replayed the night in my head, including standing half naked in my kitchen with Ewan.

The constable had access to the building. He'd also showed up to the bothy rather quickly. Had he been in the area the whole time?

My heartbeat quickened.

Was the constable trying to get away with murder?

Chapter Nine

The next morning, I headed up the mountain to the county clerk's office. Seeing my last name on the boat's title had made me more than a little curious about who Theodore McRoy might have been.

I'd had nightmares where Smithy popped up wherever I went and yelled, *"It's your fault I'm dead."* When I awoke, I was determined to shove that voice out of my head, at least for a few hours.

Abigail had drawn me a crude map, which I pulled from my pocket. The records building was up the mountain and across the street from the library. She'd drawn boxes for each of the buildings.

"You'll also find more shops," she said. Excited about the prospect of getting to know the town better and finding information about my family, I started up the mountain.

About a third of the way up, I convinced myself this was great exercise after all the pub food I'd been eating. I stopped to catch my breath. A Land Rover pulled up beside me, and the dark window rolled down.

"Are you all right, lass?"

I stopped myself from rolling my eyes. The one man I'd hoped to avoid peered out the window.

"Yes," I said breathlessly. Crud. He probably thought I was swooning for him.

"You're a wee bit pale."

"Pale is my natural color. Did you need something?"

"As a matter of fact, I do." He smiled and I wished he hadn't. What was it about these Scottish men? They were all so handsome, and I had no interest in that part of my life. My former husband had made sure of that.

After what I'd been through, I was sticking to my career. I'd travel Europe, maybe take up knitting. At some point, I'd get a dog. I'd heard dogs were full of unconditional love, and that was as far as I might go when it came to commitment.

I wasn't even ready for that yet.

"What is it?"

"Tell me where you're going, and I'll drop you off."

He didn't look like a killer, but then neither had Ted Bundy.

The last thing I wanted to do was get in a car with this man. "To the county clerk's office."

He frowned. "Get in."

My hands trembled. There was no one on the road. We were alone.

"Why were you so close to the bothy?"

"What?"

"You heard me."

"I was coming down the mountain to make sure you were sorted and ask if you needed anything."

That was a nice but handy excuse.

"Do you have an alibi for when Smithy was killed?"

He shook his head and then chuckled.

He thought all of this was so funny.

"I left the house about twenty minutes before I found you. My housekeeper will confirm the time."

"Your housekeeper, who is paid by *you*."

A giant raindrop fell on my nose.

"Get in the car before you soak," he said. "I didn't kill Smithy, and I would never hurt you. I've gone through hell trying to get a doctor to Sea Isle; I'm not about to off her."

The stinging rain pelted down. I opened the door and climbed in. The heated leather seat was a welcome warmth to my backside.

"What is it you want to know?"

He shifted the car into gear. "I heard you'd been doing an investigation into Smithy's death. I thought we'd discussed that."

"We did. You said you weren't sure it was murder. I showed you proof it was. That is, when we still had a body."

He looked at her, raising one eyebrow.

"You didn't want to investigate, so I took it upon myself. I looked up the responsibilities of a coroner, and it's within my rights to do so. And while I've discovered the victim was not exactly a celebrated town hero, his murderer should not be allowed to run free."

He grinned. "I see. I never said I wouldn't investigate. I was busy with other affairs."

"But you don't agree with me."

"I didn't say that. As the constable, I'm curious what you've found so far."

I wasn't about to mention the blackmail book that might be hidden somewhere. Secrets didn't last long in Sea Isle, so he could hear that from someone else.

"I spoke with the men who worked with him."

"You talked to them by yourself? You need to be more careful. They run in a rough crowd."

Maybe it wasn't so much being a know-it-all as it was a protector syndrome he had going on.

"I think you've forgotten the part where you weren't interested. I always carry pepper spray with me. Though it wasn't necessary. They were complete gentlemen."

That was a stretch, but I'd dealt with far worse men in far worse places.

"Gentlemen, my arse." He snorted.

"I spoke with Jasper at the tea shop, and Abigail. Oh, and Craig at the bait shop. I'm guessing you knew all of that, and I'm certain I didn't learn anything you don't already know."

"Just the same, give me the abbreviated version."

"Smithy wasn't a nice guy. He owed a great deal of money to a lot of people, including his workers. Then there is the fact he wasn't the best guardian for Abigail and Tommy, though she doesn't seem to hate him for it."

"Good work."

"Excuse me?"

"For someone with no experience, you learned a great deal in a day. I was worried about your ability to do this side of the job."

"The side of the job you hid in the fine print?"

He chuckled. "You had your barrister read the contract before you signed. It's not my fault you're forgetful."

Argh. This man.

"But in the future, it might be a good idea if myself or one of my men were with you. They know our people. That way we don't have to worry about you offending anyone."

"I wouldn't do that."

"What do you plan to do next?"

"Tomorrow, I'd like to go back to the scene. He wasn't killed in the bothy, and someone had to carry him. That means the crime scene is probably close by. Even though it rained, I might find something."

"Good. I'll pick you up at seven in the morning. We can't risk our new doctor getting lost in the Highlands."

I know someone who can get lost.

"You never said where you were going."

I glanced up to find another adorable part of the town. There were a mix of old stone buildings and the same pastel wooden ones as on the seafront.

"The records office. Someone mentioned that I had a relative who lived here years ago."

"Aye, we've had McRoys live here off and on for as long as I can remember."

"We may not be related, but I thought I might check the records."

He parked in front of an old stone building.

"Is this it?"

"Aye. Doctor?"

"Yes," I said in a huff.

"The clerk's office is closed today. It's Millie's day off, and her assistant is on maternity leave."

My jaw tightened. "And you couldn't mention this before?"

"You didn't ask."

I slammed the door before I gave into the urge to leap across the seat and punch his face. I wasn't a violent person, but he brought out the absolute worst in me.

The window rolled down again.

"Doctor?" He had the nerve to smile.

"Yes," I hissed.

"Do you need a ride down the mountain?"

"No, thank you." I said angrily and then stomped off, with no idea where I might be going.

The scent of fresh-baked bread lured me around the corner and away from the frustrating constable.

There were colorful hanging baskets in front of the shops, with planter boxes along the sidewalk. The rain had stopped, but it was much cooler up here. I put on the green sweater Abigail had insisted I bring with me.

On the corner, I turned to look down the mountain at the beautiful sea view.

None of this seemed real.

I shivered and glanced around. When would I get over the feeling that someone was watching me? Maybe my paranoia came from being in a new place. There were others on the street, but they were busy talking or watering the flowers.

The Breadery was across the street.

I crossed over at the corner. The last thing I needed was the constable writing me up for jaywalking.

"'Allo," the smiling woman at the counter said, and waved me in. "We have the fresh bread." She wasn't Scottish, but I couldn't place the accent. There was a hint of Italian mixed with something else.

"Hi," I said. "Your shop smells wonderful."

Her smile grew. *"Danka."*

German? It would be rude to ask, but I was curious. Her hair was in a black cap, and she wore a white shirt with black and white striped pants. She was probably in her late sixties, but it was her smile that drew me closer.

"We have many breads. What do you like?"

I smiled back. "Everything." Give me some bread and butter, and I was a happy woman.

She clapped her hands. "This is good for business."

I laughed. At least, she was honest.

"I'm new here, so what would you suggest I try first?"

"Is it just you?" It wasn't a rude question. She was asking about the amount I might need.

"Yes. Are there Scottish breads? Maybe I should try one of those?"

"No, no. I have something special." There were two stone ovens behind her. She took a large paddle and scooped up a round loaf.

"Fresh focaccia," she said. "Mama's recipe."

"Excellent." I wanted to eat the air it smelled so good.

The paddle dropped from her hands and clattered to the floor. She grabbed her shoulder, her face white with pain.

"What's wrong?" I moved around the side of the counter.

"Okay. It's okay. The bad pain goes away." She tried to lift her arm and grimaced. "Sorry."

She seemed to be embarrassed. "You are in a great deal of pain." I went to touch her shoulder, but she stepped back.

I held my hands up. "I'm Dr. Emilia McRoy, and I'm taking over the practice down the hill."

Her eyes opened wide. "Oh. Bless you. Bless you."

I smiled. "I'd like to help with your shoulder. If you'll let me?"

"It's okay."

"Please," I insisted. Living with the kind of pain I knew she must have was unnecessary.

She nodded.

I'd done a year with a doctor of osteopathic medicine, and had worked in orthopedics before doing my residency, and it still amazed me how many medical problems could be solved without surgery or drugs.

In the ER, I used those skills daily for pinched nerves and a variety of other aches and pains.

I probed her shoulder with my fingers. It was a mass of knots and inflamed on the right side. A quick touch down her spine, and I felt the displacement.

I stepped in front of her. "Cross your arms like this." I showed her what I wanted. "I'm going to lift you slightly from behind."

Wrapping my arms around her, I grabbed her elbows. "Take a deep breath and let it out."

She did as I asked, and I lifted her arms slightly, and the pop of her vertebrae was loud.

I let go and she stood there a moment without moving. From behind, her shoulders had already fallen back into alignment.

She lifted her arms above her head and laughed.

"Buona, Buona. Grazie." That much Italian I understood.

"You're welcome," I said. "Why don't you come by the office next week? I'd like to scan that area to make sure it doesn't pop back out on you, and maybe prescribe something to help with the inflammation."

"Si," she said.

She wrapped the bread in a blue checked cloth and tied it with rough brown twine.

I moved back to the other side of the counter. "How much do I owe you?"

"No. No. Everything is free for you. Take as much as you like." She waved my money away. "We take care of the doctor, and the doctor takes care of us."

"I know that's how it used to be, but I'd feel better if you'd let me pay you."

She waved the money away again.

"You helped me." She pointed to her shoulder. "Many years the pain. You take." She handed the bread to me.

"What's your name?"

She clapped her hands. "I am Flora. Thank you, Doctor."

After another try, I gave up on trying to pay her.

At the gourmet food store next door, I picked up some olive oil, balsamic vinegar, cheeses, feta-stuffed olives, and beautiful tomatoes. With food like this, I would not be going hungry any time soon.

There was a shop with several different types of plaid fabric in the window. The name, "Buth Feileadh," was in Gaelic across the door in gold lettering. Curious, I stepped inside.

Learning a bit of Gaelic would go on my list of things I needed to do while I was in Scotland.

"Oh, it's the doctor. I nearly came outside to pull ya in. How are you?" The woman was tall, curvy, and had royal-blue hair pulled back in a ponytail. She wore a short kilt with a sweater, tights, and Doc Martens. The punk-rock chic worked for her.

"I'm great. You have beautiful fabrics, and I thought I'd come inside to see if you have scarves."

She put her hands on her hips. "Of course, we do." She rolled her "R" and it took me a minute to figure out what she'd said.

"I'm Emilia McRoy," I said.

"Oh, everyone in town knows your name, luv. We're so happy to 'ave ya here. Let's see, was there a particular color you might want? Oh, and I'm Angie."

"Hi, Angie. I wondered if—" I stumbled over the words. "I understand that I had ancestors in the area, and I was wondering if they had particular colors."

Tapping a long blue nail against her cheek, she stood there for a few seconds. "McRoy. Let me look in the book."

She opened what seemed to be a huge Bible with a leather cover. Except inside, there were colored drawings of plaids with names in Gaelic scrawled across the top.

"Aye. MacRae, derivative. Do you know your clan?"

"No, I'm afraid I don't. I don't want to offend anyone by wearing the wrong colors. I read that in one of the books I have on Scotland. I'd hoped to do a bit of research, but the clerk's office was closed."

"Aye. It's Millie's day off, and her hips been bugging her, so she may not be in the rest of the week. Granddad," she yelled.

The shriek was so loud, my eyebrow lifted.

"'e's 'ard of 'earing," she said by way of explanation.

"Aye. Aye. Hold ye—" The stooped, white-haired man put on his glasses and stared at me like I had two heads.

"Who is this?"

"Granddad, this is the new doctor. She used to have family in the area. The McRoys. She's looking for her colors."

He frowned. "McRoy, you say?"

"Yes, sir."

"Hmm. Any relation to Teddy McRoy? Now, that was a good man. Best vicar we ever had, and he didn't bore the pants off ya with his sermons. Played a mean game of poker, that one."

"I don't know if I'm related to him, but I'd like to find out. I planned to do some research today, but I didn't know about it being Millie's day off."

"Aye, and that hip of hers is acting up. Always does this time of year."

"I did a DNA test, and some of my ancestors came through here, so I know that much."

"Good. Good. We've had McRoys in Sea Isle up until about fifty years ago. The last of them was the vicar, as far as I know. He had a brother."

He patted his long white beard. "Ricky—no, Mickey, I think they called him. Teddy stayed here with the dad, and their mother took Mickey with her to the States. Quite the scandal back in the day."

Mickey? An old memory of my parents talking in the kitchen. I was coloring. They'd been laughing at something Grandma had said. Maybe it was a joke.

"That Mickey, he had the best stories," Grandma said.

Oh. Oh.

Who was Mickey to Grandma? Did I have an ancestor who had been a vicar? And why was his name on Smithy's boat?

I wanted to find out.

Chapter Ten

While Angie's granddad looked through the enormous book, she took me around the shop to show me the different styles of kilts and outerwear they had. The tartan colors were so vibrant and beautiful, I wished I could have one of each. There were also shoes, boots, and a variety of sweaters and coats.

"Are you set for the weather?"

"I bought a coat," I said.

She laughed. "I'm not trying to sell you things you don't need, but summer ends quickly here. You'll be needing more than a coat if you want to leave your house. I'll make a list, so as you're shopping, you'll know what ya need."

"Thank you. That's kind and I appreciate it."

"Lassie, I found something that will work," her granddad said.

We headed back to the counter, and he turned the enormous book around. Then he pointed to a beautiful red tartan. Crossing the red were small lines of white, and thicker ones that looked to be royal blue. Then a few spots were green.

"That's beautiful."

"Aye," he said. "It's a modern version designed about a hundred years ago."

I bit my lip to keep from laughing. Modern was the last hundred years in Scotland. In America, many people considered something ten years old vintage.

"Oh, that's going to be a lovely color with your complexion," Angie said. "Granddad, when do you think the scarf will be done?"

"'Tis done when it's done."

Angie rolled her eyes. "That usually means a couple of weeks. Let's put the order in, and I'll call when it's ready. If you're busy, I can drop it by for you."

"Oh, you don't have to do that," I said. "And I'd love to get one of those Macs you talked about."

"We'll put the fabric inside," she said. "It will keep you warm."

I glanced at the list she'd been making for me. I didn't have a single thing on there.

"We may need to add to my order."

By the time we'd finished, I'd spent a fair amount, but I was excited about it. The idea of belonging to a group of people like the MacRaes or McRoys, was appealing for someone who considered herself an orphan.

I desperately wished Millie's hips weren't bothering her. I wanted to find out more about my ancestors.

When I left, I peered into the window of a small bookshop, but it was closed for lunch. My library at my old house had been one of my favorite places. I'd stored all my books in the USA, until I was sure it would work out in Sea Isle.

Across the street, people were busy going in and out of a large stone building. It was the biggest one I'd seen in Sea Isle.

After checking in at the front desk, and getting my library card, I headed to the historical section. I wasn't disappointed. While I couldn't find a book about the MacRae clan, I did find some history books that had facts listed about them.

Sheila the librarian smiled when I returned to the counter to check them out. "Ah, good for you. It's best to know a place if you're going to live here."

"I agree," I said.

Happy with my collection of goods, and my research, I headed back down the hill. While it was much easier than going up it, my arms ached as I set the packages down at the door of the church.

The door opened and Tommy stood there with wide eyes. "Help," he said. Then he pushed past me and picked up my bags.

"Thank you," I said softly.

Before I could step inside, he pushed past me again, carrying everything I'd brought down the mountain. I followed him.

He placed the bags and books on the kitchen table. I expected to find Abigail, but she wasn't there.

"Where is your sister?" I asked.

He stared out the window toward the cemetery.

"Shop." He pointed out the window. "Come. Garden."

My blisters on my feet hurt. I had no wish to do any more walking, but I followed him out the back door.

Besides, I hadn't taken much time to explore the grounds of my new home. When he passed the cemetery and led me through an ivy-covered arch, I couldn't have been more surprised.

The cutting garden had been beautifully planned and maintained. About a quarter of an acre, it was full of blooms, some I recognized, others I didn't.

"Sit." He pointed to one of three iron benches placed throughout. I did as he asked and waited.

"What is that one?" I pointed to a pink flower behind him.

"Our Lady's thistle," he said. Then he pulled out garden shears and clipped three of the stems. He brought them over and laid them on the bench beside me.

He walked away to a different patch of flowers. "*Hyacinthoides non-scripta*—we also say blue bells." Tommy spoke eloquently of the flowers. "*Myrica gale.*" He pointed to a small shrub that had tiny pinecones growing out of it. He went around the garden, cutting blooms and laying them on the bench, explaining each one as he went.

"*Calluna vulgaris,*" he said. That one I did recognize as a type of heather. I was terrible with plants. I loved them, but my busy schedule didn't give me time to take care of them. I envied those with a green thumb.

He gathered the flowers in his arms and walked back to the house.

I laughed, but his reaching out to me with his language of flowers was a huge step in bonding with him. I followed him.

Inside, he was already cutting the stems like a pro and putting them in a vase he'd filled with water. I sat at the table. By the time he was done, the arrangement was better than any professional one I'd seen.

Then he set them on the table. "Yours."

I smiled up at him. "Thank you. They are gorgeous. You do fantastic work."

He made eye contact for a second and then smiled.

The back door opened, and Abigail came through with her arms full of parcels.

"Is he bothering you?" she asked worriedly.

"Not at all," I said. "He made this beautiful arrangement from the cutting garden. Tommy is quite talented."

"I am," he said.

Abigail and I smiled.

"Go fetch the things in the cart," she said to her brother. He obediently left.

Abigail set her things down on the counter.

"He's so knowledgeable about the plants," I said, "and he's kept the garden so beautifully."

"In the spring and summer, he works on it constantly," she said. "In the winter, Ewan lets him work in his greenhouse. I pick up books when I can for him because he likes to memorize everything about things that grow."

"You're brilliant for fostering that talent, Abigail. You and your brother constantly surprise me by how talented you are."

She blushed. I had a feeling her life had been seriously short of praise.

"I picked up some of the orders from the post box that hadn't come in yet," she said. "And Tommy cut you some logs for the fire-place. They are just outside the back door on the right."

I looked at her, puzzled. It was so lovely out today.

"The weather is about to change. I have the chimney sweep coming tomorrow to make sure everything is cleaned up. There is heating, but the boiler is finicky. And the Aga uses gas, which keeps the kitchen warm. But we keep the fires going most of the winter."

Still sweating from my trek down the mountain, a fire was the last thing on my mind.

"Thank you," I said. "I'll take care of the inventory tonight. You've done so much already. I did want to ask if you thought it might be okay if we open early."

"The office?" she asked.

I nodded. "I thought we could do what we call a soft open on Monday. I'll let Mara and the Wilsons know. That is, if it's okay with you."

She smiled. "Doctor, you're the one who makes the decisions around here. I'm here to help you."

"No, Abigail. We are in this together. I don't know what I would have done without you and Tommy. You are a godsend."

"What makes you want to open early?"

"Do you know Flora at the Breadery?"

She smiled. "Yes, she and her son make the best bread in Scotland. Everyone knows her."

"I worked on her shoulder today and I was wondering how the doctor took care of X-rays and such. Did he send people to the hospital in Edinburgh?"

She frowned. "'Ave ya not seen it?"

"Seen what?"

"The equipment room and surgery suite?"

"Where are they?"

"I'm daft. I can't believe I didn't take ya on a tour. Apologies."

"It's okay. I'm good at showing myself around but I haven't found them."

"Follow me," she said.

We went through the house and the long hallway between the examination rooms. Then out through the lobby area where it dead-ended into several bookcases.

She shoved one of the books in, and both bookcases opened to another long hallway.

"I've always wanted a secret door," I said.

She smiled. "This house has a few. Back in the day, when the tax men came, they'd hide many of the valuables. But Ewan and Uncle helped the old doc create this new area, which is part of the carriage house. C'mon, I'll show ye."

Her brogue had slipped back in as she took me down the hallway. Most of the time she sounded more British than Scottish. I had a feeling that might be an insult, so I didn't mention it. At the end of the hall, she pushed a button on one of the walls, and the doors opened.

Inside, I blew out a breath and shook my head. The large room was beautifully organized with state-of-the-art equipment. An open MRI, CT scan, and X–ray machines were at one end, and lab equipment at the other.

"This is incredible."

She smiled. "You can thank Ewan. He feels our town deserves the best, and he sees to it we have it. Since we don't have a hospital, and it's an hour in good weather to get to one, he wanted to make sure we were outfitted.

"There are two complete surgical suites." She motioned toward some glass doors off the room.

I went to see how they were laid out and found the suites could compare with those in any large American hospital.

She motioned me to follow her to the other side of the room, where there were more glass doors. "We have three recovery rooms—or if someone needs to be kept for observation."

I shook my head. "This is nothing like I imagined a small-town practice."

"It's been updated over the years and added to as Doc saw fit. But the MRI and a couple of the other machines are brand new. Ewan wanted to make sure you could do whatever was necessary."

"Did he pay for all of this?"

She shrugged. "He did or the town might have. They are one and the same. No one cares about Sea Isle the way he does. I can't tell you how many lives he's saved by making sure we had the right equipment."

I sighed. He didn't exactly sound like a murderer.

"You'll be curious about how the doctor ran all of this without a lab tech. I've passed all the certifications for every machine. And Doc paid for me to get my phlebotomist certification as well. I can run them all. I promise I'll keep working on the pharm tech certification, now that you're here."

I stared at her. "Abigail, what are you doing cleaning my house? If you can do all of this, why don't you have a job where you can make loads of money at a bigger hospital?"

She took a step back and frowned. "Why would I be wantin' to? Ewan and the doc have invested time and money into my education. I owe them my life, and Tommy's. I make a good living. Why would I want to leave?"

"I just mean—I'm sorry. I didn't mean to insult you."

"This is our home," she said angrily. "Tommy couldn't live anywhere else. Nor could I. A big city would drive us both mad."

"You're brilliant," I said quickly. "I keep saying that, but it's true. What you can do—it's just surprising is all. At home, most of our techs only work with one or two machines. Please, forgive me. I'm impressed by you, and I feel guilty that you're cleaning my house. I can hire someone else."

"Nae, it isn't necessary. You won't be needing me all the time with the machines. It's a small village, and we seldom use them. I help with the house and the office; that's been my job since I was fifteen, and I like learnin' new things." She tapped her forehead.

"So do I." You'll have to show me some day how these machines work," I told her. "I usually send patients upstairs for whatever they need and then their scans are sent to me. I have some catching up to do."

"Happy to help," she said. "And just so you know: Ewan, in addition to payin' mine and Tommy's salaries, loans us a cottage not far up the mountain, so we are always close if you need us."

I had no desire to change my mind about the hardheaded constable, but his taking care of Abigail and her brother had really moved him over to the side of the good guys.

"I have one more question," I said.

"What's that?" She stared at me warily. I couldn't blame her. Every five minutes I stuck my foot in my mouth and insulted her.

"How do the patients make their appointments?"

She laughed. "There's been a queue since you signed your contract," she said. "They call in and leave a message, and then I put them on the computer."

"All right then. Suppose you show me how to get into the system so I can start doing some homework on my new patients. That is, if they decide to show up."

We'd gone back down the hall, and she drew the bookcases closed.

"Why wouldn't they?"

"Well, some seem to think I had something to do with your uncle, um—"

She laughed, it was more of a honk, and it made me smile. "Bunch of gossiping idgits," she said. "They know you had nothing to do with it, but we Scottish love a good story. And everyone likes to talk about the new people. Pay no mind to their silliness."

"Thank you," I said. "For believing me."

She shrugged. "The way I see it, you saved the day. His bones would have been up there for months with no one knowing where he was."

"I hope not."

"You did us all a favor," she said. "And the villagers will come around once you get to doctoring. Though, you get a bit of drink in us, and there isn't a person in Sea Isle who doesn't gossip."

She sounded as if she'd had firsthand experience with the gossips.

Tommy came in the front door. "Ewan car," he said as he stared up at the ceiling.

"Ah, it's been delivered."

"Right." Tommy nodded twice. I had no idea what was going on, but I'd become a big fan of this brother and sister.

Abigail headed outside and Tommy followed.

I went out to see what they were talking about.

Ewan stood there next to another Range Rover. This one was a dark green. How many cars did this guy have?

He walked over and stuck the keys in my hand. "The shipment had been delayed, I apologize," he said.

"For what?" I was so confused.

"Your car. It was supposed to be here the day you arrived, but they ran late."

A car? This was too much. "No."

"No?"

"I don't want a car."

He frowned and then crossed his arms. "How do you plan on making house calls?"

"Let me guess, that's in the contract?"

"Aye." He nodded.

In my defense, the contract had been thirty pages long. Martha, my lawyer, had said everything was in order, and the benefits were wonderful. I'd skimmed it, but obviously I'd missed a few things.

"Well, then. I guess I have a car."

"Aye." He looked so smug.

"There's just one problem."

"What's that?"

"I don't know how to drive."

Chapter Eleven

By seven that night, I'd completed the inventory of the meds, glanced through patient files, and familiarized myself with the operating system Abigail had put in place for patient care.

At some point, I'd have a conversation with the laird to make certain Abigail and Tommy were being properly compensated. She did the job of ten or more people. I'd never met anyone like her.

What Ewan had said about this being a rural area, and that some of my patients might not be able to come into the office, made sense. I'd turned down his offer for driving lessons, which meant I had to find a teacher.

My phone dinged. It was a text from Mara to meet her upstairs at the pub.

This time when I went in the front door of the pub, no one stopped talking. They were all busy playing darts, and the music was ear splitting. I quickly snuck to the back and up the stairs.

The door was shut at the top of the stairs, and I knocked.

Mara opened it quickly and pulled me inside. "I have so much to tell ya."

I laughed. More from the joy of having someone so excited to see me than anything else.

"I made us decaf and brought up a friend of mine." She held up a bottle of Irish whiskey.

"Isn't Irish anything blasphemy around here?"

She waved a hand. "Never in a pub or a tourist town. My grand-dad says everyone does something well, and the Irish make a great whiskey."

We chuckled and then clinked cups.

"Slainte mhath," she said.

"Someday I'll learn how to say that. Now, tell me what's going on."

"Sean and Grady were in earlier," she said. "They were fussin' about how the laird wouldn't let them take Smithy's boat out. The pair of them were whispering when I delivered their lunch, and I overheard them talking about Smithy and blackmail."

"Really?" I acted surprised. Craig from the tackle shop had mentioned there was a possibility Smithy might be blackmailing people in town.

"Did you hear anything else?"

"Something about a book and that they needed to find it. Like most men, they whisper loud. Do you think old Smithy might have been doing that for real? I bet the person who killed him is in that book. We need to find it."

I agreed. "Any chance you know where Smithy's cottage is? When I talked to the brothers, they said he lived by the Glen. I wasn't sure where that was."

"I have a fair estimation. I'll help you if you wait until my day off. It's tricky around that area to get around. Did you find out anything about your ancestors?"

I shook my head. "The clerk's office was closed. But I went to a kilt store and discovered the tartan used for the MacRae and McRoy clans."

"Oh, well, that's quite something. Was Angie there? She's a hoot. We used to play together when I spent summers with the grandparents. She always got me into so much trouble, but we had fun. She's marrying an earl—or maybe it's a marquis; I can't remember. He's got a stick up his ass, but he seems to adore her."

"She helped me a great deal. Wait—she's marrying into royalty?"

Mara giggled. "I know, she doesn't seem the type, especially the way she dresses. But her family has gobs of money. Her dad's an investment banker, and her mom's a famous barrister. Like me, though, she spent her summers here. She bought the three shops—the one here and the others in Edinburgh and Glasgow—from her granddad when she was just out of university. She's smart, and she's turned the whole business into something huge on the internet."

The judging-books-by-their-covers idea never worked. I'd certainly learned that lesson coming to Sea Isle, but I was still surprised.

"Did you overhear anything else?" I asked.

"There is a rumor that the reason Margie's dog, Fred, was found with Smithy is that he might have stolen him. That dog is an annoying little thing, but he's a champion. He was worth a lot of money. The other side of that rumor is they were having an affair. Though, the affair is more likely with Lulu. And is it an affair if they are both single?"

I'd have to add Margie to my list of suspects.

"Who is Lulu?"

"Owns an adorable shop down the way. I stay out of there or I spend way too much money."

"You learned a lot today."

She laughed. "I usually tune out the gossip and chattering, but it's been fun. I feel like Sherlock Holmes, or maybe Watson. Technically, you'd be Sherlock Holmes."

"Abigail said I made her feel like she was in an episode of Vera."

"Oh, I love that show. Have you seen the French one, *Candace Renior*?"

"Yes. Love that one too."

"We're going to be fast friends," she said.

"We are." I'd never met someone who spoke about friendship like this.

"Speaking of rumors," she said, "there's one going around the pub tonight that the laird gave you a car."

I sighed. "It's for work, but I have a problem."

"What's that?"

"I need a driving instructor."

She laughed. "Oh, I can help you with that—and Granddad. He's the one who taught me. I thought everyone in America had a car."

"I lived in big cities with great transit systems. I did take lessons in high school, but I never actually took the test. I graduated early and then headed to college, and I didn't need one."

"Well, I'll help you, and I promise it will all come back to you."

I chewed on my lip. "There's one more thing," I said. "What are you doing this weekend?"

Mara raised her eyebrow. "Why am I afraid to answer that question?"

We laughed.

"I've decided to open the practice—sort of a soft launch on Monday, but I want to redecorate the lobby area and exam rooms to feel more spa-like."

"I'm in. I love decorating."

I smiled. "I love how comfortable your place is here, and you inspired me to make the experience less stressful for patients."

"That's a great idea. I can come over first thing tomorrow."

"That sounds—oh, wait. Maybe later in the day. I'm revisiting the crime scene tomorrow morning."

"Do you want me to help you with that?"

I shook my head. "The constable offered. I'm hoping to find out where Smithy was killed. But maybe after lunch? I know you have work, but whatever time you can spare I'd be grateful."

"I'm happy to help."

After saying our goodbyes, I headed home. I had an early morning the next day, and today had been a long one.

As I turned the corner behind the pub, that sense of someone watching me sent a shiver down my spine again. Except for a few porch lights, the path was dark. I glanced around, but there was no one there.

I half walked, half ran up the hill to my home. Gasping for breath, I fumbled in my huge purse for my keys. I had to use the light from my phone, to see the keyhole.

When I let myself into the church, the scent of paint slammed into me. I shut the door quickly.

I fumbled around in the dark, trying to find the light switch. I flipped the lights on, and it was so bright I blinked.

The lobby area had already been painted, and the trim around the floors freshened with a creamy white.

Tommy had worked quickly and efficiently. But where had they found the paint so fast?

I checked the exam rooms. He'd started in on one of the walls. All I had to worry about for the next three days was finding the right lighting and decor.

I clapped my hands in delight. This was what I had imagined when I'd decided to open my own practice: a place where people would start the healing process as they walked in the door. I had to find a water feature and put up some speakers so I could play soothing sounds.

At some point, I hoped to open some yoga and meditation classes, both of which I'd been religious about practicing at home, but hadn't done once since I'd arrived in Scotland.

I headed into the kitchen for a snack and pulled out the olive oil and bread. After putting a bit of oil on a small plate, I cut a couple of slices of bread and sat down at the kitchen table to go through the mail.

In the pile, was an envelope that had only my name on it.

Strange.

The piece of paper inside was much smaller than the envelope and fell out.

I opened it carefully.

"Go. Home."

Stomach churning, I dropped the paper on the table.

Was the letter from the killer? Or from one of the villagers who didn't like the idea of an outsider being the doctor?

Someone didn't want me here. My stomach tightened into a knot.

Great. Just great.

Chapter Twelve

After a rough night of sleep, I had to force myself out of bed the next morning. Determined to be ready before the constable arrived, I showered. Then I dressed quickly in jeans and a sweater.

Before I went downstairs, I checked my weather app. The high would only be in the fifties. Sea Isle summers were quite cool. I added a thermal T-shirt under my sweater and then went in search of coffee.

The scent of which hit my nose as I came down the stairs. Abigail must have put a pot on already. When I rounded the corner, I slid to a stop.

The constable sat at the kitchen table, reading the letter I'd left there.

Lovely.

He glanced up at me and his eyebrow raised. "What is this?"

As he already had a cup in front of him, I poured my coffee and sat down at the table.

"It was in my mail."

"Bloody hell. Why didn't you call me?"

"There's nothing you can do."

"Like hell. I won't have anyone threatening you." He folded the letter and put it in his pocket. "I'll get to the bottom of it."

"Do you think it's from the person who killed Smithy?"

He sighed. "Who knows? But they're about to be bloody sorry."

"Can I ask you something?"

"Aye."

"Did you just walk in my house and make coffee?"

He chuckled. "I own the church. Technically, it's my house."

Counting to ten, I stared down at my hands.

"But no, I didn't just walk in. Abigail let me in the front door. She was busy setting up Tommy to paint one of the exam rooms."

Oh, I hadn't thought about that. "It's okay to paint, right? I want to make the patients feel more comfortable."

"I was joking before; it's your home to do with as you see fit. Send the bills over, and we'll get you reimbursed."

"It's just a bit of paint. I've got it. Your contract saves me so much on living expenses, I can afford to make the place what I'd like."

He started to say something but was interrupted by Abigail coming in the back door, holding a paper bag. "I picked up some blueberry scones from the bakery," she said. "Ewan mentioned you'd be heading up into the highlands to investigate, and I wanted to make sure you had some breakfast."

I jumped up to help her put them on a tray, along with clotted cream and jam.

"You didn't have to do this, Abigail, but thank you," I said.

"Truth is, Tommy was hungry as well, even though I made him a full breakfast."

"He's doing a fantastic job painting," I said. "Do you like the color?"

She stared at me for a minute and then shook her head. "I'm not sure I'll ever get used to someone being interested in my opinion. I love the color."

"So do I—not that you asked." The constable laughed.

After a bit of breakfast, I pulled on my new pink wellies. They were the only ones in stock that were my size. I was more of a gray, black, and blue person, but they were growing on me.

I grabbed several plastic baggies and stuffed them in my pocket. If we found something, which was unlikely, at least I'd have a safe way to transport it. I also loaded my pocket with tweezers, a small flashlight, and gloves from my medical kit.

By the time we made it to the bothy, I was out of breath, though I tried to keep that fact from the constable. He didn't seem bothered at all. Even though it was cool, the sun shone brightly. Ewan opened the shutters, and bright light filtered into the main living area.

The coppery scent of blood mixed with the damp mustiness of the bothy. I turned on the flashlight, to have a better look at the floor leading from the entrance to the bedroom.

There were a few drops of blood, but not as much as I would have expected from the head wound Smithy had suffered.

The same was true in the bedroom. There was a large spot against the wall, where he'd been leaning his head, but little had pooled on the bed.

"Hmm," I said.

"What is it?" he asked.

"There isn't enough blood."

"What do you mean?"

I pointed to the wall. "With the head wound he had—he would have been bleeding all over the place. If he'd stumbled in here on his own, there would have been a trail from the door to the bed, but there isn't.

"I'm certain he was injured elsewhere and carried here. Whoever did the carrying probably has a jacket or shirt covered in blood. And there would be a lot more blood at the scene of the crime."

I headed outside and glanced up and down the path. "I have so many questions," I said.

"Maybe I can help?" he asked.

He wasn't nearly as annoying as he had been the last few days.

"Why was he here? Was he meeting someone? It would be a very private place, right? I mean hikers may have been by, but this isn't a trail most tourists use. At least, that's what Mara said."

"She's right. And there was a notice that this bothy was closed, so anyone needing it for the night wouldn't have used it. As for Smithy, he was probably up to no good."

Of that, I was quite certain. "Let's look around close by to see if we can find the original crime scene. Smithy had to weigh over two hundred pounds, so it would have taken someone like you to carry him."

He laughed hard. "Was that one of those backhanded compliments you Americans like to give?

I rolled my eyes.

"I can get some more men up here to search if you like."

"Not yet. I don't think the original crime scene is far, and it's probably up the mountain a bit."

"Why do you say that?"

"Because going downhill is easier than going up." I'd learned that lesson yesterday. "Even someone as strong as you couldn't have carried him too far."

"Wouldn't the rain have washed away any evidence?"

I nodded. "There is a good chance that's true, but I still want to look. Let's head up there." I pointed up the mountain.

"Don't stray too far off the path. It's easy to get lost in this area."

I examined every tree as I headed up the mountain. My hope was that blood might have splattered and soaked into the bark of one of the trees. Not far from the bothy, there was a hemlock shaped like a Christmas tree. Several of the tightly closed cones had been knocked off in one section. In fact, the area of damage was almost like the outline of a body.

The canopy from the trees made it a bit darker in this area, so I turned the flashlight on and circled the tree. The only place where the cones had been knocked off was in the area facing the path.

Someone had fallen against it. If it were Smithy, the evidence would have been on his clothes. I didn't have those to examine, so I broke off some of the branches and put them in the baggies I'd brought.

Then I focused on the ground. It was mostly mud. Wearing surgical gloves, I scooped up a good bunch of it and put it in the bags.

Odd, though: If he'd fallen back against the tree, then why were his injuries on the back and top of his head?

I reached in and scraped some of the bark to put in the bags. At the very least, I could put the samples under a microscope to see if there were blood cells.

"Did you find anything?"

Ewan's deep baritone made me jump.

"I don't know," I said. "Several of the cones were knocked off this tree, so I've taken a few samples. But anyone could have fallen against it."

He examined the tree as if it were the most interesting specimen in the world.

"Even with the rain, will there be traces of blood if this is the crime scene?"

"It's possible," I said. "The tree is a living thing and blood could have soaked into it."

I glanced up to find him frowning.

"What's wrong?"

"I didn't want to believe someone capable of killing him," he said. "But the more I think about what you said, the more sense it makes. That letter means you'll be in danger if they find out you're investigating. You might have already come across the killer, and that letter was his warning."

I wanted to correct him and tell him we weren't sure about the gender, but I had a tough time believing a woman could carry Smithy down the hill to the bothy—not without help.

"You say that, but most of the town knows I've been talking to people about Smithy. And it shows that the killer is running scared because he hadn't planned for any of this."

His frown intensified.

"While I have no proof, I do have a strong feeling the bothy was a temporary hiding place. I think the killer was possibly waiting until it was dark to bring Smithy down and dispose of his body. Which did happen, but we did the job of getting the body down the mountain for him."

He cleared his throat. "You may have something there."

"It's a lot of supposition and no proof."

"For someone who hasn't studied criminology, you seem to know a lot about it."

I picked up the tote I'd brought along and stuffed all the plastic bags of evidence into it. "Working in the ER, you learn things. Cops ask a lot of questions when someone has been attacked or there's been some sort of altercation." I wasn't about to tell him I had my detective sergeant's degree from BritBox.

But I had picked up a great deal from watching hundreds of hours mysteries. Enough to know that everything I had was circumstantial, and I still had no idea who the killer might be.

But the brave front I'd put on for the constable wore off by the time we'd made it back down the hill.

I didn't know who the killer was, but he knew me.

Chapter Thirteen

By the time we made it back down the mountain, my mind had been through forty different scenarios about how Smithy might have died. Ewan had been quiet as well, and I wondered if he might be thinking along the same lines. My biggest problem was where I could store the new evidence without fear of it walking off.

We were just outside of the church graveyard when he stopped.

"We need to change the locks," he said. "You and Abigail should be the only ones with keys. I'll take care of that before I head to Edinburgh this afternoon."

"You don't—"

He held up a hand. "I will also have officers patrolling around the church, so if you see them, don't be frightened."

"That isn't necessary. The change of locks should be sufficient. I can take care of calling someone if there is any trouble."

He shook his head. "I'm also going to get an alarm for the church as well as the autopsy room. And please don't bother arguing. I should have done it sooner. That way you can feel safe about storing the evidence."

I smiled.

"What?"

"I'd been wondering where I can put it that would be secure."

He sighed. "I promise you this is usually a very safe village. It pains me that something like this happened so early in your stay with us."

"It's not your fault, and I appreciate the precautions you want to take."

"My men will be here to install everything later this afternoon." He handed me the bag with the evidence we'd gathered. "You have my number if something comes up."

I nodded.

He walked down the hill to his car. There was a one-way drive up the bumpy cobblestones to the church and a turnaround if patients needed to be dropped off, but no one ever parked there. Or at least not from what I'd seen.

He waved at a woman and her dog as they headed my way. She held a huge shopping bag in one hand and the leash for the dog in the other.

Was that the dog I'd seen in the bothy? He seemed so much smaller in the daylight.

"Mornin'," she said. "I have your delivery."

"Good morning. Delivery?"

She smiled and handed me the bag. "Mara called and ordered some fabric. I'm Margie Hobbs, I own A Cut Above, down the way." She pointed toward the main drag where the pub was.

I held out my hand. "It's great to meet you. I could have come and picked it up." Normally, I might have been perturbed that someone picked a fabric for my offices, but I trusted Mara. I appreciated her initiative.

"No troubles at all."

"Would you like to come in for tea? I've been up the mountain, and I could use a cup."

"I'd love to, but I have to get back to the shop." Margie wore yoga capris and a big sweatshirt that said "Made in Scotland."

"Is this Fred?" I asked.

"How did you know?" She sounded surprised.

Fred seemed perfectly friendly today as he sniffed my wellies.

"We met under some unfortunate circumstances," I said.

She frowned and then her eyes went wide. "I'd forgotten about that. I was worried he might be traumatized from all of it, but he woke up as Fred as ever." She laughed.

"I don't want to take too much of your time, but do you have any idea how he ended up with Smithy that day?"

She chewed on her lip. "They were friends," she said. "When I'm busy at the shop, I just let Fred run out the back door. He usually does his business and comes right back. But sometimes he likes to make a nuisance of himself and goes visiting. He was a fan of the jerky Smithy made."

She handed me the shopping bag and then scooped up the tiny dog. "If he wanders too far, usually one of the villagers will bring him back. That day, I was working on a big upholstery order for a client, and I let Fred out. It was hours later before I realized he hadn't come back. And then Ewan showed up with him and told me what happened."

"It's an uncomfortable question, but I have to ask. Do you think Smithy took Fred on purpose? I understand he has an excellent pedigree."

She chewed on her lip again. "I'd like to say no, but we've all heard the stories. I will say that Smithy brought him back to me more than once. I like to think he was just protecting my little guy from the rain.

"I'd better be off. Tell Mara I said hello, and come see me at the shop."

"I'll do that." I waved goodbye.

Abigail had taken everything off the desk and had a sewing machine on it, going ninety miles an hour. Tommy was on top of a huge buffet, hammering in place above it what looked like shelves, and Mara stood precariously on a ladder, hanging beautiful curtains that were an off white patterned with teal octagons.

"Wow."

Mara glanced back and smiled. "I hope you don't mind," she said over the noise. "I may have gone a little crazy at the fabric shop this morning, but once I saw the paint, I had a vision."

I laughed. "I love your vision. The curtains are perfect."

Abigail held up the piece she'd been working on. "These are going to be chair cushions," she said.

"Lovely. I feel guilty that you all are working so hard. I have some more fabric from Margie's place."

"Already?" Mara asked. "We weren't expecting that until tomorrow. Give it to Abigail."

I handed the bag to the talented Abigail.

"Tommy, what are you working on?" I asked softly.

"Shelves." He didn't bother to turn around, and then pounded more nails into the wall.

Mara stepped off the ladder. "He helped Granddad bring that old piece from the barn. They have so much furniture crammed in there, and felt good about donating it to the cause. I was thinking, since you wanted something that looked like a spa in here, you could use it as a coffee-slash-tea bar. Or for a jug of water with lemon in it."

She pointed to the tote bag on my shoulder. "What's that?"

I glanced back to find Abigail staring at me curiously.

"Um. Possible evidence from the crime scene." I didn't want to talk about it. "So, we have curtains and seat cushions. What is the other fabric for?"

"We liked the seat cushions so much that we decided to do something to cover the back of the chairs as well," Mara said.

"This is all so much more than I expected. How am I ever going to thank you enough?"

Abigail smiled. "This is the most fun I've had in a really long time."

"Well lunch and dinner are on me. You just let me know what you want."

"Fishies," Tommy said. I turned to find him setting the last of the shelves up on the wall.

We all laughed.

"I need to put this away, and then tell me what I can do to help."

Again, Mara and Abigail stared at the bag on my shoulder.

"Did you really find something?" Mara asked.

"To be honest, I'm not certain. I've taken some samples to see if I can find any traces of DNA. Anyway, it's not something I need to worry about right this minute. I'll be right back."

I decided to store the evidence in the locked room where we kept the meds. There was a cabinet that had space on the bottom shelf. I stuck the bag in there.

Once everyone went home, I'd examine the contents carefully.

If we were lucky, maybe it wouldn't just be Smithy's blood I'd find.

Finding the DNA of the killer would save a great deal of time.

* * *

By four that afternoon, the waiting area was completed and looked fabulous, thanks to Mara, Abigail, and sweet Tommy. Even with the darker walls, it felt light, airy, and spa-like.

The locks had been changed except for the one for the front door, where a deadbolt had been added that locked from the inside. The security alarm had a code I could remember, and even though I hadn't wanted any of it, a weight lifted off my shoulders.

The old church creaked a great deal at night, and I would take comfort in knowing some stranger wasn't prowling around.

Tommy came through the front door, carrying two topiaries.

"Aren't those heavy?" I rushed to help him, and he stepped away from me.

I backed up and held up my hands. "Sorry—I didn't mean to invade your space."

"Okay." He nodded twice. "Fake." Then he put them down. He stared at them like fake plants were the worst thing in the world.

I couldn't stop smiling, and I didn't have the heart to say they were the only kind I could keep alive.

"Oh, that does look nice for an entry point," Mara said behind him. "Good job, Tommy."

He stared down at his toes. "Fake, Abigail," he said.

"I explained," she said. "Real plants might make the patients sneeze. Pollen, allergies—we talked about what happens and how people get sick."

"No air with fakes."

I smiled. "You're right, which is why it's so lovely to have that beautiful garden you created. People can step outside and smell all the oxygen your plants are giving them.

"But in here, we need the air sterile. It's not as nice as having real plants, but necessary."

"Okay," he said, and then took off.

"He's so smart and talented," Mara said. "Did you know he designed the shelves from stuff he found in the old barn? I said we needed something, and he put it all together. And it looks so high end."

"He and Abigail are full of surprises," I said. Abigail blushed again.

"I can't believe how fast you pulled all of this together while I was up the mountain for a few hours. It's incredible."

"When I saw the paint color, it reminded me of one of those boutique hotels, and I just went from there. I really hope you don't mind."

"Mara, I will be forever grateful to the three of you. I didn't really know what I wanted to do, other than freshen it up a bit. It's so chic—and yet comfortable."

"I love design and aesthetics," she said. "As part of my degree, I studied art and design. I never meant to go into advertising. It just happened."

"Well, I would be lost if you took Abigail away from me, because she does so much around here, but you two should seriously consider going into business together."

Mara pulled Abigail into a hug. "I feel like I made a new friend today, and I thank you for that. Great idea for going into business—you might be on to something. Like Abigail, I haven't had this much fun in a long time."

"I'm glad," I said. "It helps me a bit with the guilt."

She laughed. "Don't feel guilty. You'll soon learn that this is the way things are done in the village. We help each other out. Let me know when you want to do the rest of the house. I'm game."

"Do you think it needs it?"

She shrugged. "I think it could use a bit of freshening. We can talk about it over dinner."

Everyone left to change for dinner. Though I couldn't imagine we needed to dress up for fish and chips. I opened the locked medicine room and double-checked that the bag was in the cabinet where I'd left it.

Thankfully, it was.

I closed everything and locked it again.

As I went upstairs, I may have said a small prayer that I'd find DNA on those branches and the cones. I might not have a body, but I could still prove there'd been a fight and that someone had shoved him hard enough to cause a dent in the stiff branches of the hemlock tree.

Smithy had been murdered, and I'd prove it.

Chapter Fourteen

My walk home from fish and chips, which had been some of the best I'd ever tasted, was chilly. I zipped up my jacket and was glad I'd remembered to carry a scarf with me.

About a hundred feet from the front door, I swore I heard footsteps behind me. I turned, but no one was there. The hair on the back of my neck stood up, and it had nothing to do with the cold.

"Hello? Is someone there?"

I didn't bother waiting for an answer and hurried to the door. The large key opened the main lock, but the security guys had installed a small machine to the right of the door where I punched in a code to open the internal locks.

Of course, I didn't put it in right the first time.

The shrubbery on the side of the church moved. Was someone there?

My hand shook as I tried again. When the locks turned, I shoved the door open, and then slammed it behind me. After making sure it was firmly locked, I put the code into the internal alarm to reset it.

Then I leaned against the door, gasping.

Had someone been watching me? After taking my cell out of my pocket, I stared at the numbers. If I called the constable, what would I say? That I thought someone had been following me?

I hadn't seen anyone. The wind could have shaken the shrubs.

And Ewan had said there would be officers patrolling the area—it could have been one of them.

Shaking my head, I moved away from the door. Since I wouldn't be going to bed any time soon, I decided to see what I could find on the evidence I'd gathered.

Without a polymerase chain reaction machine, I wouldn't be able to check the DNA, but I could see if there were different types of blood. When I'd worked on the inventory the other night, I'd noticed we had a blood grouping machine and the paper test strips that could immediately tell blood type.

I didn't have a clean sample, but if there was blood on the cones or branches, I'd be able to tell.

I gathered everything up and headed to the surgery suite, with all the equipment.

When I made it to the bookshelves, I pushed in several of the books to open the doors. Nothing happened.

After a few more tries, the door finally slid open.

Using a small, sharp knife, I sliced off a piece of one of the cones that had broken off from the tree. After turning on the microscope, I put the shavings on a slide and placed it under the scope.

"Yes!" I thrust a fist into the air. There was most definitely blood on the pinecone shavings. I used one of the test strips to see if I could type the blood. The first two strips didn't work, but the third time I did it, type AB came up.

Although I had no proof the blood belonged to Smithy, at least I'd found something. Putting the rest of the cone in a bag, to send off for DNA analysis, I went on to the next cone. Most of the samples came up with the same blood type.

When I reached the bark I'd yanked off the tree, there was a great deal of blood. In fact, the bark was soaked with it.

The tree had killed Smithy. Well, hitting his head against the bark had. And it would have taken more than stumbling—he would have had to fall backward with enough force to crater his skull.

Maybe the murderer hadn't meant to kill him, but he had.

* * *

I'd been dreaming about trees chasing me, when someone called my name.

"Dr. Emilia, are you okay?" Abigail whispered the question.

I sat straight up and realized I was on the couch.

I'd been cold after working in the autopsy room and had started a fire downstairs and snuggled up on the couch. That was the last thing I remembered.

"I'm fine. I must have fallen asleep down here."

Blinking the cobwebs away, I yawned. "I thought I told you to take today off."

"You did. I thought I'd come in and make sure I had everything ready for tomorrow morning. I like to be prepared, and Tommy has to finish the trim in the last exam room."

"You work much too hard, but I appreciate it. I'll make us some coffee. Do you know if we have any appointments for tomorrow?"

Since part of the town thought I'd killed poor Smithy, I wondered if anyone would show up.

"We do have a few," she said.

"Oh, that reminds me. I was, um, looking for your uncle's file the other day, and it was empty. Do you know what might have happened to it?"

She frowned. "On the computer?"

"I—oh. I didn't look there. That was dumb of me. I meant the paper files."

She smiled. "Our former doctor had a habit of losing files, so Ewan suggested years ago that we automate everything. You should find his file on there. I'll also flag the patients who are signed in for tomorrow."

"Perfect. I don't know what I'd do without you, Abigail."

She blushed.

After a quick shower and change of clothes, I found her in the waiting area at the front desk.

She handed me a small tablet computer. "I've loaded everything you need onto here. This way you can go to each room and just mark what you need as far as testing and any prescriptions, making notes."

"I love it. We used the same sort of system at the hospital."

"You have access to every file in the system. Let me know if you need help. Oh, and on the right side, do you see the "Menu" button? If you click on the little flag, it pulls up the appointments, and then double-click to get their files."

I spent the morning familiarizing myself with the system and going through some of the files for the patients.

There wasn't much for Smithy on the computer, but his blood test from a few years ago showed severe liver damage. The doctor had also marked signs of dementia. That had been three years ago.

The blood type matched what I'd found on the bark. I'd texted Ewan the night before that I needed a DNA sample from Smithy's home for comparison, and he'd said he would take care of it.

Smithy's dementia might explain some of his rude behavior, and he might have made up the stories about his black book. Paranoid delusions were a sad fact of dementia.

Perhaps Smithy's attacker hadn't meant to murder him. There were rumors that Smithy was a violent man, and if his mind hadn't been clear, he might have attacked the other person, who might have shoved him to get away.

But then why not come forward? The killer had gone to the trouble of putting him in the bothy to make sure he wasn't left out in the rain. Unless he meant to hide the body. But if it had been self-defense, people would understand.

The blow he'd suffered would have killed him fairly quickly.

Ugh. If I had a body, all of this would have been so much easier.

Before she left, I asked Abigail about the process for sending labs out that we couldn't do here. She showed me where the protective envelopes were and how to print labels from my tablet.

After she and Tommy went home, I ate a sandwich and then set about getting my lab samples together, to send off.

Even if the killer hadn't meant to murder Smithy, that didn't explain why the body had been stolen. Or the fact someone didn't want me to stay.

I'd been shot at and even stabbed in the ER. I had the scars to prove it.

I wasn't about to let someone scare me away with a dumb letter.

* * *

That night at the pub, it was quiet. I sat at the bar so I could talk to Mara, who was behind it, pouring pints.

"Are you excited about tomorrow?"

I nodded. "And maybe a little nervous."

"I can understand that."

She carried the pints to a couple in the corner.

"Whew, Mother Nature forgot it was summer," a man said as he pulled off his coat and hat. He set them on the barstool that was between us.

"Oh, it's you," he said.

I glanced up to find Craig staring back at me. He held up his hand. "How are you, Doctor?"

"You can call me Em, and I'm good." I pointed to the stew. "If you're cold, this seems to do the trick."

"You aren't wrong. Auntie's stew does heat you from the inside out."

Mara came up and kissed him on the cheek. "Evening cousin."

He pulled her pigtail, and she swatted his hand playfully. "Evening," he said. "I'll have what the lady's having."

Mara laughed as she headed off to the kitchen.

"Are you settling in?" He went behind the bar and poured himself a dark ale. Then he came back around and sat.

"I am. We're doing a soft launch of the practice in the morning."

"A soft launch?"

I explained what I'd planned.

"Aye, that's smart. Give people a chance to know ya and spread how much they like ya." His words were kind.

"Thank you. I hope it works."

"My uncle and Ewan are great judges of character. They knew what they were doing when they asked you here. No doubt about it."

I had been having doubts. Not in my abilities. When it came to the medicine side of things, I had no worries. When it came to fitting in, I wasn't so sure.

"Stop flirting with the doc," Mara said. She winked at him as she put a bowl down in front of him.

"How can I help it? The woman is smart and gorgeous. A dangerous combination."

"That she is," Mara said.

I laughed nervously. "Stop. Please. I appreciate the kindness, but flattery isn't necessary."

"I don't believe it's flattery if it's true." Craig took a bite of stew and closed his eyes. "Heaven."

"On that we can agree," I said.

"We were so busy yesterday, you never told me what you found up the mountain," Mara said. She wiped down the bar as she spoke.

I'd decided to keep my findings to myself for now. Not that I didn't trust Mara, but I wanted to see the DNA tests before I said anything.

I shook my head. "Nothing worth talking about," I said.

"What happened up the mountain?" Craig asked.

"She and Ewan were looking at the bothy where she found Smithy. Thought they might pick up something since the weather had cleared up. But that's too bad."

"Poor Smithy." Craig sighed. "I wasn't his biggest fan, but no one deserves to go like that." A shadow passed over his eyes.

I opened my mouth, but Mara caught my attention. She shook her head and gave me the "don't ask" look.

I wondered what that was all about.

Chapter Fifteen

On opening day, I decided to head down to the pub for a full Scottish breakfast so I'd have energy to see me through the day. I heard voices outside the front door and opened it carefully.

There was a line of about twenty people.

I glanced down at my phone to check the time. We didn't open for three more hours.

"Good morning," I said.

Everyone glanced up at me and said, "Morning, Doctor." It sounded like they'd rehearsed it, as they were all in sync.

I laughed. "We don't open until ten this morning," I said. I'd decided we'd only work from ten till two each day. That would give me time to write up any reports I needed and for Abigail to finish the filing.

"Doc used to let us come in as we pleased," an elderly gentleman at the front of the line told me. "If it was an emergency. I think I got another stone," he said. "Been paining me all night." He held his mid back.

My guess, he was talking about kidney stones, which are extremely painful.

"Briana woke up with a fever this morning." The woman behind him held a sniffling toddler. "Her nose is running like a faucet. I tried to make an appointment, but you were all booked up today and tomorrow."

I smiled. "Right. Why don't you all come in and have a seat," I said. "I guess breakfast can wait."

"I'll run down and get you some," said a teen boy as he helped an elderly lady into the doorway. "Grandmum's arthritis is giving her trouble. She didn't have an appointment, but I convinced her to come."

"Aye." the woman said. "Can barely walk."

I shook my head. "No, it's okay—I'll get breakfast later."

"I can't get the bleeding to stop." A man in his forties, dressed in a plaid shirt, held his hand up. It was covered in a blood-soaked kitchen towel.

"You're first," I said.

I was well into his stitches when Abigail came into the exam room.

"I'm sorry. I should have known they'd do this."

"Do what?" I asked. "They have emergencies."

"Well, maybe Mr. Munston here does. But the rest of them can make appointments. Except for little Clarissa. She's burning up with the fever. I made appointments for everyone else and sent them home. I bet you didn't even get breakfast."

"No," I said, and then laughed. "I could have seen them all," I said. "We have three hours before the clinic opens."

She shook her head, and Mr. Munston laughed.

"They'd be taking advantage," he said. "Abigail is right. Doc only took the ones who were true emergencies."

"Otherwise, you'll wake up to people banging on the door at all hours," Abigail said. "The people in this village need boundaries. When you finish up here, you'll have just enough time to see Clarissa and get some breakfast. I'll have it sent up from the pub."

"Thank you, Abigail. Oh, does Clarissa have a cough with that runny nose?"

"A nasty one."

"Okay. Do me a favor and wear a mask and gloves. I'll do the same. Colds and flus spread like wildfire. Let's take precautions."

*   *   *

Later that afternoon, I was exhausted and exhilarated at the same time. I'd been in my element today. And much like in the emergency room, every case was different here.

I'd treated everything from a summer flu to sprains, arthritis, and kidney disease—and the list went on.

My last patient was Caitlin, who was in the last trimester of her pregnancy. I'd met her my first day here. She'd been one of the people who welcomed me at the pub.

"This place is beautiful," she said as she walked in. "Everything is so different. I feel like I'm at a spa in Glasgow."

I laughed. "That's the point. How are you?"

She shrugged. "Very pregnant. I've started the waddling stage, and I feel like a fat penguin."

"Aw, you're gorgeous, but as your baby moves down, a little waddling isn't such a bad thing.

"Come sit down and let's get your blood pressure." I motioned to a small sofa. I found patients tended to get more nervous up on the exam tables, so I'd made sure we had cushy chairs or sofas in every room.

Her blood pressure was extremely high, almost dangerously so.

"Hey, I need you to lie down on the couch, and let's put your feet up for a minute."

Her eyes went wide. "What's wrong?"

"Your blood pressure is a little high, but we can bring it down. I'm going to show you how." I helped her shift so she could put her feet on the arm of the couch.

"Abigail?" I pushed the intercom button on my tablet, which had come in quite handy today.

"Doctor?"

"Can you bring me some pillows, please, and a fetal monitor."

"I'll be right there."

I moved my rolling stool beside the couch. Her poor hands trembled.

"Everything is going to be all right," I said. "I want you to close your eyes and take a deep breath. Hold it for two seconds, and then let it out like a big sigh. Do those three times in a row for me."

By the time she'd finished the breathing exercise, Abigail was there, helping me prop her up with pillows. I positioned the fetal monitor on her belly.

The baby wasn't in distress, which was a great sign.

I took her pressure again. "Excellent. Keep doing that for a minute, and let's see if we can bring it down even further. I'm going to listen to the baby's heartbeat."

I smiled when we caught the beat. While I never planned to have kids of my own because I was married to my job, I still loved babies and children.

"That little human is going strong."

She breathed out a shaky breath. "Thank goodness."

Tears dripped down her cheeks.

I took her hands in mine. "Hey, it's okay. I didn't mean to scare you."

"It's not just that." The last word came out as a sob.

"I've seen this sort of thing before." My throat clogged. "I'm your doctor. Everything you tell me is confidential. You're upset about something, and it's showing up in your body."

She closed her eyes. "I don't even know where to begin."

"Why don't I start by raising a question that we ask anyone under duress: Are you afraid someone at home might hurt you? Or have they hurt you?"

She half laughed and half cried. "No. It isn't that."

"Has someone threatened your life? Even if it seemed like a joke at the time, we take these matters seriously."

My sanity took a hit every time I worked with an abused child or woman. It happened more often than most people would ever realize, and the victims were groomed to keep the worst of it from everyone else.

She shook her head. "Oh, I see what you're saying. No. I'm married to Mike, who is just lovely. He treats me like a princess. That's part of the problem."

Then she sat up and wrapped her arms around me. She sobbed while I patted her back. She stopped and took a deep breath.

"I'm so sorry. You probably think I'm an idiot."

"Not at all. It's obvious something is really bothering you. Why are you so upset? Just spit it out. I find that the easiest way to do it and maybe I can help sort things out. And crying is a part of the pregnancy hormone parade you're in. It may help you release some of your fears, so never be embarrassed about crying."

She gave me a watery smile. "You really are quite kind."

I chuckled. "I try. Now, tell me what's going on."

She blew out a breath. "At my hen party, I got really, really tits over ass. I don't even remember that night. All I remember is waking up the next morning in the bed of a man I didn't know. His boat was moored in the harbor.

"I got out of there as quick as I could, but when I made it onto the dock, Smithy was carrying some stuff to his ship. He looked at me and then the boat, and said, "That one is going to cost you, lassie."

Smithy? I'm not sure what I'd expected her to say, but it wasn't this.

"He said he was going to blackmail me," she sobbed. "That he had a black book and kept a record of everything. He was wild-eyed and scary."

She closed her eyes and then continued. "I thought maybe he was just giving me a hard time. I'd heard the stories about him and saw him lose his mind at Harry's Pub once. That day I walked away, and then it was the wedding, and I forgot.

"A month after Mike and I were married, Smithy knocked on our door. Mike was working in Edinburgh. Smithy said if I didn't give him a thousand dollars, he was going to tell my husband, Mike."

"That's terrible," I said. "Here, lie back down. Your blood pressure is going up again. Take deep breaths."

She did as I asked, and her breathing evened out. "So, what happened?"

"I ended up telling Mike the truth. I don't care what anyone else thinks of me, but I do care about him."

"What did he say?"

"That he loves me and that he knows I love him. He wasn't happy, but we worked through it. Turned out he couldn't remember his bachelor night either. He said it felt like someone had drugged him he was so out of it. I told him it was the same way for me. What if someone did that to us on purpose?"

My mind went a hundred miles a minute. What if Smithy had conspired with someone else? That person might have killed him or one of the people they were blackmailing.

"Are you worried about the baby not belonging to your husband?"

"No. Yes. I don't know. My periods have always been weird. I honestly don't think I had sex. You know, there are ways a woman can tell if that happened. My panties were on, and maybe he could have used a condom, but . . . I don't know."

"Do you think you could recognize the man or his boat?"

"No. It was like I was still drugged. I wouldn't have remembered talking to Smithy if he hadn't knocked on my door. I thought the whole thing was a bad dream."

"Well, Smithy is gone now. But I have one question: Do you think Mike might have hurt him?"

"I want to say no. He's a big teddy bear of a man, but he's also very protective of me. I can't see him killing someone, though. I can't believe I said that out loud. You can't say anything—you promised."

"I did and I will keep my promise."

"But what if the police find Smithy's blackmail book?"

I'd just have to find it first.

"Is there any way you can bring Mike in with you? We also need to talk about your diet and work on your breathing to keep that blood pressure down."

"He's working in Edinburgh during the week, and he's only home on the weekends. He's making extra money for the baby."

"Well, let's set up an appointment on a Saturday so I can talk to you both about your pregnancy."

*   *   *

By the time Caitlin left, her blood pressure was normal, and I was exhausted. The day couldn't have gone better as far as the patients were concerned. I'd been grateful people showed up.

Too tired to head down to the pub, I made myself a sandwich with the focaccia and sat down with my laptop at the kitchen table. Curious about what Caitlin had said about her husband, Mike, I checked out social media. Through one of her accounts, I found him.

Caitlin was at least five seven, and he towered over her. He was a giant of a man and could have very easily caused the injuries Smithy had suffered.

He certainly had motive, but had he been in the vicinity? She'd said he'd been out of town during the week, so that would be something I had to check up on.

I did a search for his name and found he'd been charged with an assault and battery. They called it GBH here. She'd said he was a teddy bear of a man, but he obviously had a violent history.

After another search, I found an article about a pub brawl, the one where Mike had been charged with a GBH. He'd been let off because he'd been protecting a woman and her child from the men brawling.

Oh. That made him more of a hero, but if he loved his wife as much as she believed he did, there was no telling what he might do to protect her.

I made some notes in the journal I'd been keeping. I'd have a chance to talk to Mike in person on Saturday, when he came in with Caitlin for her follow-up.

An ad came up for a find-your-heritage site. After getting my DNA results several months ago, I'd thought about joining one of the sites to do more research, but there hadn't been time.

I grabbed my billfold and pulled out my credit card. If I wanted to learn more about my father's side of the family, now was the time.

Besides, I had to know if I was related to the man who had owned Smithy's boat. Could it be a coincidence?

A few minutes and forty dollars later, I found out there were a million McRoys.

After an hour, I'd narrowed it down to about two thousand. I only had my dad's name. There was a bible with his parents' names, but it was in storage with the rest of my books. I'd sold all my furniture, but there was no way I'd part with my books.

"Duh." I typed in Theodore's name, and he came up. He had been a vicar here up until twenty years ago and had died under mysterious circumstances, according to a newspaper article that had been written about him.

The obit talked about how many organizations he'd helped through the years and how beloved he was. It was quite sweet.

But the local newspaper had run a front-page story about his sudden death at Miller's Pond. He'd been found by a Mr. Brown.

Smithy?

The coroner had listed the death as unexplained. Some of the townspeople had given quotes on how they thought the vicar's death was mysterious.

I found another article from one of the Edinburgh newspapers. *"Vicar Dies Suddenly"* was the title of the story. There wasn't a great deal of information other than that he'd seemed to be in perfect health but had died during a festival in Sea Isle. He'd been judging a pie contest an hour before he was found dead.

The former doctor might have performed more than a cursory autopsy since the circumstances were unusual.

I went to my office and grabbed the tablet. I thumbed through the records but didn't find any McRoys in the mix.

I pursed my lips. There had to be a death certificate on file. What the heck was that about?

Maybe, the body had been sent to Edinburgh. I did another search to see if I had access to those files. I didn't.

Darn.

I wonder how Millie's hips are doing. It was time to do a deep dive into the county records. And perhaps a trip to Edinburgh was in order.

Chapter Sixteen

The second-best place for information was the pub. Even though I was tired, I decided to head down there. Mara's granddad had known the vicar. He might be aware of the circumstances of his death.

There were only a few people in the pub. Mara was behind the bar, loading bottles of ale into the fridge.

"Oh, I'm glad you came down. How was the first day for ya?"

I smiled. "Great. I was surprised by how many people showed up."

"We've been without a doctor for so long, I'm sure the town will keep you busy. Driving to Edinburgh is such a pain. And while there are a few doctors in towns around here, Sea Isle folks are a bit fussy when it comes to that. Are you hungry? I have some stew left over from lunch."

"No, thanks. I came for information this time."

She smiled and leaned her elbows on the bar. "Do tell."

"I think I told you I was curious about my family. I don't know much of anything about my dad's side."

"Right."

"Well, I found some information on the vicar who was named Theodore. I think I mentioned him to you?" I honestly couldn't remember if I had.

"Oh, I meant to ask Granddad about him. Sorry, I forgot. He goes to bed when the sun gets low, but I'll try to remember tomorrow."

"Can you also ask him about Mickey? I think that was the vicar's brother. I did a search on an ancestry site, but Mickey's name wasn't related to Teddy's. I did find a niece, Ellen McRoy, but her father wasn't listed."

Her eyes went wide.

"What?"

"That's the name of Craig's wife," she whispered.

"I thought you said he was single."

"He is now. She left without a word years ago. He finally got a divorce or something when she didn't show up in court to contest it. I was off at university at the time, so I don't remember all the facts. Just that her leaving devastated him. We don't ever talk about her, especially to him."

Had he recognized my name? Odd that he wouldn't say anything, although in a way I understood. I never talked about my former husband. The memories were just too painful.

"Is there someone I could talk to about her?"

"I'm sure Gran would spill what she knows. Maybe we can ask tomorrow morning?"

The man at the far end of the bar waved at Mara.

"You go ahead and serve him. I think I'll take a walk."

I'm not sure why I headed toward Craig's shop. He'd said he closed in the early afternoon, and it was nearing six.

But I forced myself down the steps.

The closed sign on his door, said it all.

What were you going to say? Hey, was your ex-wife related to me?

I'm sure that would have gone well. The detectives on television made it look so easy.

"Bummer."

I was surprised to find the tea shop was still open.

"Hey luv," Jasper said. "I was just about to lock up when I saw you heading this way."

"Oh." I stopped. "I can go."

"Not at all. What can I get you?"

"Why don't I get something to go?"

"Do you want an Americano?"

"Nah. I better stick with some sort of herbal tea. Caffeine late in the day can keep me up at night. I've had enough trouble sleeping since I arrived."

"Our sea air isn't putting you out?"

I laughed. "I think it's living in an older home. I'm not used to all the creaks and moans."

Then there was the fact that someone had come into my home while I'd been sleeping and had stolen a body, but I couldn't tell him that part.

"Did you have a new place in Seattle?"

I nodded. "A little house close to the hospital, and it was brand new when I bought it." I frowned. Funny, I hadn't really thought much about my old life since I'd arrived in Sea Isle.

"Is that the face of regret?" he asked. And then he handed me a paper cup of tea.

"No. Not at all. I love it here. It's a bit of a learning curve, but the people, for the most part, are kind. And even though some folks are a little nosy, I like that everyone seems to care about each other."

"I forgot, today was your first day at the doctor's office. How did it go?" He knocked his paper cup against mine in cheers.

"Great, really. I was busy before the doors even opened."

He laughed hard. "I'm not surprised. We should celebrate with treats. What kind would you like? I have some petit fours left over, and some chocolate croissants."

"I'll take some of both," I said.

I sipped my tea while he put my purchases in a beautiful pink carryout box. Then he handed it over.

"Where are you off to next?"

"Maybe the beach for a walk? That way I won't feel guilty about eating my treats later."

"Hold up and I'll come with you. That is, if you don't mind company. I'm going to eat an early dinner at the pub tonight. I get tired of my own cooking, and Mara texted that shepherd's pie is on the menu."

"I haven't had a bad meal there," I said. "And I'd love the company. How much do I owe you?"

He laughed. "You know the rules."

"Yes, but I'm not one to follow rules, especially ones the constable has set up."

"Well, I am. I don't want him getting wind that I made you pay for something."

I rolled my eyes. "Whatever." I put some bills on the counter. "Consider this a tip."

He laughed again but didn't fight me. "Let me grab my coat."

With Jasper by my side, we headed down the steps to the beach. Thankfully, I'd worn my duck shoes that Angie, from the kilt store, had said I'd need, so walking in the sand wasn't so tough.

We chatted about everything, as two new friends do. He made me laugh several times. Since the tide hadn't come in yet, we were just about to the stairs that led up to the pub, when I spotted something in the water.

I put my hand over my eyes, to cut the glare of the sun.

"What is it?" he asked.

A wave picked up the object, and it was more than clear that it was a body, floating facedown.

"Oh. My. God," he said.

I tossed my phone toward him and stripped faster than I thought possible.

"Call the constable," I ordered before diving into the frigid sea in my bra and boy shorts.

"Crap." It was stinging cold, and the body was still out there several more yards. I fought against the waves and tried to grab hold, but the body was slick and bloated. That it was naked made it even tougher to get a grip. I had to hook my hand under the armpit and half drag it back.

I'd made it to where I could stand, and found Ewan wading out to help. He hadn't bothered to take off his clothes.

The face was as bloated as the body, and fish had nibbled at him, but the big bashed-in skull was more than evident.

More men arrived to help us get the body on a stretcher.

Then someone wrapped a foil blanket around me. Even though my teeth chattered from the cold, I pulled it off and put it over the body. No one needed to see this. It was enough that Ewan and I had seen Smithy in this condition. The autopsy was going to be a bear.

"Looks like you found him," Ewan said, but his voice was a mere whisper.

Another blanket went around my shoulders.

"Yep."

"You could have hypothermia."

"I'm okay. Let's get him to the lab." I ran over and pulled my jeans and sweater over my wet body. It helped. Then I slid my feet into the shoes.

"I need to a—" My teeth chattered so hard I couldn't get the words out to Jasper.

"Don't worry." He handed me the pink box of treats. Then he pulled his jacket off and wrapped it around my shoulders.

His body heat had stayed in the warm wool, and I wasn't about to turn it away.

"Thannnks."

"No problem. Let me know if you need anything—or I can bring food up from the pub later."

I'm not squeamish at all, but then again, I'd never worked on a body with that much deterioration. The last thing I was worried about was food.

I nodded.

Ewan and his men carried the body to the church and went around the side to the back. They waited as I input the new alarm code.

With my brain frozen, along with my body, no one was more surprised than I was that I managed it on the first try. Ewan had positioned himself between me and the other men, so they couldn't see me do it.

Inside, I opened the doors for them to carry him in and put him on the slab.

Ewan came out to the kitchen and frowned. "You should shower in warm water, and change," he said.

My body shivered from the cold, and I was sniffling.

"I will if you promise not to leave the body unattended until I get back."

"Done."

"I'm going to help the doctor," he said to his men. "Get the boats and do a search to see if there is any other evidence in the water. I doubt it, but you never know."

They left, and the doors shut behind them.

"I meant what I said." I pointed a finger at him.

"I'm going to lock the door," he said, "and make some coffee. No one will take him away."

I'm not sure why I trusted him, but I did.

"I'll be right back."

Ten minutes later, I dried my hair with a towel. He'd been right about the warm shower, and I hadn't wanted to get out. Unfortunately, the hot water only lasted for so long.

Downstairs, I caught Ewan eating one of the chocolate croissants.

For once, he appeared embarrassed. "Sorry. I missed lunch, and I probably won't be able to eat after watching what's about to happen."

"It's okay," I said. "Take whatever you want."

He pointed to a cup of coffee. "I don't see the point of decaf, but I remembered Abigail saying you don't drink the real stuff past a certain time."

Abigail and I might need to chat over sharing information with the constable.

"Thanks."

I held the warm cup in my hands as I sipped.

Ewan grabbed a petit four out of the box.

"Would you like a sandwich? I don't have much else in the fridge, but I can manage that."

He shook his head. "No, this will do, thanks."

"Smithy probably isn't going to tell us much in his state. Any sort of DNA has been washed off."

"I'd say he's told us a great deal," he said.

I blinked. "Are you agreeing that he's been murdered? I mean, you hinted at it the other day but didn't come out and say it."

"Aye," he said. "And the person who dumped the body forgot something important that happens around August."

"What's that?"

"The currents change, but not in the normal way. Usually, the water is much warmer this time of year, and the body would have floated out to sea, but that isn't the case. We've had a cold summer, and the water temperature has been below normal."

"So, maybe the person who killed him isn't an experienced sailor?" That might knock off the men who worked with him.

He shrugged. "Perhaps. Although it could be the person had a smaller boat and didn't have time to take him out far or was worried about getting caught. They had to be in a rush when they took him that night."

"Well, let me see if Smithy is willing to give us any clues. Meanwhile, you need to think of a good story."

"What do ya mean, lass?"

"One that explains how he ended up in the ocean when he was supposed be here in my lab."

He grinned. "Fair point."

We put our cups in the sink and headed toward the lab, where the body had been laid.

I zipped into a protective suit over my clothes and handed one to Ewan.

"Are you really worried about contamination? Poor Smithy's been floating for days."

I sighed. "Did you see the bloat? There's no telling what will happen when I cut into the body. And you need to wear this." I handed him a mask. "Noxious gases have formed, and we need to protect ourselves. Be prepared for one of the worst smells of your life."

Ewan appeared surprised. I put a bit of Mentholatum under my nose and handed the small tube to him before I put on my mask.

"What's this?"

"Like I said, the smell will be worse."

He nodded solemnly.

"You ready for this?"

"No, lass. I don't think I am."

Chapter Seventeen

The sea had washed away most of the evidence, and an hour later I was almost finished with Smithy's autopsy. There had been marks where his body had been bound by rope, and small bits of plastic from the sheet he'd been lying on were still in the rope.

The odd thing was, he was naked. When we'd left him here that night, he'd been fully dressed.

"Do you think the killer was afraid of DNA evidence, so they took his clothes?"

Ewan nodded. "Probably burned them."

He had been extremely helpful as an assistant, which surprised me. He took measurements and packed samples of lab work to be sent off to Edinburgh. I'd found bark deeply embedded in Smithy's skull, but it was sheer dumb luck that small piece was still there.

"I'll have to send it to a lab, but this confirms what I thought about him being pushed into the tree. But the amount of force we're looking at here, the person would have been tall and very strong."

Caitlin's husband, Mike, came to mind. Though he had a strong motive, I had no proof or evidence it was him. The brothers also fit the bill, and they had access to boats.

Ewan nodded.

I pulled a sheet over Smithy. "There's something I need to tell you," I said.

He put down the clipboard he'd been holding.

"What is it?"

"There is a rumor concerning Smithy blackmailing people."

"Aye, I've heard the same, but no one has come forward."

"Well, they wouldn't, right? Especially, now that he's gone. No one wants their dirty laundry aired in public."

"And your point?"

"I'm sure the rumor is true."

Ewan frowned. "How's that?"

I stepped right into that one. Dumb, Em. Dumb.

He crossed his arms. "Who is it?"

"I spoke to them under doctor–patient confidentiality. It would be physically impossible for this person to have killed Smithy." That much was true, and it did no good to throw Caitlin's husband under the bus if he had an alibi.

"We're talking about murder. It could have been someone this person knows," Ewan said.

"What I'm more interested in is finding a book that was mentioned more than once when I was talking to people about Smithy."

He sighed. "What I'm more interested in is who told you they were being blackmailed. They are prime suspects in this investigation."

This time I sighed. "Ewan, I took an oath, and I'm not going to break it. If I thought this person was a danger to society, I would find a way to share the information, but they aren't. We need to search Smithy's home. His employees said he has a place by the glen, but I don't know where that is."

He cleared his throat. "We've searched there as well as on his ship," he said.

"When?"

"When the body disappeared, my men and I searched everywhere. We didn't find any sort of blackmail book."

It wouldn't have been out in the open, and Ewan's men hadn't known to look for one. I had to search Smithy's place myself.

"Okay, good to know. I appreciate your help tonight."

"It's my job to oversee autopsies." He wasn't happy.

"Please, don't be angry. I wouldn't have brought it up at all, but I want to share information with you in the hopes that you might do the same. Is there anything you haven't told me?"

"No. And as far as the coroner's job goes, you're done. You've found out how he was killed. My men and I will take over from here."

"What?"

"Your job is discovery and to write the death certificate. Now, we have that information. We'll take it from here."

I had to stop myself from rolling my eyes.

His phone buzzed. "I'll be off. Police business."

And then he was gone.

My part of the investigation may have been done in his eyes, but one way or the other, I'd be making my way up to Smithy's home.

* * *

The next morning, I was ready for Mara when she arrived at seven for my driving lesson. When we sat in the car, it felt odd to be behind the wheel. I hadn't driven since I was sixteen and in high school.

I had been reading through Scotland's driver's manual that was available online. What I hadn't counted on was driving on the left side of the road.

"This feels weird," I said from the driver's seat.

She smiled. "Buckle up and we'll go over the basics. Luckily, you won't have to worry about shifting gears in this car. It will automatically do it for you."

The Land Rover still had the new leather smell, and it only had twenty miles on it.

She went over the rudiments of driving, most of which came back to me quickly. I reversed out of the gravel parking area.

"Let's go down the main stretch," she said. "It's not so hilly."

I did as she asked, though slowly.

"See? You've got this."

"We've only gone a hundred feet."

She laughed, and so did I. My shoulders dropped and I took a deep breath.

"Okay, now, as you pull out, you know to look both ways before going."

"Right." It wasn't long before we were cruising along. I might have slammed on the brakes a little too hard when we came to a pedestrian crossing, but overall, my first trip out wasn't so bad.

"Do you by chance know where the glen is?"

"Aye. Make a U-turn, and we'll head up the mountain. What's there?"

I shrugged and then turned the car around the other way.

"I heard someone mention it the other day."

She laughed. "It's where Smithy lived."

"Yes, that's probably where I heard about it."

"I'll show you."

We headed up the mountain, past the main part of town.

"Slow down a bit—it's a dirt road that leads out to the glen."

We finally made it down the bumpy road, and I stopped at a crossroads.

"Up on the hill is Ewan's place," she said. "Actually, this land is all of his for several hundred acres and all the way down to the sea."

The home was a stately country home that looked like something out of *Town & Country* magazine. Was that even in circulation anymore?

"Wow."

"It's just as gorgeous inside," she said. "The man has an eye for detail and has kept up his family legacy and built upon it."

I had no idea he was so wealthy. Not that a person's financial security was important to me. It was just unexpected.

"Over to the right and down that road"—she pointed to another dirt path that didn't look wide enough for a car—"is where Smithy lived. I think his was the third house on the lane."

"Ah. Thank you. Just in case I need to do a house call, I wanted to familiarize myself with some of the area."

"Right. You can tell me the truth, you know."

"Nothing to tell," I said. "I was just curious, and I had no idea Ewan's house was so big."

"Word is he's richer than God, but we don't say that because it's blasphemy." She laughed. "Truth is, he's happy to share his wealth. He may own most of the town, but he also takes responsibility for just about everyone who lives here."

"Doesn't that come with being the laird?"

"I suppose, but he does a lot no one knows about. He's a good man."

"Do I detect a crush?" I smiled as I turned the car around. I had a full load of patients later in the morning, and by now, there were probably more waiting outside the door.

"Ah, no. He's not my type. I prefer men to be arseholes, or at least that's my pattern. I've not dated since I moved here to live above the pub."

"The dating pool can't be too large in a town this small," I said.

"True, unless you count the summer tourists. You missed the main part of that. From May until mid-August, we have a fair amount of sailors, divers, and beach lovers come through. After Saturday, most of them will be gone until next year."

"What happens Saturday?"

"Did I not tell ya? We have a town tradition called the Gathering. It started hundreds of years ago, and it's tied around fall harvest and such. Basically, these days it's an excuse for a big party. Takes place right here in the glen, in front of Ewan's home."

"I don't think I was invited."

She laughed. "Don't be silly. The whole village is invited. It's casual and we build a bonfire. Everyone brings food and drink. There are carnival games for the kids. That sort of thing."

"It sounds fun."

I'd also be in close proximity to Smithy's house.

If there was a blackmail book, I was sure I'd find it there.

Chapter Eighteen

M ike, Caitlin's husband, was adorable. She'd been right about him being a teddy bear of a man. His love for her poured out of him, as evidenced by everything from making sure she was comfortable to recording our conversation about her care on his phone.

"I want to make sure I don't forget anything," he said, and then smiled.

They were cute together and finished each other's sentences.

I hope he's not a murderer.

If possible, children deserved to grow up with both parents. I understood that better than most people. I'd grown up without either one until my mother returned. And then she died, leaving me again.

"You can do short walks, but if your ankles swell or you feel dizzy, I want you to lie down and put your feet up. Do you understand?"

She nodded.

"Stay away from salty foods because they make you retain water," I instructed her. "Speaking of which, increase your water intake. That will help. But most of all, keep your stress levels low. When you're pregnant, your hormones think it's a party.

"When you feel yourself spiraling, take deep breaths and count to ten as many times as you need to. It's scary stuff having a baby—I get it. But you two are going to be awesome parents—we just need to get you through this last month and half."

I printed out some sheets on meditation and breathing for them.

Caitlin had waddled out to the waiting room for some water.

"Mike, can I ask you something?" I whispered.

"Yes," he replied, eyeing me warily.

"She told me about Smithy," I said.

His face turned red.

"Don't get upset with her, please. That was part of what sent her blood pressure so high. As the coroner, I've been investigating his death. I wondered if there was anything else you could share with me."

He frowned. "What do you mean?"

"Did he contact you? Or threaten you?"

"No. The coward. I wish he had. I'm glad he's dead. I'm not sure what I might have done if I'd come across the smarmy bastard."

"So, you never met him face-to-face?"

He shook his head. "Seemed he knew I was working out of town and would bother her when I wasn't here. When I'm in town, I'm with her all the time. But it did cross my mind to go and find him when she told me."

Something passed across his face.

"What is it?"

He sighed. "She wasn't the only one who can't remember that night. I think that bastard set us up. I don't know how, but I don't remember drinking enough to pass out, and yet I did. Woke up in a place where I didn't belong, much like she did. That's why I don't blame her at all. I blame Smithy."

Had he set them up? That would have been premeditated and a horrible thing to do to a bride and groom. However, that type of incident seemed well within his character.

"So, the day he was killed, can you tell me where you were?"

"Working late. If you give me a pen and paper, I'll give you the number of my boss. He'll confirm what I said."

I handed him the paper and pen, and he wrote down the number.

"Thanks for telling me, and don't worry. Your words are confidential with your doctor. "Now, back to Caitlin. She won't always be in control of her emotions. Whatever you do, don't tell her to calm down. Nothing angers a woman faster. Remind her to breathe, okay? And just agree with whatever she says, but help her find a way to calm down."

He nodded.

Caitlin came back in. "Are we doing the sonogram?"

"Yes. Are you ready?"

* * *

Parking, I'd been told, was limited, and Ewan wanted to make sure everyone made it home safely. Luckily, for me, the shuttle was picking people up down the hill, at the back of the pub.

There were a few people already waiting.

"We have five more minutes before we leave," the driver said.

I sat down in one of the seats near the front. A minute later, Jasper joined me. He sat in the aisle seat across from mine.

"How are you?" he asked as he set several boxes on the seat beside him.

"I'm great. How are you, and what is all that?"

"I'm ready to party, and that, my friend, is the last of the macarons and eclairs."

"Aren't you worried about someone mugging you?"

He laughed. "You're talking about yourself, aren't you?

"Truer words have never been spoken. I forgot about bringing some food," I said.

"Not to worry, we'll say one of these boxes is from you."

"I haven't been in town long, but I have a feeling everyone will know that isn't true. And what is everyone else going to eat, since I've decided all of those belong to me?"

He laughed, as did the driver, who I recognized as one of the men who worked with Ewan.

"I brought a full van up this afternoon. So there should be plenty for everyone. Any news on poor Smithy?" Jasper asked.

I shook my head. After my slip with Ewan, I'd decided to keep the information I'd gathered to myself. There were enough rumors spreading about the murder.

"Nothing, other than that Abigail has the wake planned for Monday night."

"Aye. I promised to help Mara with that."

"That's kind of you."

He shrugged. "Abigail was more accepting of me than other kids when we were in school together." He whispered that last part. "I'll do whatever I can to help her."

"You're a good man, Jasper."

"I try. Are you excited about your first Gathering?"

"Truth is," I whispered, "I'm nervous. Tell me what to expect."

He laughed. "Booze, food, and dancing around the bonfire."

After a few more people joined us, the driver pulled up the hill. He stopped by the library, where more people got on the shuttle. I scooted over to make more room for an elderly gentleman I didn't recognize. In the past week, I'd been certain I'd met everyone over seventy in Sea Isle. I guess that wasn't the case.

As was expected in a small town like this, most of my patients were at least seventy and older.

Everyone chatted and the excitement was palpable. Many of the men—and women—wore kilts.

I'd forgotten to check in with Angie about my scarf and other purchases at her shop. I'd ordered a great deal, and they handcrafted their products.

When we arrived, there was a large, striped tent, and then off in the distance was a huge stack of wood for the bonfire.

"Wow."

"It is a sight," Jasper said as he followed me off the bus.

"Are you sure I can't carry one of those?"

He shook his head. "Pastries aren't that heavy. Besides, I don't trust you." He chuckled.

"You are a smart man."

Mara had said it was informal, but the decor inside the tent was beautiful. There were flowers everywhere, and crystal chandeliers hung down throughout. There was a dance floor in the middle, where couples mingled. The tables laden with food had been lined up along one wall.

There were carving stations as well as several tables of homemade goods and casseroles.

I helped Jasper set out his wares, and it only cost him three mouth-watering macarons.

"I don't know if anyone has said this, but you should probably open a patisserie."

"Really?"

We laughed.

"Those were better than any I had in France."

He waved away the compliment. "I'm still perfecting my recipe," he said.

"Tasted perfect to me."

Mara raced up. She was dressed in a beautiful kilt and a lacy white blouse. Her curls were piled on top of her head and dotted with small flowers.

She kissed Jasper on the cheek and gave him a hug. "I'm so glad you're here."

"You only love me for my eclairs," he joked.

"My sweet friend, there are far worse reasons to love a man." She popped one of the miniature treats into her mouth.

"I thought you said this was a casual party."

She frowned. "It is. Why?"

I pointed to her and Jasper. "You're both dressed in beautiful kilts," I said.

In my big fluffy sweater, dark jeans, and boots, I felt a little underdressed.

"It's not like we're wearing our formal ones, silly."

There were formal kilts? I had so much to learn.

"Come on, I have some people I want you to meet," she said.

Jasper came with us as Mara introduced me around. The tent was filling up, and as it grew more crowded, I found myself sticking to the edges of the canvas.

I have a thing about crowds—as in, I'm not a big fan.

I'd been backing away toward the entrance when I bumped into someone.

"Sorry," I said as I turned.

Craig smiled down on me. "You okay, Doc?" His hands were on my shoulders, steadying me. He was dressed in a kilt and white shirt, and looked very handsome. So much so, I had to force myself to breathe.

"Sorry about that."

"Was someone bothering you?" He glanced over my shoulder.

"Not at all. I—I'm not a big fan of being in the center of a crowd."

"Aye, I understand that."

"You do?"

He let go of my shoulders. "I feel the same as you. Though, I hope you'll chance it and dance with me later."

My stomach fluttered. "I'd like that."

A large horn sounded, and everyone filed out of the tent.

"What's going on?" I asked Craig as we followed the crowd.

"It's time for the bonfire ceremony," he said.

"Doctor Em?" Abigail ran up beside us, and Mara was right behind her.

"Where's Tommy?"

She smiled. "He's up at the house with the children, playing games. They have caregivers who trade off every few hours so parents can enjoy the festivities, as well as those of us who care for adults."

"That's a brilliant idea."

"I finished my shift, and I thought I'd come find you."

She looked so much younger in her kilt and with her hair tied in braids. Flowers were woven into the braids.

"I'm glad you did. Do you know Craig? Craig, this is my friend Abigail, who works with me at the office."

"Happy to meet you," Craig said.

"Hi," she said shyly, and her eyes went wide.

"What?" I whispered.

"You look happy," she whispered back.

"She's right." Mara put an arm around both of us. "Are you having fun?"

I nodded.

"We're just getting started," Mara said. Jasper joined our little group, and we made room for him in the circle around the bonfire.

"The laird will speak," someone said through the speakers that had been set up outside.

I hadn't seen Ewan, and I'd wondered where he was. Not that I cared—I was just curious.

He stood on a large box next to the pile of wood and held a book. Another man held a flashlight on the pages, as well as the microphone.

Ewan glanced out at the crowd and then focused on me for a split second. Something passed across his face, but then he bowed his head.

The words were in Gaelic, and I didn't understand them. But his warm, deep baritone nearly sang them, and chills slid down my spine.

Then he chanted, and others did the same before they broke out in the most beautiful song. As much as I wanted to know what they sang about, I didn't interrupt. I swayed with them and even joined hands. I had Mara on one side and Craig on the other.

And while I had no idea what was going on, I was caught up in the moment as the music of their voices moved through me.

Then the fire was lit, and the chant grew louder, and the vibration of it went through my body. The people here probably didn't see it as a collective meditation. Chanting like this could be healing for the soul and good for the body. Many of the ancients knew what they were doing when they'd set up these rituals.

* * *

The chant died down, and everyone threw up their hands and cheered as the bonfire was lit with torches.

No one really spoke for the longest time as we gazed at the flames. When they reached the top, another cheer went up, and people began dancing and singing.

I lost sight of my friends as they were pulled away by others to join the revelry. It was just as well. I had a plan for tonight that had nothing to do with drinking or dancing.

The fire illuminated the area. I spotted the road where Mara said Smithy had lived.

I glanced around as I stepped behind the tent and into the cover of darkness. If I was quick about it, I could get down there and back with no one the wiser.

I'm going to find that book if it kills me.

Chapter Nineteen

What I hadn't counted on was the complete and utter darkness I ran into the further I moved away from the party. I tripped twice on divots, and I finally turned on my flashlight.

After meeting Smithy, and hearing so much about him from other people, I hadn't expected the quaint little cottage that had been well maintained on the outside. There was a garden and even flower boxes in the windows.

Had that been Ewan's doing because it was on his property?

The front door was locked.

Dumb. I didn't even think about how I'd get inside. I laughed.

This wasn't one of my brightest ideas.

The wind picked up, and the hair on my neck rose again. I turned quickly and shone the flashlight on the side of the house. No one was there.

Get a grip.

I'd never tried breaking and entering. On the other hand, this could still be considered a part of the investigation.

Finding that book might lead to Smithy's killer, and Ewan's men had already searched here. There was no reason I couldn't take a gander.

The subterfuge was necessary so I wouldn't insult Ewan and his men.

I walked around the back of the house and found a sliding glass door, which opened easily.

Inside, the kitchen was small but neat. Not a dirty dish in sight.

But the living area was a different story. Books were strewn all over the floor, and the sofa cushions were topsy-turvy.

Had Ewan's men made this mess?

I knelt on the floor to go through the books. I made neat stacks as I opened them and checked the pages.

Nothing looked like a journal or someplace where he might keep a list, and I had a feeling this was a big waste of time.

While some people hid things in plain sight, others created places to store their most valuable possessions.

After checking for a loose brick on the fireplace—I'd seen that on one of my mysteries—I decided to look elsewhere.

I checked the bathroom and even looked under the toilet lid.

There was a weird thud, but I had no idea if it had come from inside the house or the outside. I turned off my flashlight and made my way down the dark hallway.

At the door of Smithy's bedroom, I thought I heard footsteps.

"Is someone there?"

Silence greeted me.

Nerves on edge, I checked under the mattress and remade the bed. The closet was empty save for a couple of jackets. The small chest of drawers was a bust.

There were no secret treasure boxes under the bed, and I felt like a fool. Ewan's men had already done a thorough search, and he was right: nothing was here.

I glanced at my phone and realized I'd been gone much longer than I'd expected.

As I passed the bathroom on my way out, I paused.

"Is someone here?" I asked nervously.

And then everything went black.

* * *

Light flashed, but I couldn't open my eyes. I tried to wave it away.

"She's conscious," someone said.

"Sir, you'll have to leave while we examine her."

"I'm not leaving her," Ewan said gruffly.

"Stop. Yelling. Hurts." The hoarse whisper came out as more of a croak.

"Ms. McRoy, can you open your eyes for me?" That was a different male voice.

"Hurts," I said again.

"It's *Dr. McRoy*," Ewan said.

"What happened?" I croaked again.

"You suffered a head injury," a man said. "Luckily, there's not much swelling on the brain, although we weren't so sure of that when you first came in. Do you remember what happened?"

I tried to shake my head, but I couldn't move.

"Paralyzed?" I forced my eyes open just as a bright light blinded me. I shut them again.

"What? No. I'm Dr. O'Brien. We have you in a neck brace to keep your head still. You took quite a blow. You're lucky the damage wasn't worse."

"Hard head," I joked.

The doctor chuckled.

"Bloody truth." Ewan whispered the words.

"We'll need to watch you overnight. You do have a concussion and a fair-sized lump on the side of your head."

"I'm fine," I said.

"No, you're bloody not," Ewan said angrily.

I sighed.

He wasn't wrong. My head ached and my throat felt like I'd swallowed gravel.

Finally, I blinked my eyes open.

The doctor leaned over the side of the bed and smiled.

"There you are."

I tried to smile, but it hurt.

Ewan was on the other side of the bed, and a nurse was working around him as she slid a pulse monitor onto my finger.

He did not look happy about life.

"What's wrong?"

His eyebrows drew together. "You could have been killed, that's what's wrong. What were you bloody thinking?"

One of the monitors beeped loudly.

"Ewan, if you're going to stay, you must keep her calm," the doctor said. "We can't have her blood pressure going up like that."

Ewan stepped away and went to stare out a window. At least, I thought that was where he was. He'd gone out of my peripheral vison.

What had I been doing? I tried to remember, but it hurt my head.

"As I said, we'll keep an eye on you tonight. I'll be back to check on you before I end my rounds."

"Throat."

The nurse hand me a cup with a straw. "Small sips," she said.

"They incubated you before they flew you here," the doctor said as he put the chart on a hook at the end of the bed. "From what I understand, your breathing was quite shallow. Probably due to the blood loss. Those head injuries can be a mess."

I reached up to find my head bandaged all the way around.

"Yeah, it's going to hurt. We're going to give you something for the pain now, but you have at least a week before you'll feel anywhere close to normal," the doctor said before leaving.

"Someone hit me."

There was a heavy sigh, and then Ewan came back over. He pulled a chair next to the bed and sat down.

"Yes. Though more likely they knocked you so hard against the wall that you hit your head. There was so much blood we thought you were dead."

"Didn't see him."

"Him?"

I closed my eyes. "The footsteps were fast but heavy."

"I told you my men searched the place. Why were you there?"

"I needed to see for myself," I said. "I had to see the case through, and your men didn't know about the book when they searched."

He opened his mouth and then closed it again. His eyes cut up to the machines monitoring my health.

"If you feel that way in the future, please ask for assistance. You could have been killed tonight."

"How did you find me?"

"Mara and Craig said they hadn't seen you and were worried. It was as if you had disappeared after the bonfire started. They were worried. None of the shuttles had taken you down the mountain."

"But how did you find me at the cottage?"

"Millie had complained about a prowler disturbing her chickens. I had a feeling it was you."

I'd yet to meet Millie, but all the angry words I'd thought about her dissipated. She'd probably saved my life.

The books. "Hey, did your guys leave a mess at Smithy's? There were books all over the floor."

He frowned. "No. We left the place as clean as we'd found it. Why?"

"I wonder if I interrupted the prowler. I'm the one who stacked the books. That means he was hiding the whole time I was there." A shiver went down my spine.

The painkillers hit, and my eyes shut of their own accord.

"Bedroom."

"What, lass?"

The pain in my head lessened, and I sank back into the blessed darkness.

Chapter Twenty

After checking out of the hospital, Ewan flew me back to Sea Isle in his helicopter. Thankfully, it was a short trip. I'd flown in one before, but never with a head injury and a belly full of painkillers.

I'd never been so happy to feel the ground under my feet. It was an easy trip in the Land Rover, down the mountain to the church. He pulled into the roundabout and stopped.

"Thank you, for all of this. I could have managed to get myself home."

And it had become home, even if someone had tried to kill me.

"I've arranged for Abigail to see after ya during the day."

I tried to shake my head, but it hurt.

"Abigail has to plan Smithy's wake. It's—" A stabbing pain went through my head, and I closed my eyes. I fell back against the seat of the car.

"Hey, hey." Ewan's warm hand wrapped around my wrist. "Your pulse is high. Bloody doctor, he should have kept you there. I'll be having words."

I laughed, even though it hurt.

"Are you like this with everyone in town?"

"What do you mean?"

"The overbearing and overprotective laird? I'm a doctor, and I can take care of myself. I don't want to bother anyone. You can't order people around to do your bidding."

When he didn't say anything, I opened my eyes to find him staring at me like I had three heads.

"I didn't order anyone. We made a list and several people volunteered. Mara thought it best if we kept it to people you were already comfortable with, so she and Abigail decided to look after you.

"As for me wanting to protect the people here, I owe them. Many a town is suffering because the young and old move away. The people who live in Sea Isle chose to stay. So, yes, I care for them like my family. Without them, we'd be a ghost town."

"Oh. I—my head hurts. I should get inside."

I let him help me out of the car and into the church. Mara met us at the door.

"Oh, luv. You look like you've been to the wars." She took my purse and led us into the living area.

"Where's Abigail?" Ewan asked.

"Organizing the kitchen. Everyone and their sister have dropped off something to eat. Granddad is back in the surgery, trying to make sure the Jacuzzi bath mechanics are working, in case she needs a good soak."

"I'm fine, guys. Really. I took a good conk to the head, and it hurts a little, but I'm okay."

"You"—she pointed at me—"sit down and shush. You scared the livin' breath out of me when we couldn't find you. And then to see Ewan carrying you up that hill with all the blood."

Ewan carried me. I'd hardly made it down the hill on my own two feet earlier.

She bit her lip. "I was worried we lost you." She sniffed.

I'm not a hugger, but I reached my arms around her and squeezed. "Thank you for caring," I said.

"Oh, Mara you thank, but I'm an overprotective, bossy laird." Ewan chuckled. "I'll see if I can help your granddad."

"She's not wrong," Mara called out after him. "Tell me how you really are and what you were doing in Smithy's cottage." She pointed a finger. "And spare no details."

"I'm fine except a headache. And I was looking for evidence," I said. That was true.

"Ewan was white as a sheet last night. I think he thought you'd die on him before he could get ya to the hospital.

"We had a long caravan of people who went to the hospital. The lobby waiting area was a sight. The toughest part was finding someone sober to drive."

"Wait, people were at the hospital? No one told me that."

"Wasn't worth worrying you. Ewan came and gave us the news that you were going to be okay—though he didn't look like he believed it. Then he sent us all home. I was so mad. I mean, I consider myself your best friend."

I smiled. "You are."

"Right? Pigheaded man. I was so drunk I didn't remember how I got to the hospital, so it was probably a good idea to keep me away from you. I do remember crying all the way home."

"Please, tell me you didn't drive."

"Nae. Craig drove."

"I feel so guilty for pulling everyone away from the party," I said.

"Eh, all you did was save us from some end-of-night drunken brawls. A free bar in this town is basically an invitation to fight."

"That's so wrong." I laughed.

"Aye, but true. Now tell me what do you need?"

"You don't have to stay," I said as she sat on the couch.

"Nonsense, I want to. So does Abigail. There's enough food in the kitchen to feed a few armies. Others have put together a watch party. Someone tried to kill our doctor, and we don't take that sort of thing lightly."

It was hard to wrap my head—no pun intended—around all of this. "It's strange for me to have so many people who care."

"Isn't that why you moved here? We look after our own."

I'm not someone who cries much. Comes from being an ER doc for so long and shoving all those emotions down into what we called the pit. But my eyes watered, and I sniffled.

I'd had friends in Seattle, but not like this. These people genuinely cared about my safety and well-being.

"Now tell me what you need."

"Coffee. Something sweet. And a new head."

She laughed. "The first two I've got waiting for you. The third, we're going to have to order out."

I smiled.

She went off to the kitchen. My purse was on the coffee table, and I opened it to find my aftercare instructions. It had been difficult to focus on the words as the nurse checked off the steps.

My head throbbed.

I found my pills, but something was missing—I couldn't quite place what it was. I dumped the contents on the large ottoman in front of the couch.

"Oh. No."

Mara came in with my treats. "What's wrong?"

"I need Ewan."

She put the tray down and ran off. They came back quickly.

I stared down at the contents and tried to focus.

"Are you hurt? Did they give you the wrong meds?" Ewan asked.

"Where did you find my bag?"

"What?" Ewan stared at me like I'd gone mad.

"I put it down on Smithy's kitchen table while I was searching through his house. Is that where you found it?"

"I don't understand," Ewan said.

Probably because I wasn't making much sense.

"Was my bag still in the kitchen?"

He shook his head. "My men found it on the ground near the chicken coop. Why?"

"My notebook is missing."

"Did it have doctor stuff in it?" Mara asked.

I sighed. "I'd written down everything I'd learned so far about Smithy's death, from notes about the autopsy, to observations made by people I've talked to along the way. Everything, and everyone, is in that notebook."

Mara's eyes went wide.

"And now the killer has it," Ewan said.

I nodded solemnly.

Chapter Twenty-One

Smithy's wake was an odd affair. He hadn't been a religious man and had requested in his will to be cremated. His ashes, along with a picture of him as a young man, had been placed on the bar of the Pig & Whistle. From my spot at one of the round tables in the corner, I could see it all.

Abigail sat next to me. Tommy had stayed with a caregiver Ewan had hired to help. Tommy wasn't much for crowds, and I understood that better than most.

A woman stood near the picture of Smithy and clinked her glass.

"Who's that?" I asked Abigail.

"Vicar Veronica," she said. "I would have asked my priest, but uncle didn't care for him."

"Abigail and her family appreciate you showing up to say goodbye to Smithy," the vicar said. "As we all know, he was an interesting character. He took in his niece and nephew when they needed a home, and he did his best."

She looked to Abigail, who nodded and smiled.

"May he find peace wherever he lands." She held up a glass, as did everyone else. "We send you off in style, Smithy."

And that was it.

Abigail chuckled.

"What's so funny?" I whispered.

"Poor vicar. I was just thinking about how tough it must have been to even say that many nice words about my uncle."

At least she had a sense of humor about the situation.

Craig sat next to her. "Can I give you a hug, Abs?"

She nodded.

He hugged her gently. "I'm sorry you're having to go through this," he said, and it was obvious from his tone he meant it. "If you need help with anything, you let me know. I mean it."

"Thank you, Craig."

He glanced over at me. "How you feelin', Doc?"

"I'm good, thanks."

I'd pulled my hair up into a messy bun to hide the stitches on my head, but I also had two black eyes, and one of my cheeks was an odd shade of green mixed with black. No amount of makeup could hide the damage, so I hadn't bothered.

"Given your troubles, I'm surprised you were able to come."

"I wanted to be here for Abigail," I said. It had been tough, though. I'd expended a great deal of energy just getting here, and I was already tired.

"Ewan told me that you and Mara searched for me. Thanks for that."

"Aye. You gave us all a fright. Glad you're okay."

Caitlin and Mike came over and waited patiently while Craig said a few more words to Abigail.

Then he left, and they sat down.

Caitlin hugged Abigail and they started talking.

Mike kept looking at me and shaking his head.

"I'm fine," I said.

"Can't stand someone beating a woman," he said. "I hope Ewan catches the bastard fast."

His words were harsh and caring at the same time. They did not sound like the words of a guilty man.

"Me too."

Jasper came over and sat on the other side of me. He put a plate in front of me with several macarons. Then he handed me a cup of coffee.

"Decaf," he said.

"It's like you know me or something," I said before popping one of the macarons in my mouth.

He and Mike laughed.

"Way I see it, we have to keep your energy up," Jasper said. "Sea Isle needs her doctor."

"Well, I'm doing a half day tomorrow. Let folks know for me, okay?"

Jasper frowned. "That's way too soon, right? You're still black and blue."

I rolled my eyes. "I'm fine." I desperately wanted to lie down. Still, I wasn't leaving. Abigail had done so much for me, and I could tell she needed me.

Someone started singing and the whole bar joined in except for me and Abigail. I put my arm around her shoulder, and she leaned into me.

"I sometimes forget the kindness of our village," she said softly.

"It is quite amazing." I didn't recognize the haunting song they sang about lost souls at sea, but the beauty of the blended voices swept through me.

Music was intertwined deeply in the Scottish culture. No one was embarrassed about singing. It was a part of their lives as much as eating and sleeping might be.

A few hours later, my eyes drooped, and I had to shake myself awake.

"You're exhausted," Abigail said. "Let me see you home."

The music had become lively, and people danced.

"No. You stay, but I think I'll say my goodbyes." I hugged her and she rested her head on my shoulder.

"Thank ya for being here with me."

"I was happy to do so. I'm grateful to have you as a friend."

She smiled sweetly. "I feel the same way about you."

"Is there anything I can do before I leave?"

She shook her head.

I said my goodbyes as I made my way through the crowd. "I'll walk you home," Craig said as he pushed open the door.

"You don't have to do that," I said. "It's a short walk."

He shrugged. "I can use some air. Too many people for me in here."

"We have that in common," I said.

The wind had picked up again, and the temperature was a good twenty degrees cooler than when the wake had started. I pulled my sweater tightly around my shoulders.

"Here," Craig said, draping his navy peacoat over my back.

"You're going to freeze," I said. He wore a beautiful red, blue, and green kilt, with a white shirt.

"Nae. This weather is nothing to a Scotsman."

I smiled. "If I'm this chilly during the summer, I'm a bit worried about winter," I said.

"I'd say you'd get used to it, but we have a bone-chillin' cold here with the wind off the sea. Trick is to wear layers. You'll start to think everyone is gaining weight, and then come summer, you realize it was only the clothes they were putting on."

We laughed.

"Angie at the kilt shop told me that as well. I ordered quite a few things from them."

"Aye, that's a good idea. I can't remember what you Yanks call it, but you may want one of those long puffy coats for the dead of winter. That and a fur-lined pair of boots will get you through most days."

"I'll have to look into that."

As we neared the church, he cleared his throat.

"I wondered if I might ask you something, Doctor."

"Call me Em, and sure."

"I understand you still feel poorly, but when you're better, would you like to go out to dinner some time?"

I stopped. I thought he might want to ask about something medical.

"I—uh."

He waved a hand. "Sorry, that was too forward of me. You barely know me, and it's been a while since I've asked someone out. I'm sure I've messed it up."

"Oh, don't be sorry. The question was unexpected is all, and dating isn't something I'm interested in right now. With the practice and settling in, I've been busy."

"Forgive me," he said. "Why would you even be interested in someone like me?"

"Please, Craig. It's not that at all. You're a handsome and kind man. I'm just saying I can't offer anything beyond friendship."

He smiled down at me. "A man can never have too many friends."

"Neither can a woman."

"I'm all right with taking a friend to dinner if you are."

"That would be fun."

After punching in the code, I fumbled in my purse for my key, and my hand hit an envelope.

What was that?

"Thank you for walking me home." I handed him the coat.

"My pleasure. See you soon."

I slipped into the door, turned on the lights, and pulled the envelope from my purse.

When had someone had time to put this in here? My bag had hung on the back of my chair.

Heading into one of the exam offices, I found some latex gloves.

Carefully, I opened the letter.

"I should have hit you harder."

The words sent my stomach plummeting, and the hair on my arms rose.

Someone definitely wanted me dead.

Chapter
Twenty-Two

By Wednesday, I no longer needed Tylenol and had managed to work a full day. Crazy enough, I still had some energy left. The killer may have thought trying to scare me with threatening letters was the way to go, but it only made me more determined to find out who was behind these terrible actions.

It wasn't just about Smithy anymore. The murderer was after me. Finding Smithy's blackmail book was high on my list of things to accomplish.

If the killer had found it the other night, then he wouldn't be worried about my investigation.

My only problem was keeping my snooping from the laird, who had forbidden any more sleuthing on my part.

What he didn't know wouldn't hurt him.

I called Mara.

"Are you busy?"

"Truth?" she asked.

"Always."

"I just woke up from a glorious midweek nap. I'm ready for anything."

"Good. Feel like doing some snooping with me?"

She laughed. "I seem to remember the laird laying down the law about that."

"I have a job to do, and I don't take orders from the laird."

"Technically, I believe you should, but I'm in. I've wanted to play Watson to your Sherlock since this all began. Speaking of which, *Sherlock* or *Elementary*? Be careful how you answer: the state of our friendship depends on it."

This time I chuckled. "They are both great shows, but I'm a big Benedict Cumberbatch fan."

"Ding. You win, friend. What do I need to bring? I bought a black sweater and leggings in case you needed me to break in somewhere. I like to dress for success."

We laughed.

"Maybe a flashlight. I have gloves for us. Meet me at the car in ten minutes."

I changed quickly and grabbed a warm jacket for later.

"Heading out?" Abigail asked. She'd been working on updating the patient records.

"I'm going for a drive," I said. No way I'd tell her where because, as much as I adored her, she was far too loyal to Ewan.

"I can drive you," she said. "Tommy needs another hour or so in the garden. He says we'll have snow soon, and I tend to believe him."

"You stay here," I said. "Mara is taking me."

"Okay." She opened her mouth and closed it.

"What?"

"Nothing," she said. "Just be careful on your *drive*."

Darn she was perceptive. "Thanks."

At the car, Mara wore her jeans with a black sweater, black Doc Martens, and a beret.

I may have chewed on my lip to keep from smiling.

"This is my Watson outfit, what do you think?"

"Perfect," I said.

"Thanks. I'll drive. You're a great driver, but better safe than sorry with that bump on your head."

Even though I needed the practice for my test in a few weeks, I handed her the keys.

At least, I didn't have to face Smithy's house alone.

When we arrived, the chickens next door squawked.

"Hush, you, or I'll steal you for pie," Mara said.

The chickens stopped and stared at her, and then went about pecking the ground.

"Who knew you were a chicken whisperer," I said.

She grinned. "The trick is to mean what you say. They seem to understand when their lives are in danger."

We tried the front door, but it was locked, as were all the windows and the back door.

I'd ordered a lock-picking kit online, but it hadn't arrived yet.

"Hmm," I said.

"Ewan probably locked it up tight after what happened to you."

"At the very least, I should be allowed to view the scene where the crime committed against me happened."

"I watch a lot of mystery shows, and I'm pretty sure there are rules about that. But I'm happy to call Ewan if you want."

"No." The word was sharp. "I don't want him to know I'm here."

Mara laughed. "I was kidding. If he knew I drove you here, he'd have my head."

I turned in a circle. There was an old shed behind the house. At least we could try to see if it was open.

We walked toward the structure, and that strange feeling that someone might be watching us crawled down my spine.

I glanced around.

"What is it?" Mara whispered.

"I have this weird sense that someone has been watching me."

She stepped away and looked on the other side of the house. When she came back, she shook her head. "I don't see anyone."

"Do you think there's a chance the neighbor next door might have called Ewan?" I gazed over at the house. Other than the chickens, there was no sign of life.

"Millie? She's probably at the archives." She glanced at her phone. "She'll be closing soon, though. We should hurry."

"I still need to research my ancestors," I said.

"Let me know when you do, and I'll help you."

I shook off the sense of dread curled in my stomach. "Thank you, Mara. You're the best."

She blushed. "I feel the same way about you. Funny, how sometimes we connect better with strangers than our own families. It's like I grew up with you and have known you all my life."

"Exactly the same for me. Okay, let's see if we can get in here."

I was surprised when the knob turned in my hand. But the door stuck. Mara put her hands on mine, and we both pulled.

The door creaked as it swung open. It happened so fast we almost fell.

The overhead light didn't work when I pulled the chain. We took out our flashlights, or torches, as Mara called them.

The wooden building was more like a workshop. There were all kinds of rusty boat ornaments as well as tools. Hooks hung down from the rafters like scary implements of death.

"This isn't creepy or anything," I said.

Mara giggled. "I'm certain I've seen this place in an American horror film. Be careful." She ran into a table with her hip. "Ouch." The shack rumbled around us, as tools and hooks clanked together.

"I vote we just take a quick look," she said.

"Right there with you."

"Just one thing."

"What's that?"

"What are we trying to find?"

"Some sort of log or book that has notes in it. Maybe he wrote about the killer somewhere."

"You think Smithy kept a journal?" She dropped her flashlight. "Wait. You think there is a blackmail book somewhere? The one the brothers were talking about?"

I shrugged. "I don't know, but I have to check."

I had to step over a few boxes, but I headed toward an old file cabinet. My grandma had one like it in her office. She'd been a practicing general practitioner until she'd received her ALS diagnosis. She'd gone quickly after that, and I'd lost the center of my world. The one person who had always been there for me.

This file cabinet was slightly warped—probably from sitting outside in a shed.

After pulling on a few of the file doors and finding them locked tight, I went in search of a key. "Keep your eye out for a file drawer key," I said.

Mara snorted. "Tiny, flat key—I'm sure we'll find that in here."

She had a point. The shelves and benches were covered in odds and ends. The old metal desk in front of the file cabinet was piled with old books and magazines. I picked up the stacks and looked underneath.

Meanwhile, Mara had bent down and was staring at something under one of the workbenches.

"See anything?"

"Just some old ship lanterns. I wonder if Abigail and Tommy will inherit all this stuff. Or maybe Smithy left it to his sons."

"Is it odd that they didn't show up for the wake?"

"Not from what Granddad said. Something about bad business a long time ago when Smithy's wife left him and took their sons. None of them have ever come back."

"Maybe I'm nosy but I wonder why? I mean, I can understand the wife, but the sons?"

She clicked her tongue. "I don't know exactly, but I do believe violence was involved."

"Ah, that makes sense. Poor woman."

"Yeah. When he started in on Tommy, Ewan put a stop to it. That's why Abigail is so loyal to the laird. He probably saved their lives."

Abigail had said the same sort of thing.

A hardback book slipped out of my hand and thudded on the ground.

"Eek," Mara startled and then laughed.

"Sorry, it was heavier than I expected."

"I'm just jumpy," she said. "This place is spooky."

I sneezed, which made the bump on my head hurt. "And it's full of dust. Let's call it a day," I said. "You go on out—I'll be right behind you."

I bent down to pick up the book and something fell out of it. A small gray notebook.

"Ewan's coming down the hill," Mara said. "Warning! Ewan's coming down the hill."

I tucked the notebook into my bag. It was probably nothing. At home, I wouldn't have to worry about the constable staring over my shoulder.

As I came out of the shed, he pulled his Range Rover in front of Smithy's house.

"What are you doing here?" He didn't sound angry, but his eyebrow arched up.

"Her job," Mara said bravely. Then she turned and made a face at me.

"I told you we searched the premises and found nothing."

More than anything I wanted to wave the notebook in front of his face and say, "Oh, really?" But I had no idea what was in it.

"I came to investigate the crime scene," I said. "I do remember you saying something about it being my job."

"But Smithy wasn't killed here," he said smugly.

"I wasn't talking about *that* crime." I stared at him pointedly.

He frowned. "Why would you need to see where you were attacked?"

"Blood spray might tell me the height. Whoever it was left some pretty good bruises on my shoulders," and they still hurt when I moved my arms. The person had used great force to slam me against the wall, hard enough to knock me out.

"You can't investigate your own incident," he said.

"Is someone else taking care of it?" I crossed my arms.

"Me," he said.

"Oh? And what have you discovered so far?"

"That the suspect is large and male, judging from the handprints on your shoulders," he said. "The doctor pointed them out to me, and they took pictures. Unfortunately, they didn't find any DNA. The arsehole probably wore gloves.

"From the bruising, the doctor said it appeared the suspect slammed you against the wall and then punched you with his left hand, which was what caused the bruising on your chin.

"As for the blood splatter, there wasn't much. Most of it pooled beneath you when you hit the floor."

My headache returned. I'd guessed as much given my injuries, but having someone confirm it turned my stomach.

"I see," I said.

"But none of that explains why you were in the shed."

I cleared my throat. "My notebook," I said.

"You said you were only in the house that night?"

"Did I? It's all a bit fuzzy," I said. I rubbed my head and winced when my hand hit my stitches.

"I should probably get the doc home. She worked the whole day and needs her rest. But you know how she is—she couldn't rest until she looked for her notebook. Bye, Ewan."

Mara half dragged me to the car before I even realized what she'd said.

Partway down the hill, I started laughing.

"What is it?" she asked, but she was smiling.

"You may be the best Watson ever."

"I am. Did you see his face?"

"It's burned in my brain." I laughed again.

She pulled into the parking place at the bottom of the hill. "Since you're down here, do you want to grab dinner at the pub?"

I yawned. "No, I think I'll turn in very early tonight."

An American in Scotland

"Are you sure?"
"Yes, I'll see you in the morning, Watson."
"Okay, Sherlock."
Once inside, I pulled out the notebook.
"Okay, Smithy, tell me all your secrets."

Chapter
Twenty-Three

There may have been secrets contained in Smithy's notebook, but by nine that night, I was no closer to discerning them. There were initials and then a series of marks. I'd seen Morse code, but this was a derivative.

The Wi-Fi had stopped working. We only had so much bandwidth each day. I took it as a sign that it was time for bed.

That first night after the hospital, Jasper had dropped off a gift basket with several kinds of teas. One of them he swore by for sleep, so I made a cup and headed upstairs.

I'd just sat down on the bed when the house alarm screeched. The cup and saucer clattered to the nightstand. My heart in my throat, I reached in the drawer to get the pepper spray I kept there. I'd been leaving them all over the house since the last break-in.

Downstairs, I flipped the lights on in the den and carefully made my way down to the front office. I tried the door, and it was firmly locked.

I was just about to head to the back door when there was a loud bang on the front one.

"Emilia it's me," Ewan shouted. "Are you okay? I'm using the code to come in."

Before I could answer, he was inside, and the screeching of the alarm stopped.

I stood in a defensive pose with the pepper spray ready to go.

"I'm here. You're all right," he said.

"I know. I'm fine. Did you set the alarm off?"

He shook his head. "I was walking home from the pub when I heard the bloody thing. Let's check the back door."

I followed him into the kitchen. After flipping the locks, which were still in place, he opened the back door.

"Do you have a torch?"

It took a minute for my tired mind to compute what he meant. "Yes."

On my way back to the kitchen, I realized the notebook was out and slid it into my purse. Then I grabbed the flashlight I had in there.

"Hmm," he said. I glanced down to see what he'd been looking at.

"Arsehole tried to pry the door open, but the new locks held."

I breathed deeply. "Do you think it was the killer? Or maybe they were after drugs?"

He stared at me pointedly. "We can only hope it was drugs."

I frowned. "At least the alarm scared them away."

"True. Still, I'll order a new steel-enforced door to replace the wood one."

"But it's a beautiful door and may be historically significant to the house."

"I don't give a bloody care how historically accurate it might be. The damn thing would splinter with a good kick. If you aren't worried for your own safety, perhaps think about how much safer the medicines you keep will be."

"Right. Sorry. I'm tired and I'm not thinking straight."

He reached out as if he were going to touch me, and then stuck his hand in his pocket. "I'll stay here with you."

I shook my head. "You don't need to do that. I'm sure we've scared them off."

The last thing I wanted was a sleepover with the laird. Okay, maybe I might have dreamed it once, but that was when I'd been in the hospital, and I had a concussion.

"Just the same, I'll be taking the couch." He stated it as if there was no arguing.

"I'll grab you a pillow and a blanket."

After making sure he had what he needed, I went upstairs and sat on the side of my bed and sipped the tea.

Even though I'd been nervous about Ewan being downstairs, five minutes later I couldn't keep my eyes open.

* * *

The next morning the laird was gone when I went downstairs. Abigail was in the front office, working on some filing.

"Morning," she said. "I heard about your scare last night."

"Yeah, good thing Ewan was close. I think the alarm, which sears through your brain, was probably enough to scare the person off. I'm sure half the village heard it."

"I'd told you about the kids breaking in for drugs a few years ago. Nothing too bad, but that's when we put the locks on the door to the medicines. Could be they thought they could take advantage of the new doc."

"Maybe, so," I said. There was no reason to worry Abigail about the killer. She'd been through enough the last few weeks.

"When is our first appointment? The internet went down last night before I could check. I think we ran out of bandwidth."

She smiled. "Nae. Ewan upgraded our system day before yesterday so you wouldn't have to worry about it. It's the finicky router. Let me show you how to reboot it. Once you do that, it should come back on. It's a good router, just sensitive to the power surges the church gets now and then, especially when there is any kind of weather."

"Good to know," I said.

"I actually marked you down for a day off," she said. "Ewan wanted you to have one day off a week, as well as the weekends. Though you're always on call."

Ewan. Ewan. Ewan. I should have been grateful, but the last thing I wanted was some guy dictating how I ran my practice.

"Before we schedule for next week, let's talk about it first." The words came out in a harsh tone that was meant for the laird, not Abigail.

"I'm sorry. I should have asked you first," she said.

I was being a pain.

I forced myself to smile. "Abigail, don't worry. I'm just saying, the day I need off may change from week to week. That's all."

"I understand." But she didn't look like she believed me. "Do you know what day you need off next week?"

"Is there a day that works best for you?"

She stared at me with a mask of confusion.

"What?" *Did I insult her again?*

"It's embarrassing, but I'm not used to my boss asking my opinion."

I put a hand on her shoulder. "Let's get something straight. I think of you as more of a partner in this practice. I'm not sure what I'd do without you. Ewan is technically your boss. He pays you. And if you want to further your education, I'm happy to help with that. I said this before, but I'm really amazed by all you do and how you care for Tommy."

She frowned. "He's my brother."

"Exactly, and you don't think twice about taking care of him, or ever complain. I count myself lucky to have you both on my team. What day works best for you next week?"

"Wednesdays are good. I help with the kids' study group at the church in the early evening."

"Wednesdays are great for me as well. I came here for a less stressful way of life, and I never want the practice to overwhelm us or for either of us to suffer burnout like I had in Seattle."

"You came here for peace, and then some maniac hurts you."

I laughed. "Well, it hasn't been without excitement, I give you that. But so far, I love working with the patients and you."

"I can't believe I was afraid of you when you first arrived," she said.

"You were?"

"Ewan kept talking about how we had to make the fancy doctor feel welcome and that you were used to a certain way of working. He made it seem like you were an ogre out of a storybook or something, but that you were great at being a doctor."

I laughed. "I don't think I've ever been called an ogre before. Though, some of my residents at the hospital nicknamed me the witch doctor ."

"No." She clapped a hand over her mouth.

"I took it as a compliment. They named me that because I'm good at coming up with solutions when others are out of them, but I also demanded near perfection from my staff. In emergency medicine there is no time to second-guess or make the wrong decision."

"That's very true. I've admired how quickly your mind works," she said. "I'm learning a great deal from just reading your reports and running the labs."

"I'm sorry if I've been abrupt with you. I promise I never mean to be."

Her face turned red. "You aren't an ogre. Not at all. You're kind and thoughtful. And I'm grateful that you include me in the decisions."

"I'm going to head to the library. There's no reason for you to hang out here. Unless Tommy is busy with the garden."

"He is," she said. "He's preparing the garden for winter. He has a sense that there's a bad storm coming later in the week. Like I said, he is never wrong."

Tommy was just as much a wonder as his sister.

I pulled out some bills and put them on the desk.

"Take him to get Fishies when he's done. Tell him it's my treat."

She shook her head. "You don't have to—"

"I know, but I want to."

"I may use the time to look at courses. Are there any you'd like to suggest?"

"Tell me what you've done so far."

She turned the computer screen toward me. The list of classes she'd already taken online were impressive. She had almost enough credits, and with just a few more, she might be able to become an RN, or whatever the equivalent might be in Scotland.

But what surprised me most was her psychology credits.

"Do you want to be a therapist?"

"What do you mean?"

I pointed to the list. "You have as many psychology classes as you do medical ones."

She pursed her lips. "I never realized that. Some of the classes I took so I could find better ways to work with Tommy on his skills. That, and I wanted to help us both through—"

"Through what?"

Her cheeks turned pink again. "Uncle wasn't the only person who gave us a hard time when our parents died."

"Was it kids at school?"

"Aye," she said. "Tommy hadn't been diagnosed back then. Everyone thought he was slow because he didn't talk at all. The kids at his school—he'd been beaten more than once before I brought him to Doc.

"He took us both for testing in Edinburgh."

Her hands shook.

I sat down on the desk and took her hands in mine.

"If it's too upsetting, you don't have to share."

"No. It's just that other than Ewan, I've never told anyone what happened." Her voice trembled with unshed tears.

I swallowed hard.

"The decision to share is yours."

She nodded. "Tommy may not have been able to speak, but he understood incredibly complex constructs far beyond anything we could have expected. He read at a much higher level, and you've seen his interest in the natural world."

Tommy had an amazing knowledge of zoology and, evidently, weather.

"And what about you?"

She ducked her head. "I'd always been good at school. Things came more easily to me than most. But when my parents died, my grades suffered."

"That's understandable."

"I tested high in the sciences," she said, "and above average in the other subjects."

"That doesn't surprise me, Abigail. I don't think you understand how brilliant you are. Your knowledge, and ability to do so many things around here, is way above normal."

She smiled. "You said that before, but I thought you were being nice."

"I was being honest. What happened after the testing?"

"Ewan hired a tutor to work with Tommy," she said. "Even back then, he looked after us. He'd finished his law degree and had come back to Sea Isle to settle."

Ewan was a barrister?

"I continued with regular school. Once Ewan sorted Uncle, things were a bit easier at home, and I had more time to study. When I was thirteen, Doc let me work here in the afternoons. Tommy worked on the garden, and Doc taught him how to fix things around the church."

"Thirteen? Aren't there child labor laws in Scotland?"

"Aye. But it wasn't like that. I bugged poor Doc until he showed me how to run some of the machines. When I turned fifteen, he set me up with some courses. And I've been studying ever since."

"And the psychology courses?"

"I used them to help me communicate with Tommy," she said. She folded her hands on the desk. "His tutor, Mr. Gregory, taught me a great deal as well. He worked with special students like Tommy."

"How lucky you are that Ewan found him."

She chuckled. "You have no idea. Two years later, I was able to communicate with Tommy in a way that worked for him. I don't know what either of us would have done without Ewan's and Doc's help."

As much as I hated to admit it, Ewan was a good guy.

Darn.

"Oh, I've been running my mouth, and I've kept you from your day off."

"Abigail, I like spending time with you. And I'm grateful you shared all of this with me. I am curious about something, though."

"What's that?"

"Is there a career you really want for yourself? Maybe even something you've only allowed yourself to dream about?"

"I would like to be a therapist," she said quickly. "I've always wanted to help kids and families get through the rough times."

"Then you should do it."

She frowned. "I can't go away to school. Tommy will live with me the rest of my life, and I won't move him from the one place he is comfortable."

"Oh, I wouldn't ask that of you. I'm thinking there may be a way to roll all these credits toward some type of degree. At most schools, you already have enough for a minor in psychology."

I smiled at her, hoping to encourage her dreams.

"Do some research on schools and see what you can find. I have a great many friends in academia, and they'd welcome a mind like yours. Almost every major university has online coursework now. If that's what you want, we'll make it happen."

"Really?" She wore the brightest smile, as if the weight of the world had just been lifted from her shoulders.

"Yes. Do you think, once you have your degree in therapy, you might like to join the practice? I mean, you're already a partner, but you know what I mean. I like the idea of having a professional who could help with mental health as well."

She clapped her hands together. "I—yes."

"Do not do any more work today. That's an order. But you are welcome to use the computers to research schools. Do you need anything from the library or from up the mountain?"

"Nae. But thank you, Doctor Em."

"You could just call me Em."

"Maybe, when I'm a therapist," she said confidently. Her back was straighter, and her chin lifted.

"Okay, amazing Abigail. I'll see you and Tommy later."

* * *

I texted Mara, who agreed to meet me at the car.

A few minutes later, I pulled up in front of the beautiful stone library. It was large for a town this size, and I mentioned the fact to Mara.

"Oh, that is Ewan's great-great-grandfather's doing. He was a barrister, and he loved books. The estate library wasn't big enough, and he had the idea that educating the town would make everyone more prosperous.

"So, he built this building, and there are financial resources for at least three or four hundred more years of maintenance, growth, and to buy books. It rivals even the largest libraries in Scotland."

"Wow."

"I know. I almost always find what I need here, and if you don't, they will order it."

We had to wait a bit at the front desk while the librarian helped another patron.

"What are we looking for exactly?" Mara asked.

"I'm not sure why I didn't tell you, but I found this yesterday." I pulled Smithy's notebook out.

"Is that what I think it is?" she whispered back to me. "That's evidence and you should give it to Ewan."

"I will. Eventually. But I want to make sure it's pertinent to the case first."

Mara smirked. "Or at least, that's what you're telling yourself."

"Exactly. Swear you won't say a word to anyone."

"Swear," she said.

"I think it's Morse code, but it has weird initials in it, so I want to make sure I read it correctly. I'm no expert, but my gut says it's a mix of two types of code."

I was silent for a moment, and Mara waited patiently, then I continued on another topic, my family ancestry: "I picked these up a few days ago, but they weren't helpful. I learned a great deal about the origins of the clan MacRae, but I'm trying to find something more specific. And Millie never seems to be available when I have time off."

Mara laughed. "You aren't the first person to run into problems with Millie being at work. From what I understand, she organized the place when she started working there in the seventies. But she's up there in age, and the town council gives her a lot of leeway. When her assistant comes back from maternity leave, we should be able to get in there and check things out."

"I hope so," I said wistfully. There wasn't much online about my specific branch of the family. I needed to see those old records.

The librarian returned and checked my books back in, and then she directed us to the rows with code books.

All seven rows. My chest tightened.

"I had no idea there were so many kinds of code," Mara said.

"Well, we'll start with the Morse code books and then see if we can figure out what the other part of it is."

We systematically went through each book. While there were several that had information about Morse code, none of them looked like what was in the journal.

I found a book that had information on all types of code. Mara pulled down some others, and we went back to the table.

I was about to give up when she shoved her book in front of me.

"I bet you're right."

The paragraph was about how Morse was often mixed with other codes to create a personalized one that only the person writing it, or someone with the key, could read.

"Interesting," I said. "The problem is finding the other type of code."

My stomach growled, and the back of my head throbbed. We'd been at it for hours. "I'm starving. How about we check some of these out, and I buy you dinner?"

171

"Yes." She did a fist pump. "I didn't want to be rude, but I skipped lunch."

As we were checking out the books, I sensed someone might be watching us. I turned, just in time to see someone ducking behind a bookcase.

"What's wrong?" Mara said over my shoulder.

I wasn't about to say someone is watching us in front of the librarian.

"Nothing," I said. But I glanced over my shoulder again to make sure. No one was there.

You're being paranoid.

Am I?

By the time we ate lunch at a small Italian restaurant, I was ready for a nap.

We were halfway to the car when Mara stopped and glanced behind her.

"What is it?" Had she seen someone watching us?

A shiver ran down my spine.

She gently grabbed my shoulders and turned me around. "Millie's 'Open' sign is out. Let's go see if she can help you with your family."

I half walked, half jogged over. My pasta brain was gone. My hand shook with excitement when I pushed down on the handle, but the door didn't budge.

"Maybe she forgot to change the sign," I said.

Mara snorted. "Even though she's older, Millie doesn't forget things. When people say she's committed the archives to memory, they aren't joking."

She knocked.

A key turned in the door, and it opened.

"I'm headin' home," an older woman with a head full of white curls said. She had cat-eye glasses pushed on top of her head, and she wore the favorite outfit of women around here: khaki slacks, a plaid shirt, and a giant scarf around her neck. None of the colors matched.

"Oh, Millie. I wanted to introduce you to Dr. McRoy. She's been trying to get in to see the archives. She's curious about her ancestors."

Millie pulled her glasses down and eyed me from head to toe. "You the one who broke into Smithy's house?"

"I didn't break in," I said. "I was investigating."

Her eyebrows went up.

"Fine, but right now I'm going to lunch." She gently shoved Mara to the side and shut the door.

"Is there a day that might be better?" I asked politely.

"I'm busy cataloging," she said. After locking the door, she bustled past us much faster than one might expect for a woman of a certain age.

"Sorry." Mara sighed. "I swear she's normally nice."

"Probably thinks I'm a thief," I said. "I can't be mad. If she hadn't reported the break-in to Ewan, I might not be here right now."

"Don't say that." Mara put an arm around my shoulders, which were much better, as we walked to the car.

I had to make time to figure out the past, but right now I was on the hunt for a killer.

After parking, Mara helped me carry the heavy books up to the church.

I unlocked the door and turned off the security system.

She slipped as she came in, and nearly fell over.

"What was that?"

I leaned down to pick it up. There was nothing on the outside of the letter.

I didn't want to worry Mara.

"Probably something a patient dropped off, let's take the books to the kitchen."

I folded the letter and slipped it into the back pocket of my jeans.

The killer probably thought he scared me with these letters, but they only infuriated me.

I followed Mara into the kitchen, and we set everything down. "Do you want some help?"

"No, you've done so much already. Truly. I'm so grateful you're my friend."

She waved a hand. "I feel the same way about you. I have to work a double shift tomorrow. How about we do a girls' night Friday? We can eat trashy food and work on these codes or watch movies. I want you to have fun, so you'll stay."

I laughed. "You don't have to worry about that, Mara. I mean it."

She smiled. "I worry sometimes because of what happened with Smithy and someone hitting you on the head. And then Millie being so rude."

"You forget that I worked in the ER. I'm used to rude and people half out of their minds with pain, trying to get medical care. I can tell from meeting her that Millie is a woman set her in ways. I don't have a problem with that."

"Okay. But do you still want to do a girls' night? I'll bring the nail polish and whiskey."

"How do you feel about pizza?"

"Love it."

"Then it's a date."

She took off through the back door, which had been replaced while I was gone. The new one looked like old wood, but it was steel.

"Ewan." I snorted.

After setting the alarm, I sat down at the kitchen table and pulled the letter out of my pocket.

Don't read it, I thought to myself.

That was a good idea. The killer didn't seem particularly clever when it came to language. The contents would be the same. Of that, I was certain.

Why was the killer warning me?

An American in Scotland

That never made sense when I saw it in murder shows.

I'd received two letters in two days.

After grabbing some gloves from my purse, I used a nail file to open the envelope.

I unfolded the note.

You are dead.

"Not if I find you first."

Chapter
Twenty-Four

I sat straight up in bed and couldn't figure out where I was for a minute. Sleep had not been my friend since I'd moved to Scotland. I had no idea if it was because someone had broken in and stolen a body from my mortuary or if it was the constant creaking and groaning of the old church.

But for once, I'd been sound asleep until something woke me up. I listened carefully.

Silence. I shivered and it wasn't from the cold. I'd ordered a baseball bat online, as well as more pepper spray and a Taser, the last of which wasn't exactly legal here in Scotland.

I'd had one in Seattle, and it had saved lives, including mine when things went wrong in the ER one night, but it was in storage. I never thought that I'd need it here.

There were footsteps downstairs.

I gulped.

I carefully unplugged the lamp from the bed side. After taking off the shade, and unscrewing the lightbulb, I held it by the heavy iron base.

I slipped my phone in the pocket of my sleep shorts. Carefully, I tiptoed down the stairs.

The living area was dark.

My flashlight was in my purse in the kitchen.

I snuck through the living room. The wind whipped through the trees, and the branches scraped against the stained-glass windows.

Trees, I don't need the atmosphere any scarier.

Noises came from the office area. The footsteps were heavy, which meant someone big.

This is a dumb idea.

I headed back to the stairs to my bedroom and locked the door that led up to it.

What use was having the constable on call if I couldn't wake him up in the middle of the night?

Someone is in my house, I texted.

You're fine.

Arrogant jerk.

I heard them, I wrote back.

I saw them. They are gone now.

What?

Ewan, where are you?

In your office, double-checking everything.

I'm going to murder him. The headline would read: *"American Doctor Kills Beloved Town Hero."*

I was okay with that.

Furious, I whipped open the door to the living room. He'd turned on one of the side table lamps, and I blinked as my eyes adjusted to the light.

"What do you mean you saw them?"

I lifted the lid on the ottoman, which I hadn't known was there until I saw Abigail putting the clean blanket and pillows back in there.

"As I passed, it looked like someone had entered your back door. What good is it to have an alarm if you don't set it?"

I closed my eyes and counted to ten. As infuriating as he was, he may have saved my life tonight.

"When Mara left earlier, I set it."

He frowned. "That means someone knows your code."

My body quivered, and I wrapped my arms around my waist. "Maybe Abigail came back because she forgot something."

"It was definitely a man, well over six foot. The question is, where did he go? I thought I heard him in the office, but no one was there."

The house alarm buzzed loudly, and I may have jumped and screamed a little.

Before I had time to take a breath, Ewan ran to the front door. I followed him.

The front door was open, and he was gone.

I stared at the opening for a full minute. Then, I closed the door and locked it. Whoever it was had hidden where Ewan couldn't find him.

That meant it was someone who knew this place.

I glanced around my office and then the waiting area.

The bookcase stood open.

I flipped on all the lights. Breathing in more courage than I had, I went down the long hallway to the treatment rooms. The only weapon I carried was my fury. I'd grown tired of these games.

* * *

I flipped the light on in the main room. Then I proceeded to check the operating areas. I'm sure Ewan had done the same. Maybe he had been the one to leave the bookcase open.

Then I headed over to the whirlpool. At the bottom were several dirt clods, though no footprints. Had the culprit been hiding here? And if so, why were there no footprints if the dirt had come from his or her shoes?

There was dirt on the floor, but someone had wiped up any footprints they might have left.

This wasn't kids.

I swallowed hard.

I grabbed evidence bags from one of the storage cabinets. I scraped up the dirt and put it in the bags.

The front door opened just as I returned to the waiting area.

"Argh," I screamed.

Ewan stepped in and held up his hands as I tried to beat him with the plastic bags. "It's me, lass. I lost him."

"Would it hurt to knock or ring that weird doorbell before you come in? Do you have to walk in every time like you own the place? I mean, yes, of course you own it, but . . . yeah."

He had the nerve to chuckle.

"I'm sorry I scared you. What are you doing with those?" He pointed to the evidence bags.

"I found some dirt in the whirlpool and on the floor. Abigail scrubs every bit of this place daily. I thought I'd gather it just in case."

"I didn't see tracks." He ran his hand through his hair. "Maybe we can get a footprint."

I shook my head. "They wiped them up. The dirt clods and smears are all that is left."

"There wasn't anything on the floor or I would have noticed." He set the alarm again, and then headed back toward the surgical suite.

After so many scares, my legs were a bit wobbly, but I followed.

"There's a toe of a boot," he said. Using his cell, he took a picture. "Strange. There are only prints going out. This one is smeared, but the outline is still there. I'd say he's a size forty-five; I'm forty-six, and it's a bit shorter."

I didn't have the brains left to convert that into American sizes, but it was large.

"I'll have my men take a better look at this in the morning."

"If he was in here, how did you miss him? Wait. That came out wrong."

He shook his head. "No idea. Is there water in the bath?"

"A small puddle," I said.

"Aye, that's why we only see the prints going out."

"That makes sense."

He glanced into one of the operating rooms. "Might be he hid in the bath while I checked out one of the other rooms. I can't believe I missed him."

"You're sure it's a male?"

"If it was a woman, she'd have the widest shoulders I'd ever seen, and be nearly as tall as me. He was fast—lost sight of him as soon as we hit the main path up the mountain."

Hard to imagine Ewan, who looked as fit as any man I'd ever met, being outrun by anyone.

He rubbed his chin. "Don't know how I lost him."

"It's okay." I smiled.

"Why are you grinning like that?"

Because you aren't perfect.

"We have more clues substantiating what we had before. It's probably a large man who has access and knowledge of my alarm system. He's fast and he wanted something that was in my office. The footsteps never came close to the stairs of my bedroom. My guess is he was trying to get in and out without me ever knowing."

His eyebrow rose. "Did you tell anyone the code to the alarm?"

He did that a great deal.

"Of course not," I grunted. "Maybe, it's one of the guys who installed the alarm."

"It is not one of my men," he said sternly. Then he pulled out his cell and dialed a number.

"Yes, I bloody well know what time it is. I'm at the doc's place. She had an intruder who knew the code."

There was silence on the other end.

"Cole, answer me."

There was a garbled sound, and I couldn't make out what the other guy said.

"What? Check and see if that was used tonight."

No one said anything, and then the unintelligible voice spoke quickly.

"We'll discuss this in the morning. I want you here first thing to change the override code, and this had better never happen again. Do you understand?" I'd never seen Ewan so angry.

"What happened?"

"Bloody Cole left his toolkit in his truck while he was at the pub. Someone cleaned him out."

"What does that have to do with my alarm?"

"He writes the override codes in a small book he keeps in his tool kit, in case he's ever without his computer when a client calls him. Bloody idiot had to be driven home tonight from Harry's. He was drunk, and he can't remember who it bloody was. Might not be the person who stole his kit, anyway.

"I'm sorry about this."

I liked people who took responsibility for their actions, but this was too much.

"It's not your fault," Ewan said. "And though it scared the heck out of me, at least we have a better idea of who the person is, and we know that he was probably at Harry's Pub tonight. This guy is clever and knows the church and the mountain well enough to hide and get away quickly."

My investigation must have hit a nerve if the killer was worried enough to go to such lengths. What if Cole's memory returned, and he remembered who had driven him home?

"Did you find something at Smithy's? Is that what they were after?"

His question caught me off guard.

Come clean. Ewan had experience with the law, and it was time to hand the journal over.

But did he have the time to decipher the code? The book could say just about anything. I had to make sure that it was the blackmail book first.

My protective nature took over. If Smithy had written something down about Caitlin, I had to protect her. I'd called Mike's boss, and his alibi checked out.

"No," the word came out as a croak. "You were there. I could use a snack. Are you hungry?"

I hated lying, but I had to make sure the book was real evidence. In a way, I was doing Ewan a favor by not wasting his time.

Keep telling yourself that.

Tomorrow, I'd head to Harry's Pub to have a chat.

Someone might have seen Smithy's killer.

Chapter Twenty-Five

Harry's Pub had to wait longer than I'd expected. My patients were stacked up the next morning and long into the afternoon. We had four last-minute emergencies, most of them broken bones on some teens who thought it was cool to jump rocks in the Highlands. One had fallen, and as the others tried to save him, they had injured themselves too.

I'd been surprised they made it down the mountain with all the broken bones.

Their parents were out in the lobby, but I was busy bandaging the broken wrist of one of the boys.

"Why would you do something so dangerous?" I asked.

He had a Harry Potter vibe going on, though his round spectacles had been scratched and twisted during his fall.

"It was a lark."

"A lark worth dying over?"

He sighed deeply, as only teens can do. "We saw a scarf, and we were worried there might be someone down there," he said.

I smiled at him. "I'm not judging," I said.

He glanced at me as if he didn't believe me.

"Might be hard to imagine, but I was once a teen. I mean it was like a thousand years ago."

He laughed.

"Couldn't you tell it was just a scarf?"

"Nae. The edge was poking out under one of the long rocks. People sometimes use the ledges to get out of the rain, but the rocks are slippery, and it's easy to hurt yourself."

"Oh. Really?"

"Yeah. You made a joke. Funny, Doc."

"Next time you're worried about someone being hurt, call emergency services."

He sighed. "It was Amos's idea to climb down. But then he fell. Some of the smaller rocks slid down the mountain, and we worried there wasn't time to get help."

They'd been stupid, but also brave.

"All of you have broken bones because of a scarf. It'll be months before you're healed, and then physical therapy."

"Physical therapy. Like the footballers? Cool."

I turned away to grab some more tape, so he didn't see me smile.

"If one of you had died, would you think it was cool?"

"No, Doctor. I promise. We won't do anything like that again."

He was a teen boy, and I had my suspicions that what he was saying was far from true, but he seemed to believe it in the moment.

"Okay. What color cast do you want?"

"What color did the other lads get?"

I told him.

"Aye, then I'll take purple."

They weren't bad kids. They were around fifteen, and they'd all been much more respectful than any teen I'd come across in America. One of the boys told me they were in the area looking for treasure.

While I'd been too busy trying to get into college early when I was fifteen, I'd run across my fair share of smart young people who had made dumb decisions.

After plastering the cast, I walked him back into the lobby, where I found Ewan talking calmly with the parents and boys I'd already treated.

"You all know that area is off limits. You could have been killed. Use your bony heads next time. We've found more than one dead body right where you fell.

"I'll let you off with a warning. If I catch you up there, I'll have the lot of you in the *barlinne* before your next breath. Understood?"

I'd have to look up *barlinne*, but I had a feeling it was jail.

"Yes, sir, Mr. Constable," the boys said in unison. I had to hide a grin. Ewan's stern expression had the young men shaking in their sneakers.

Amos, the boy who had broken his leg, turned gray and then he swayed. "Sit down," I said as I helped him into the chair behind him. "Look at me, Amos. Breathe deep, like I am."

His body shook. "Ewan, I need a blanket from the storage closet in the surgical suite." He ran off before I finished the sentence.

"What's wrong with him?" his mom asked.

"Shock, though not a bad case," I said. The boy's breathing had already deepened, and color came back to his cheeks.

The other boys sat down in the chairs around us.

"Oh, Amos," his mom cried out.

One of the other mothers shook her head and pointed a finger at her son. "You ever scare me like this again, and I'll let your dad send you to St. Francis's."

The boy's eyes went wide.

The rest of them ducked their heads and stared at their muddy boots, then left with their parents.

Not long after, Amos's dad showed up. He was a huge man, and his voice boomed. "You could have died." I was about to intervene, but then the man wrapped his arms around his son and sobbed.

The boy patted his back like he was consoling a child. "Sorry, Da. Sorry, I scared you." His color was back.

"I've printed out some aftercare instructions." I handed them to his mom. "And I wrote my number on the bottom. If you have any questions or he starts to show symptoms of shock, call me. But I think he's going to be okay."

A half hour later, the boy's father carried him out to their car.

"What is St. Francis's?" I asked as I shut the door.

Ewan grinned. "A boarding school run by the most ruthless nuns you've ever met."

"Sounds scary."

He chuckled. "It was, but those women gave me a fine education."

"Did they beat you?"

"Oh no. It wasn't like the movies—although I might have preferred it. The sisters were masterful at using the wrath of God on us. One look from the nuns, and you'd be offering to do extra chores."

I laughed.

"But the scariest bit of punishment was the silent condemnation. As if they were giving you time to go through every stupid thing you'd ever done and how God might punish you when it was your time."

"I kind of like these nuns."

He chuckled. "There isn't a boy who went there who isn't grateful. I'm running late. I've got to go."

Then he left.

On the desk was the scarf the boys had risked their lives to pick up. It looked a bit worse for wear, but nothing a good cleaning wouldn't do for it.

I flicked away some of the mud and then found a label for the tartan plaid. The boys had fallen thirty feet away from where Smithy had been killed. The trees were dense in that area, and I hadn't noticed the ledge just beyond them.

Wait. Could this belong to the killer or Smithy? There had been a fight before he hit that tree.

"That's a reach." I said.

"What's that?" Abigail asked. She carried a mop and a bucket. I'd offer to help clean up, but she wouldn't let me. Cleaning was her thing, and I wasn't about to interrupt.

She'd done the X-rays and even ran the MRI on Amos, who had hit his head in addition to breaking his leg.

"This is the scarf the boys found. Do you know what clan the plaid is from, by chance? Did it maybe belong to your uncle?"

She stared at it and then shook her head. "No. I don't think so. Why?"

I shrugged. "That's the same area—uh, it's close to the bothy," I said. Bringing up her uncle's murder would only cause her grief. "I thought he might have dropped it."

She frowned and then shook her head.

"Nae. He didn't like wide scarves like that."

"Thanks," I said. "Oh, there's something I wanted to ask you."

She looked at me, waiting.

"I was wondering if you might want to join Mara and me for an impromptu girls' night out tomorrow."

She smiled shyly. "You want to invite me?"

"Of course. We're friends, right?"

She nodded and then sniffed. "Yes, but Mara's closer to—"

"My age?" I finished for her. Abigail was about fifteen years younger, but she had the soul of someone much older.

She gasped. "No. Not at all. I meant, you're closer to her, I dinna want to impose."

"It's not imposing if you're invited."

"I'd be honored," she said. "I'll see if I can find someone to watch Tommy for me."

"Great. If need be, you can bring him with you, and we can set him up in my room upstairs or in the kitchen with his books and video games."

Over the past few weeks, I'd discovered gardening wasn't Tommy's only talent. He was well read and belonged to a team that played some sort of game with warriors online. He never spoke when he played. That's what Abigail had said.

I thought of Tommy and her as family, as in I only ever wanted the very best for them. Funny how these Scots had opened my cold, dead heart in just a few weeks.

"Thanks."

"I need to run some errands. You mind locking up?"

"Not at all."

"Oh, and don't forget the new code. Please don't share it with anyone."

"Ewan gave me the same lecture he did you," she said.

I laughed. "He is a careful man."

"Aye," she said. "But it gives me the willies that someone just walked right in."

The hair rose on my neck, but I refused to think about the intruder being so close while I'd been sleeping.

"Me too."

* * *

The reason for my first stop at Buth Feileadh was twofold. I'd put the scarf the boys had found in a plastic evidence bag, and I hoped Angie's grandfather might help me identify the owner.

"Emilia," Angie said as I walked in the door, "it's good to see you."

I smiled. "I didn't expect you to be here," I said.

She laughed. "I just arrived with a shipment from Edinburgh, which includes your order."

"Look at me with the good timing."

Angie grinned. "I can't wait to show you everything."

"I'm excited," I said. "Before that, I was wondering if your grandfather might help me identify what clan this tartan belongs to?"

Her eyes opened wide when I put the plastic evidence bag on the counter.

"Is it from the incident?"

"No. Some of my patients today found it wedged into a cliff, and I wanted to return it to the owner."

She eyed me suspiciously, as if she didn't believe my words. "Needs a cleaning."

She pursed her lips. "Even muddy, I can tell it isn't one of ours. We use a tighter weave, but I'll ask Granddad to identify the pattern."

While she was in the back of the shop, I looked around again at their beautiful clothing.

When Angie came back, I met her at the counter. Her arms were loaded with green boxes tied with gold ribbon. "These are all yours. Let me get the rest."

I'd gone a little crazy when I was here last and had forgotten how much I'd bought.

By the time she returned, the counter was full of boxes.

Her granddad followed her out with more. He handed me the plastic baggie. "Wilsons," he said. "But I'm not sure which clan. They each have their own version of the weave."

"Thanks," I said. Mara's grandparents were Wilsons. Could the scarf belong to someone in her family?

"Are you okay? You look pale."

"Did I really buy all this? I'm kidding." I laughed a little too loud.

They chuckled.

"Don't worry, you'll use everything for years to come," Angie said. "Do you want to try them on here to make sure everything fits? Tailoring is free."

I glanced at my phone, to see the time, and then I made a face. "I don't really have time today. I have so many errands to run before the shops close."

"We'll help you load them in your car," she said. Ewan had said it was okay to drive without my license, but I'd kept my solo trips to a minimum.

"Thank you."

Angie made jokes with her granddad as they helped me, and I mentioned they should play comedy clubs.

"This is only for my own enjoyment," her grandfather said. Then he winked at me. I hadn't laughed this hard in a long time.

The grandfather was quick and sharp-tongued, but Angie gave right back to him.

"Angie, before you go . . ."

"What is it?" she asked.

"Do you know Mara and Abigail?"

She blinked. "Mara and I are friends. I know about Abigail and Tommy. I'm friends with Ewan, and he looks after them."

Angie was so bold, I had a difficult time imagining her being friends with the overprotective Ewan.

"You probably have plans, but I'd love for you to come to girls' night with Mara and me, and possibly Abigail."

She smiled. "Oh?"

"You don't know me well, and it's a last-minute sort of thing."

"What can I bring?" she asked excitedly. "And here I thought I'd be bored this weekend, planning wedding stuff."

"Wedding?"

"Aye. I'm getting married in a few months." She held up her hand. She wore a huge sapphire and diamond ring.

"That is gorgeous."

"It is. Been in Sully's family for ages. Tell me, what I can bring?"

"Just yourself."

"Oh no. In Scotland, if you don't bring food, wine, or a gift to a party, people will talk about how ungrateful you are for years, and it's considered bad luck."

"We can't have that." I laughed. "Bring whatever you think we might enjoy. Maybe around seven or so? It's super low key. Pizza and movies, or whatever else we might come up with, and feel free to wear what's most comfortable."

"This is my kind of party," she said. "Don't get me wrong, I love to dress up for a do, but casual is just as fun."

* * *

By the time I finished my errands, I realized I'd forgotten to tell Mara I'd invited more people.

I texted her the info, and she sent me a message back: *Yay! The more, the merrier.* I was glad she felt that way.

An American in Scotland

Since I was alone and had so many packages, I drove up to the circle in front of the church. After unloading everything, I was exhausted.

But I had one more stop, and I wouldn't be able to sleep until I went there.

Chapter
Twenty-Six

After a quick shower and a change of clothes, I put on one of my new coats. It fit perfectly. I was grateful for the hood as I walked to Harry's Pub. A heavy mist fell from the mountains, and it almost felt like night since the sun was blocked.

Even though my driving skills had improved, I had no wish to practice in the rain. I'd also seen one too many accident victims come through the ER from drunk driving.

I planned to sip a pint while I snooped at Harry's. My stomach growled. Maybe I'd have a few snacks.

Inside was quite different from Mara's pub. This one had dead deer heads all over the walls, and everything was hunter green. The occupants were mostly male, with a few women sprinkled about.

"Em?"

Between the music and conversations, the place was loud. I turned in a circle to see who had called my name, and then decided I must have imagined it.

I made my way around the crowd near the door and was almost to the bar, when there was another big crowd of people.

It was a Thursday night, and I hadn't expected it to be so busy.

The Pig & Whistle had been equally crowded when I walked by. What happens on Thursday nights?

"Em. Behind you." A voice said over the din.

I turned and ran straight into Jasper.

"Eek."

He steadied me with his hands. "Didn't mean to frighten you, luv."

"Surprised," I said. I grinned. "What are you doing here?"

"Having a pint with some friends. We have a pitcher—why don't you join us?" Even though he was right in front of me, it was difficult to hear. Any investigating would have to wait until a slower night.

"Sure," I said.

He led me back toward the door to a booth. Craig was there, and Cole, who I'd met when he installed my alarm. Poor guy had to hear it again from Ewan this morning when he'd come back to give me a new code.

He'd been so loud that I'd gone outside to tell him to be quiet. He had disturbed my patients.

I didn't hear him after that.

"You, I owe a pint," Cole said—although what he was drinking looked like a soda. People here didn't like ice in their drinks, so it was hard to tell.

I took my coat off and folded it between Craig and me, while Jasper sat next to Cole.

"Hello, Doc." Craig smiled.

"Hey. Nice to see you again. Why is it so crowded?"

The men laughed.

"Thursday is trivia night, and the pubs are connected, so it doesn't matter which one you're at," Jasper said.

"Shouldn't you be supporting the Wilsons?" I asked Craig.

They laughed again.

"We compete as teams," Craig said. "And a third of all the proceeds from the bar go to a local children's charity. We're all doing our part. Well, Cole is our designated driver tonight, so he's keeping a clear head."

"After last night, and today, I won't be drinkin' for a while." He laughed. "I am so sorry, Doc. I didn't have a chance to apologize."

"Don't worry about it. Someone stole your stuff. You couldn't help it. Did you remember who drove you home?"

Craig pointed to himself. "That was me. I'd walked to the pub, and he lives close. I drove him home. I was so busy getting him into his house, I can't say that I locked up his lorry. I feel awful about it."

Jasper picked up the pitcher in the middle of the table and nodded toward me.

"Yes, please." I sipped the ale.

"I feel out of the loop. What happened?" Jasper asked.

"Someone used my code book to break into the doc's place," Cole said. "I can't apologize enough, Doctor."

"Cole. Stop. I mean it. No harm was done. Ewan scared whoever it was away."

"Ewan was there?" Craig asked.

"Saw them going in," Cole answered. "Male, about as tall as he is."

"You must have been scared to death," Jasper said. "I'm sorry you had to go through that."

"I agree," Craig added. "I thought you guys were doing a watch." He seemed upset.

Cole sighed. "We were between shifts. Mal had a family emergency and ran home. That's why he called Ewan. He couldn't get in touch with anyone else. It was only ten minutes between when he left and when Ewan arrived."

No one had mentioned any of that, and I'd forgotten Ewan's men were keeping an eye on the church.

The timing was weird, though. The intruder had entered just as one of Ewan's men left. That had to be someone on his team.

"I'll come stay with you until they catch the arsehole," Jasper said.

"You are sweet, my friend, but I'm fine. The intruder came nowhere near me. He was in my office. For all we know, it could have been a teen, trying to find drugs. Abigail said that has happened before."

"True," Craig said. "Still, you have my number. If you are ever afraid, don't be afraid to call."

"Why does she have your number?" Cole asked. "You two . . .?"

"No," Craig and I said at the same time. Then we laughed hard. The other guys joined in.

"I was following up on some alibis," I said. That seemed like years ago. "Craig was helping me out. I'm curious how you all know one another." I was desperate to change the subject.

"It's a small town," Jasper said. "I went to school with Cole. He used to keep the footballers from beating me to death."

Cole punched Jasper in the arm. "My ma was sick back then. This man and his parents kept me, and my brothers and sisters, fed. It was the least I could do."

I didn't know Cole well, but my estimation of him rose by several degrees.

"Now, Doc, for the important question," Craig said.

"What's that?"

"How good are you at trivia?"

"Unless it has something to do with medicine or bones, you do not want me on your team. I've never won a game of trivia in my life."

It wasn't until I was much older that I had even watched television or went to movies. My husband had made it his mission to teach me all about pop culture.

He had always worried that I took life too seriously.

My stomach knotted. It was the first time I'd thought about him in a few days.

In Seattle, memories of him had been everywhere. Even two years later, it had come to a point where it had been impossible to forget what he'd done.

I wasn't sure if it was the burnout or the fact that I couldn't reconcile what he'd done with the man I knew him to be, and I ran away.

"Em, you okay?" Craig's voice was in my ear. I'd been holding my pint halfway to my mouth and hadn't realized it.

"Oh, my mouth. That's where this was going?" I sipped the beer. "Are you guys sure you want me on your team?"

They laughed.

* * *

A few hours later, our team had come in third, and I'd been able to contribute far more than I'd imagined. One of the categories was mystery shows. I nailed every answer.

The guys fist-bumped over the table as they cheered.

"That's the best we've ever done," Cole said. "Doc, you're our lucky charm. Can I buy another around? I owe you at least that."

"You don't owe me anything," I said. "I ate half your nachos and a good portion of whatever hot cheese thing that is." I pointed to the bowl. It was several kinds of cheeses, with different kinds of shellfish mixed in. It had been served with toast points, and I would be back to order that again. "Besides, I have early appointments tomorrow. I'm going to head out."

Before they could argue, I slid from the booth.

"I'll walk you home," Craig said.

"Nae. I've got it," Jasper said. "Those cakes don't make themselves at three in the morning."

We all laughed.

We stepped outside. The rain fell in sheets now. I felt guilty about him walking me all the way home when his shop was right there.

"Jasper, you are sweet, but I'll be fine. I promise. The sidewalk is well lit."

"Nae. I'll be walking you to the door. You're my friend, Em. I don't want anything to happen to you."

"You're going to be soaked."

He laughed. "A bit of water never hurt a Scotsman." He had a coat that was made like mine, and he pulled a cap from its pocket. We talked about some of the questions that had come up and the funny answers others had given in the pub.

"Ya know, I think Craig might be sweet on you." We'd reached the bottom of the hill. I slipped a bit, and he held my arm.

"What? He was just being nice."

"Nae. You were so focused on the game; I don't think you noticed the way he looked at you. All lovey-dovey."

I snorted. "He drank a lot of beer. I think he was trying to focus."

Jasper helped me up the hill. The rain pounded down hard, and it was useless to try and talk. When we reached the portico over the circular drive, it was a relief.

I'd lived in Seattle a long time and was used to rain, but not like this.

The flood lights came on, and the door became visible.

"What is that?" Jasper asked.

I stopped. "Don't touch it."

He jumped back.

I pulled my phone out of my purse.

"Who are you calling?" he asked.

"The constable."

Chapter Twenty-Seven

Friday went by in a blur of patients. We'd had several emergencies come by early in the morning. And it was nearing four by the time we'd finished for the day.

Thankfully, I had bought pizza fixings from the gourmet store and ready-made dough from the bread shop. That way everyone could make their own pizza.

After getting everything organized, I ran upstairs to shower before my guests arrived. I'd stepped out of the shower when the alarm buzzed on my phone.

I glanced out the window and saw Mara, her arms full of bags.

I wrapped my robe around me quickly.

"Coming," I shouted into the speaker, and I ran downstairs.

My feet slipped a bit when I went from the wood floors to the slate ones in the entry. I made a full stop just before reaching the door.

A note card was on the floor. The same kind of paper as before.

I picked it up and then ran to my office. I stuck it under some files there.

"You are not ruining my fun tonight," I said aloud.

"Couldn't hear you," Mara said when I opened the door. "What were you saying?"

Abigail and Angie weren't far behind her. They too had their arms full of food.

I smiled. "That I was coming. What is all this?"

"Everything we need for a good party," Angie said.

Abigail smiled sweetly. "I wasn't sure what people might like, so I made a lot of different things."

"Well, we definitely won't go hungry."

I led them into the kitchen.

By the time the food was unloaded, the counters were full, as well as the long wooden table.

"Maybe we should make it a girls' week," Mara joked.

"We do have enough food for an army," I said.

"I think it looks a little bit like heaven," Angie piped in. "Abigail— wine or Scotch?"

"I'll start with wine," Abigail said.

"Where's Tommy?" Mara asked.

"He went to Edinburgh with Ewan, who had to pick something up," she said. "He loves riding in the car, and Ewan is his favorite person."

"I keep trying to convince Em that Ewan is a good guy, but I'm not sure she believes me," Mara said. "You tell her, Angie. You used to date him."

Angie rolled her eyes. "When we did our A levels. It didn't last long. He thought I was too dramatic, can you imagine?" She snorted.

Like the rest of them, she wore jeans, but her magenta blouse had ruffles from the neckline to the waist, and down the arms. And she wore black boots with six-inch heels. I had no idea how she'd made it up the muddy hill without a speck on them, but she had.

"I was so insulted by his comment, I didn't speak to him for years. Then he came into the shop in Edinburgh. We got to talking, and he helped me figure out how to grow my business. Not sure what I would have done without him. Also, he's responsible for introducing me to Sully."

I remembered Sully was her fiancé.

"And I'm jabbering," she said. "I just wanted you to know there wasn't ever anything romantic between Ewan and me. Except for a peck on the cheek, I don't think we even kissed."

"Well, considering your dating history, that is surprising," Mara joked.

"Cow." Angie playfully swatted Mara's shoulder. "True, but the good doc doesn't need to know all the sordid details—at least until we have a few more drinks in us."

"Why would I care about Ewan's dating history?"

The women burst out laughing.

"What?"

"Let's just say, Ewan has taken more than a passing interest in you," Mara said.

"No." I waved a hand at her. "It's not like that. His only worry is that I'll decide to run away again."

"Again?" Abigail asked. The jovial fun had taken a turn into the uncomfortable.

Freudian slip, anyone? "I mean, I did leave a promising career to move across the world and hang out with you guys."

That lightened the mood. After that, we joked with one another as we set about getting the food ready. Abigail took it upon herself to put everything in order so it would be easier to tell who had what.

After I burned the first pizza round, Mara decided she'd be the one to bake them.

When everything was heated, we sat around the big table in the kitchen, sharing a bottle of wine, and then another.

"And Ewan is letting us use the castle in Edinburgh for the wedding. Not many exes would do that."

I'd been asking about her wedding details.

"No, they wouldn't," I said. "And for the record, I never said he was a bad guy—just that he annoys me."

"Oh, that I understand," Angie said. "I'm not sure there's a more protective man on the planet. He treats everyone in this town like family, and he's so bossy."

We laughed.

"He just walks into the church like he owns the place," I said. "I mean, technically he does, but I deserve some privacy."

"Does he?" Abigail asked.

"Aye," Mara answered. "Scared her to death more than once. Says he's only looking out after her, but he hasn't been sleeping in the pub looking after me." She waggled her eyebrows, and we all laughed.

"I told you. He just doesn't want someone to murder me. It's hard to get a doctor to live here. At least, that's what he told me."

"Someone is trying to kill you?" Angie's eyes went wide.

"Conked her hard on the head and sent her to the hospital," Mara said. "You must have left before all that happened at the Gathering."

"I did leave early. I had to get back to Edinburgh. I can't believe someone attacked her at the party."

"Was at my uncle's," Abigail said.

"We're only on our second bottle of wine, but I'm so confused."

Mara explained what had happened that night. Thankfully, she left out what I'd been looking for when I'd snuck away.

"Oh. You poor thing," Angie said. "I'm so glad you're okay."

"Wait. Back up," I said. "Ewan has a castle?"

They stared at one another.

"You don't know about Ewan, do you?" Angie asked.

"Other than that he's the laird, constable, mayor—and extremely bossy—what do I need to know?"

"He's one of the richest men in Scotland," Abigail said. "At least, that's what they said in one of the magazines."

"He's so private, no one knows exactly how much he's worth, but the companies he owns are extremely successful," Mara added.

"We're talking more than a hundred billion," Angie said.

I had a mouth full of wine and spit it back in my cup to keep from choking on it.

My friends laughed so hard, I thought they might fall on the floor. The giggling went on for a good ten minutes. Poor Abigail was gasping for breath.

I'd been to the country house estate, where the festival had been thrown, so I knew Ewan had money, but hadn't realized how much. And I certainly didn't know about a castle.

All that money and he was taking Tommy with him so Abigail could have some girl time.

"Fine. I'll say he's a good man if we change the subject. Angie, tell us more about your wedding."

She shook her head. "Are you sure? I tend to get a little crazy when I start talking about it."

Mara patted her shoulder. "Of course, we want to hear. It isn't every day royalty gets married."

"Why do I feel so out of the loop? Royalty?"

Other than sometimes being involved with the same charities, I'd never paid much attention to royals.

"It's not like what they have in England," Angie said. "My grandpa on my dad's side is a marquis. The title was given to our family two hundred years ago when we helped with something. I can't remember what."

I smiled.

"Angie, you should know your family history," Mara chided.

"Anyway, my soon-to-be husband is a duke. And while we'd both rather have a small, intimate gathering, there are certain things that must happen when royals marry."

"Tell us." Abigail said. "I only know what I've read in the paper.

"Really? My fiancé is one of those guys who doesn't mind tasting the cake, but after that, he wants me to make the rest of the decisions and says all the details give him a headache."

Angie shook her head, then continued.

"I know I should mind and want him to be more a part of it, but he's right. It is easier this way. Besides, if he's involved, then his mother is, and that's a very long and involved story no one wants to hear. She doesn't approve of my style—or anything else I do."

"Oh no," I said. "That's not good."

"Luckily, Sully thinks I'm the grandest broad who ever lived."

"I've never been married, but the details for a royal wedding must be overwhelming," Abigail said.

I'd been married in a courthouse. Big weddings never had the appeal for me that they did for other women. My husband and I didn't have much family, and we'd thought doing it on our own was best.

"Not if you have my ma." Angie smiled. "She gets me like no one else in our family. She made everyone in the wedding party binders with checklists, which is what makes her such a great CFO for our business."

I had a little twinge of jealousy when I remembered my own mother leaving me.

"She sends me reminder texts explaining when I need to do something, and I just do it. The great thing is, I know she has opinions—she's never lacked for them. But she lets me do exactly what I want."

"A wedding at a castle . . . it has to be a fairy-tale theme," I said.

Angie smiled. "Well, more of a punk rock fairy tale. That's the reason my mom stays out of the decision making. My dress is red, and I promised my guy he wouldn't have to wear a tux, but he's wearing his sexy kilt and a black shirt and jacket I bought him. Black is his favorite color.

"And his company designed sneakers for him and the groomsmen."

This guy didn't sound like any duke I'd ever heard of.

"I like that you're doing it your way," Mara said.

"Me too," I said.

"The reception will be more of a party. The only thing we caved to was that we'd use the chapel at the castle for the vows. My mother is strong when it comes to her faith. Nearly killed her when she had to get her marriage to dad annulled."

"I'm sorry to hear that," I said.

"Long story," Angie said, took a breath, then continued to talk about her wedding. "Then the reception will be held in the ballroom."

I thought most castles were small, especially ones in Scotland. Not that I was an expert, but I had done some reading.

"And this is Ewan's castle?"

She nodded excitedly. "The big one in Edinburgh. We thought about the one he has in the highlands, but it won't accommodate everyone Sully's mom needs to invite. So, Ewan offered. Did I mention he and Sully are friends? Anyway, that's what we're doing. Now, someone else talk."

Ewan had more than one castle? No wonder he was so bossy.

The wine flowed freely as we talked about life.

"Oh, did you remember to ask Mara about the scarf?" Angie asked. "She's a Wilson, she might know."

"What scarf?" Mara asked.

"The one the boys found up the mountain over by the falls," Abigail answered. She'd been so much more outgoing tonight. I couldn't have been happier.

"Let me see it. Why do you think it's someone in my family?"

I went in the laundry room to find my purse, where I'd stashed it, but the scarf wasn't in there.

"Huh."

"What's wrong?" Mara asked.

"It must have fallen out in the car."

"I'll go get it," Abigail said.

"No, it's okay. You three keep an eye on the pie. God forbid we don't have a sample of every dessert known to man."

They laughed.

I used the key fob to turn the alarm off and headed down the hill to the car.

I searched all over, but I couldn't find it. I shut the door and swore I saw someone move in the garden. A shiver ran down my spine.

"Is someone there? Come out and face me, you coward." The wine had made me much braver than I felt.

"Who are you talking to?" Mara whispered by my side.

My attention had been so focused on the garden, I hadn't seen her come out.

I might have screamed.

Then she screamed.

Then I screamed again.

Abigail and Angie ran out. Angie held a broom like a sword. Abigail had a huge iron frying pan. They looked so fierce, and I laughed.

A nervous titter at first, and then everything came out as a big cackle. I couldn't stop, no matter how hard I tried.

"What's wrong with her?" Abigail said. "We heard screams."

Mara shrugged, and I laughed so hard tears streamed from my eyes.

"She's gone mad," Angie said. "Or she's drunk. How many glasses did she have? That merlot did go kind of quick."

"Aye," Mara said. They were so serious, and I couldn't stop.

I managed to point toward the garden.

"Someone was in the garden?" Mara surmised.

I nodded, and then the laughter spilled out again.

What is wrong with me?

"Do you think it's the killer?" Abigail stared menacingly at the flowers and held her frying pan higher.

I giggled even louder.

"The killer? Let's get back inside," Angie said seriously.

I felt bad that they were so worried, and I couldn't stop giggling long enough to speak.

"I agree," Mara said. "I think maybe I scared Em, and then she scared me, and yeah, we were kind of loud. Maybe this is her way of letting off steam."

I finally caught my breath. "What she said?"

"Should we check it out?" Mara puffed out her chest. I forced myself to look away, so I didn't start laughing again.

"We probably scared them off with our screams."

"Why would someone be lurking in your garden?" Angie asked.

"Do you think it has anything to do with those horrible letters you've been getting?" Abigail asked.

"How did you know?"

She sighed. "You left them in a stack on your desk, and I thought you wanted them sent out, but they were open. And I, uh, peeked, so I could address them for you. Does Ewan know about them?"

"Some," I said.

"I think my feelings are hurt," Mara said. "Why didn't you tell me about the threatening letters?"

"I vote we go inside and force her to tell us everything," Angie said.

"Agreed," the other women said in unison.

"I couldn't find it," I said as we made our way into the living area.

"The scarf?" Angie asked.

"Maybe I accidentally left it at the store?"

"Nae, I sent Granddad to the pub a bit early, and I cleaned up. It wasn't there."

I frowned. "Maybe it fell out when we were loading the boxes, but I've lost it."

"Why did you want to ask me about it?" Mara asked.

"It was Wilson tartan, but not the kind you and your grand folks wear," Angie said. "But maybe someone wore it into the pub."

"After we eat, I could draw it for you," Abigail said.

We all turned toward her.

"I forgot about that," Mara said.

"What?" I asked.

"Abigail can draw anything," Angie added. "She's a brilliant artist and won all the awards in school."

"You never cease to surprise me in good ways," I said to Abigail.

She blushed.

"If you draw the pattern, I might remember it," Mara said. "But be warned—lots of tourists wear scarves. Why are you so interested in it?" she asked me.

"It was found near a crime scene."

Her eyes went wide. "And you think it belongs to someone in my family?"

"Of course not." I said abruptly. "And it may have nothing to do with the case. I'm just curious."

"Oh. Okay." She took a deep breath.

"His killer is most likely someone close to him," I said.

Abigail's face paled. "Like me?" she whispered.

"I've had waaaay too much wine. No. No. Not at all. No one in this room killed Smithy. I'm the queen of foot-in-mouth disease. I didn't intend to—we should eat dessert."

Mara cracked a smile. "Just messing with you, Em."

Abigail giggled.

I put my hand on my chest. "Thank God."

"But you need to tell us everything," Angie said. "I can keep a secret better than most, and I know these two can." She pointed to our friends.

"I haven't been doing the coroner job long, but I have a strong feeling that would be inappropriate."

"Well, I'm Watson. And these two are like those lovely secondary characters in the show, who say something and all the pieces fall together in Sherlock's head."

"Why do you get to be Watson? I look great in hats," Angie said.

The women snorted with laughter.

"Seriously, Em. You have someone related to Smithy. You have someone who knows a lot about what happened. And someone who is coming in with very little knowledge of the case."

Angie frowned. "Oh, that's why I'm not Watson. Fair enough."

"Brainstorming is good psychologically," Abigail said.

"Not you too. I wanted this to be a fun night for everyone," I said. "And I need a break from the crazy stuff that's been happening to me."

"Right," Mara said. "Like Abigail said, it's good to discuss things and get them out in the open. You're a doctor—you know that. And maybe one of these ladies is a code breaker. How will we know if you don't ask?"

"Code breaker?" Angie and Abigail said at the same time.

I leaned my head into my hands. My stomach still hurt from laughing, and I didn't want to ruin our night.

"Come on, Em," Mara urged.

"Fine. But we're going to set a time for one hour, and then it's back to the fun stuff. Deal?"

They nodded.

A bell went off, and we all screamed.

"It's the pie," Abigail said.

We laughed again.

"Great. We'll load up on sugar, and then we'll put our new mystery club to work," Mara said.

"Only *you* would turn it into a club," I said. She made everything fun, and it was one of the things I adored most about her.

"I'll go get the letters," Abigail said.

"There's a new one under the files on my desk."

They stopped and turned toward me.

"What did it say?" Abigail asked. There was a slight tremble in her voice.

"I don't know. I didn't look."

She ran to the front, and I helped Angie and Mara organize the desserts. Everyone had brought two of their favorite things.

By the time we sat down at the table with our plates loaded with sweets, Abigail had found the letters and put them on the table.

"You should open it," Mara said. "What if it's some sort of clue?"

"They aren't that kind of letters," I said.

She frowned. "Do you want me to open it?"

I shrugged. "If you want."

Abigail handed her a pair of gloves. "Do I really need these if they've just been sitting on your desk?"

"I ran tests on the ones that I'd opened. Other than that the same paper and ink is used every time, there haven't been any other clues.

Abigail's cell buzzed on the table. "Good news," she said after reading it.

"What?" Mara asked.

"Ewan says that was one of his security guys in the garden. He heard the screams and came running, but then you were laughing. The guy thought we were playing a game."

"The game of murder." Angie said it in a deep, devilish voice, and we cracked up.

"Read the letter, Mara," Abigail said. "Ewan wants to know what it says."

I sighed. "Abigail, please stop texting with the constable. I know you are close to him, but what happens in the church stays in the church."

I meant it as a joke, but her eyes watered. "I'm sorry," she murmured.

"A wee bit harsh, Em. She's just trying to keep you safe," Mara said.

I reached across the table and grabbed Abigail's hands. "I didn't mean it like that. If something happens, I'd like to be the one who tells him. Otherwise, I get lectures, and as you know, I'm not a fan."

She nodded.

"See? This is why I didn't want to do this tonight. I made sweet Abigail cry."

"I'm not crying." She sniffled and wiped her nose with a tissue. "I was scared earlier. That's why I texted him."

"I'm surprised he isn't here already," Mara said.

"He's still in Edinburgh," Abigail replied. "But he's heading back now."

Her phone buzzed again.

She swallowed hard. "He says if I don't tell him what the letter says, I'm fired."

Mara picked it up quickly and opened it.

She paled and made a weird squeaking sound.

"What does it say?" Angie asked.

Mara lay it on the table.

"'You will die tonight,'" she squeaked.

209

Chapter
Twenty-Eight

If the note the killer had written hadn't sent a shiver down my spine, I might have laughed at the expressions on my friends' faces. Mara's fists tightened on the table, and she sneered. Abigail's eyes were wide, and her lip trembled.

"I'd like to see him try. Arsehole," Angie broke the silence.

"I bet he has no idea we're here," Mara said. "We could trap him."

"Can I tell Ewan what the letter said?" Abigail asked.

"Yes. I don't want you to lose your job, but tell him that we are all here and we are safe."

As the last word left my mouth, thunder boomed above, and the lights flickered.

We all screamed at once and then fell into hysterical laughter.

"Now, you know how it feels," I said. "That's what happened to me in the garden."

"I don't understand why we're laughing," Abigail said. "Your life is in danger. What if the killer shows up tonight?"

"We'll trap him," Mara said. "It's four of us against him."

"I don't think he'll try anything," I said. "There are too many witnesses. So far, this guy likes to threaten from afar."

"But he's been in your house," Angie said.

"We changed all the codes to the alarm, and I have steel doors now. The best way to end this is to find out who he is."

"Let's get the books and figure out that code," Mara said. "We have four smart, talented women. We can do this."

An hour later, the code books were piled on the table.

"This code is hurting my head," Angie said. "My brother used to make up codes with his friends. He loved keeping things from me and my sisters. But I can't make sense of this. I feel like you need to tell us everything," she said.

"She's right," Mara chimed in. "Close your eyes and take us through each step. Maybe you'll remember something that has slipped by."

Everything fell out of my mouth in a waterfall of words, including not being able to sleep well since I'd arrived.

When I finished, they stared at me with wide eyes and open mouths.

"Well, that was embarrassing."

"Are you kidding," Mara said. "I knew about the investigation, but why didn't you tell me the rest? I can't believe you haven't packed and headed back to the States."

I blew out a breath. "I've thought about it more than once."

"No," Abigail said forcefully. "I'm sorry." She grabbed my hands and folded them into hers. "You're the best thing that has happened to me and Tommy. Please don't leave."

I smiled. Thinking one might be making a difference and knowing it were two very different things. Tears formed in her eyes.

"That's selfish of me, but I promise we won't let anything happen to you."

"She's right," Angie added. "I don't know you as well as these two, but I'd sorely miss your friendship. Besides, you have to come to my wedding. Look, I just made this all about me. I really am what you Yanks call a bridezilla."

We laughed.

"I love it here," I said, and it was the truth. "Except for the fact that someone may be trying to kill me, I don't even mind the investigating part. It's almost like trying to diagnose someone in the

ER. You go through the steps, and each one rules out what might be wrong." I smiled. "The people here are so much nicer than I'd expected, and I love everything else about Scotland."

"Wait until winter," Angie said.

We laughed again.

"From now on, I'll be here at night until the danger is over. Abigail will be here during the days with Tommy. Until we catch this guy, we're never going to leave you alone," Mara said.

I shook my head. "Then I'm putting you in danger. I don't feel good about that."

"There is no arguing," Mara said sternly. "We are doing this together."

"Tell me what I can do," Angie said. "I want to help."

"You are busy planning your wedding and running your company. I'll be fine, I promise."

"Nope. That won't do," she said. "I feel closer to you three than I do my friends who are in my wedding. I love them, but they are very much about what's the latest fashion, and they're the "I'm totally going to steal that handbag kind of friends." You three are the real deal. I want to be a part of this."

Mara laughed. "She won't leave you alone until you give her a job. Angie isn't one to let things go."

"Keep an eye out for that scarf," I said. "Maybe I dropped it on the ground outside your store. Someone may have stolen it out of my car. The last time I remember seeing it was when it was in my purse. I don't know, but if the killer wore it, maybe he didn't want me to find DNA. I could kick myself for losing it."

"I say we turn this into a sleepover," Angie said. "And I can stay here on the weekends to help Mara out at nights. That is if you don't mind having a guest."

"We don't really have a guest room," I said. "Ewan's been staying on the couch at night."

Mara coughed and held a napkin to her mouth to keep her wine from spraying over the rest of us.

"What?" Angie asked.

"Well, he keeps breaking in at night to catch whoever is doing this to me, and then he won't leave. He's been sleeping on my couch."

They laughed.

"No wonder he's looked so tired in the morning," Mara said. "The last few days when he comes to the pub for breakfast, I thought he'd been working or partying a lot."

"Ewan? Partying?" Angie crossed her eyes. "Really, Mara?"

"Could be our Ewan fancies you," Angie said. "He could have had his men watch the house. But he's choosing to stay with you. Aye. I think the laird has a crush."

My cheeks must have turned crimson. The women around me giggled.

"No. I mean, he's always—never mind."

They laughed again, and I joined in.

"I so needed this tonight," I said when I caught my breath.

There was a round of "me too's."

"Let's come up with a plan," Angie said. "Like they do on *Scooby-Doo*."

"You had that show here? I loved it when I was a kid," I said. It was something my dad and I had watched together on Saturday mornings while eating huge bowls of sugary cereal.

"We still do," Angie said. "Though I'd rather be Scooby than Shaggy, if we're handing out roles."

"I think we are all Velmas and Daphnes," Mara said. "We're smart, capable women, and we can do this."

"What she said," Abigail added.

"The first order of business is to figure out the code in this book." I pointed to the journal. "I know it's Morse code for part of it, but when I try to decipher the letters, it makes no sense. But it's hurting my brain. I'd rather watch a movie."

"Let's research for a bit, and then we can watch a movie," Mara offered. "After all the scares, none of us will be sleeping any time soon."

"I like that plan," Angie said. "Besides, I love puzzles. I dinna like to speak ill of the dead, but Smithy wasn't the smartest man I've ever met. My guess is the letters are the key. Once you figure out how to read the key, then you can use it to decipher the code."

"I agree," I said. "The problem is, I've been through most of these books, and I haven't seen anything that would help figure out the key."

Everyone picked up one of the library books I'd left skimmed throughout the table.

Thunder rattled the windows, and we all looked at one another and smiled.

The wine wasn't helping my thought process, and I had a difficult time focusing. I was about to call it quits, when I thought I heard the alarm beep on and then off, like someone was coming in.

Abigail must have heard it as well. She was already on her feet.

"What are you doing?" A male voice boomed at the entry to the kitchen.

This time, we all screamed.

Chapter
Twenty-Nine

I mmediately after screaming, we jumped up and each of us held up our book as a weapon. Ewan stared at us as if we'd gone mad.

"What have I said about knocking or ringing the buzzer before just walking in?" I said angrily. "You scared us to death."

"She's not wrong." Mara pointed a finger at him. "What would your mother say about you walking into a woman's house unannounced?"

I swear his cheeks turned a light shade of pink. Ewan blushing was a sight to behold.

Who knew the laird might be afraid of his mother?

I smiled.

"I thought you were having a party," he said gruffly. "When I didn't see or hear you, I was worried. How was I to know you were doing a book club?"

"Were you invited to the party?" Angie asked.

I started laughing and they joined in.

He sighed. "I only stopped to see if Abigail wanted me to take Tommy home with me. He's asleep in the car, and Mrs. Garrity loves to look after him."

Abigail had bent over laughing. "That's kind of you, Ewan. We've decided to do a sleep over. We won't be leaving Em alone until you catch the killer."

"What?" He was right back in protective mode.

Mara waved a hand at him. "Since your men have done such a poor job looking out for our friend, we're taking over. Now out with you and stop interrupting our fun."

He glanced at the books we held and then back at us. Then he turned toward the waiting area. "Strangest party I've ever seen," he said under his breath.

We laughed again. My stomach would hurt in the morning from all the giggles.

"Who is Mrs. Garrity?" I asked when he left.

"His house manager," Abigail said. "She's tough but she taught me everything I know about cleaning and mending things. That said, she has a soft spot for Tommy. She dotes on him, and she's one of the few people he can stand for any length of time."

"Well, then she can't be too bad," I said. "Tommy is awesome."

"That he is," Mara added.

Abigail's eyes went wide. "No one ever says nice things about my brother. He bothers most people."

"If you ask me, most people are dumb," Angie added.

Abigail blinked away tears. "I've never had friends like you."

"Well, you do now," I said. "How about we take a break and watch a movie?"

"Don't you want to figure out your puzzle?" Angie asked.

"It can wait. What are you in the mood to watch?"

"I say we get some snacks," Mara said. "It's been a whole hour since we last ate."

Abigail giggled.

"Snacks it is."

* * *

Two and a half hours later, we were curled up on the big sofa as the credits ran on the Rob Pattinson version of *Batman*. I sometimes felt a bit weird over my love of the actor. He was much younger than me, but I especially thought he was wonderful in this role.

No one else had argued when I suggested the film, and it was a go-to for me when I needed to shove the world aside for a bit.

The women were right. I did feel safer with all of us here. Ewan had texted Abigail that we could go up to his house, but I refused to allow someone to scare me out of my home. I loved this old church, even though it creaked and moaned regularly. Even now, the wind whipped around, rattling the windows.

Mara snored softly in the middle of the couch. Angie was snuggled in the corner, with her eyes mere slits. Poor Abigail had fallen asleep on the large ottoman a half hour into the movie.

I hadn't known them for long, and yet these women had become friends who were willing to face a killer for me. I smiled, thinking of Angie with her broomstick and Abigail with the frying pan.

A person could go their whole lives without finding friends like them.

I'm so lucky.

* * *

At some point, I must have dozed off. When I opened my eyes, daylight streamed through the stained glass, and the scent of coffee hit my nose.

I yawned and stretched.

Angie was sound asleep in the same position from last night, but the other two must have been in the kitchen.

After running upstairs and washing my face, I headed down to the kitchen.

Mara was at the stove, making eggs and sausages.

"Morning," she said.

"Good morning. You don't have to do that. I bought some pastries for breakfast."

"After all that wine and whiskey last night, I thought we might need a bit more." She smiled.

"I won't argue. Besides, it's nice to see someone using the stove. I have no idea how it works."

She laughed. "I'll show you some basics after breakfast. But these Aga stoves are the best, especially in the winter. They stay warm all the time, and you'll find yourself at the kitchen table because it will be the warmest place in the house."

"Abigail said kind of the same thing," I said.

"Did you want to work on the code again? I've an hour before I need to help Gran at the pub."

"Nah," I said. "I've decided to give my brain a break the rest of the weekend. Maybe, if I get away from all of this, it will make more sense on Monday."

"That's a grand idea. We have live music at the pub tonight. Will you come and hang out with me?"

"I will," Angie said sleepily from the doorway.

"Of course, I will," I said. "That sounds like fun, and I love Scottish music. Well, maybe not the bagpipes, but I'm sure I'll learn to love them as well."

They laughed.

"What?"

"Scottish music runs the gamut," Angie said. "Everything from punk and rock, to the old songs of our people."

"Tonight's band has a lead singer who sounds like Lewis Capaldi," Mara said, then lifted the pan. "I made a full Scottish breakfast."

"Yes, please," Angie said. "Where is Abigail?"

"Off to check on Tommy," Mara said.

* * *

After breakfast, I decided to go shopping to find something new to wear, and Angie went with me.

We walked along the sidewalk in front of the seawall shops.

"You don't have to do this," I said.

She shrugged. "To be honest, I'm enjoying spending time with you and the girls. And I haven't been shopping here in ages. For a small town, Sea Isle is well equipped. You can find most anything you need here or up on the mountain. Have you been in Lulu's yet?"

I shook my head. "What kind of shop is it?"

"She has a bit of everything. I promise you'll find something you absolutely need every time you walk in there."

I didn't need anything except to find Smithy's killer.

No. Stop thinking about him.

"Oh, and you might want to have a chat with Lulu about Smithy."

I frowned. "Why?"

"They, uh, dated? I'm not sure you'd call it that. Sometimes she takes him home from the pub, and I think she was sweet on him for years. I have no idea why. The few times I've seen them together, he didn't pay much attention to her. I don't want to say too much. She's a grand lady, and I adore her."

"Okay, let's go."

Walking in the shop was like being transported to another world. There were beautiful pieces of art, mixed in with clocks and knick-knacks, on the walls. But it was all arranged so that it was a bit like walking into Wonderland.

We'd only gone a few feet inside when I found a small painting that would be perfect for the space over my bed.

"Mornin', ladies," a woman, who may have been in her sixties or eighties, said from behind the counter. Her platinum wig was teased to the max, and she wore a psychedelic pantsuit right out of the 1960s, with green and blue swirls. She had deep blue eye shadow and a full face of makeup.

I liked her instantly. I couldn't explain it if I tried, but I felt a connection.

"Angie!" She screamed and jumped over the counter and hugged her.

Yes, *jumped*. Maybe she wasn't in her sixties.

"Auntie." Angie squeezed her hard. "I've missed you."

Ah, so they are related. Maybe love of clothing genes—and eras— ran in the family. Angie swung the way of eighties punk, and her Aunt Lulu seemed to like the sixties.

"Oh, luv. It's been too long. How are you? How are the wedding plans going?"

"I'll tell you everything, I promise, but I want you to meet my friend, Dr. Emilia McRoy. She's the new doctor in town."

The woman let go of her niece and reached out her hand. I shook it. "Angie said you have a great shop, and she was right."

She put her arm around Angie's shoulders. "Thanks, luv. You always have been my best press agent. Why don't you have a look while I catch up with this one?"

I wandered off, but I listened to everything they said. I may have tuned out for a bit when Angie talked about the drama with the wedding.

The front half of the shop was filled with small gifts that would be perfect for any situation. The back half was stacked with vintage-looking clothing, but everything was brand new. Lulu's name was on the labels.

Most of the clothes weren't my style, but they were beautifully made.

An emerald cocktail dress caught my eye. I picked it up off the rack. The lacy top had three-quarter-length sleeves, and the chiffon skirt flared out.

Please be my size.

I peeked at the tag and then smiled. The designer was Talbot Runhof. I had no idea who that was, but they'd made one beautiful dress. Without even trying it on, I took it to the counter.

"That's going to be gorgeous on you," Lulu said.

"I agree," Angie said, lightly touching the lacy top. "Don't you want to try it on?"

I shook my head. "Even if all I can do is stare at it hanging on the closet door, I'm okay with that."

The women laughed.

"Remember, I said you'd find something that you'd need."

I smiled. "You were right, and I'm not done. Is it okay if I take the painting I want off the wall?"

"Of course, luv. Grab whatever you want and bring it to the counter."

On the way to get the painting, I found some silver clothing hooks that had different types of flowers on the end of each one. They'd be perfect for the laundry room so that I could hang up my winter gear.

Then I stopped to look at emerald earrings and a matching necklace in a locked case. By the time I made it back to the counter to buy everything, I had several bags' worth.

"Auntie says it's okay if you want to ask about Smithy." Angie leaned on the counter.

Her aunt pointed a finger. "First, I need to make a confession."

Angie and I glanced at one another, wide-eyed.

"We fought the night before he died," she said. "The old coot said my psychedelic suit was giving him a migraine. You can insult any other part of my life, but not my fashion sense. I have a vibe."

"You're beautiful," Angie said. "Shame on him."

"I agree. What happened?" I asked.

"I'd dressed up special because he said he wanted to go on a date. Said he'd come into a windfall. It was the first time in a long time he didn't just show up for a booty call. Do the kids still call it that?"

Angie coughed to hide her laugh.

I shrugged like I didn't know the answer.

"But he made a comment about your outfit?" I asked.

"Yes. As if he was any judge of fashion. I told him to sod off. He apologized and said he hadn't meant it as an insult, but more of a joke."

"Right," Angie said.

"Usually, we'd fight and go our separate ways. It wasn't like him to apologize like that. Said he had a lot on his mind and wasn't thinking. I forgave him, and we went off to the pub."

"Anything else happen?"

"He didn't want to stay the night." Lulu sighed. "He had a business meeting at ten. I said the only thing that happens that late at night is monkey business."

"Is there anything else you remember about that night?"

She patted her wig as if she was nervous.

"What's wrong?" Angie asked.

Lulu stared down at her hands, which were flat against the glass counter. "I'm not proud of what I did."

Was she the killer?

My heart raced.

He wasn't killed until the next afternoon, but she could have lured him to the woods. She was tall, but so thin, I couldn't imagine her having enough strength to cause the injuries Smithy sustained. But people did surprising things when they were pushed too hard.

"This is confidential," I said. "You can tell me anything."

"I followed him to the docks. I had to see if he was meeting up with Margie. He didn't think I knew, but he sometimes visited her as well. If you know what I mean."

I nodded. Margie. I'd forgotten about her.

"But it was a man he met."

"Any chance you recognized him?"

"Nae, it was dark and cloudy that night. Even with the sea-wall lights, it was hard to see, and my eyesight isn't that great for distances."

Darn.

"Anything out of the ordinary you might have noticed—or his clothing? Did the other person see you?"

Her head popped up. "Do you think it was the killer? He might have seen me. Great. Now, I'm dead."

Angie cleared her throat. "He seems more interested in Emilia at the moment."

"What?" Lulu asked.

"Just make sure you lock your doors at night," I said. "About the clothing the other person wore?"

Lulu closed her eyes for almost a full minute. "He wore a scarf. I only noticed it because it was lighter than the rest of his clothing. White background with some kind of plaid."

I pulled the drawing Abigail had done of the lost scarf out of my giant bag.

"Was it this?"

She stared at it for a few seconds and then shook her head. "Could be. They were too far away, and once they met up, they walked off quickly toward Smithy's boat. I came home."

"Did he ever talk about . . ." How did one ask about blackmail? "Other business?"

She looked confused. "What do you mean, like his boat?"

"No, Auntie. You've heard the rumors about him blackmailing folks around here," Angie interjected.

Her aunt's eyebrow went up. "If I knew for sure about that, I'd've turned the bastard in to the constable. I'm all about live and let live, but you start making people pay for their secrets and you belong with the devil."

Well, at least she wasn't complicit in that.

We soon said our goodbyes. After all that shopping, we decided to head down to Jasper's tea shop. It was a bit early for a full tea, but I needed sugar in my system.

When we arrived, there was a note on the door that said he'd be opening at noon.

"There he is." Angie knocked on the glass door and waved.

Jasper squinted and then smiled.

After opening the door, he led us inside.

Our arms were full of shopping bags.

"Someone has been to Lulu's," he said as he guided us to a table near the counter.

"It's my new favorite place," I said. "I apologize for us being so early. I'm sure you have tons to do, and we don't want to keep you."

He waved a hand. "I needed a lie-in this morning, which means I slept until five AM and then came in to work."

"What time do you usually come in?" Angie asked.

He shrugged. "Somewhere between two or three in the morning. It's a lot of work for one person, and I'll be hiring help soon."

"You really must love what you do," I said.

Lucy Connelly

"I do. Every morning it's a challenge to create one new thing. It's a game and I love it. What would you like to try? I assume you're hungry."

"I can always eat," Angie said.

"I'm with her, especially if the treats are as good as yours. I'd love to try whatever the new thing is that you made today."

"I'll take the same, and one of your raspberry scones, if you have them."

"Tea or coffee?" Jasper asked.

"Coffee," we said in unison. He laughed.

Soon he had small plates of sugary goodness and three cups of coffee.

"I've been curious how your case is going," he said, and then sipped his coffee.

"I haven't made much progress except that I've learned Smithy had a lot of enemies, all of whom seem to have alibis."

"The scarf is a lead," Angie said.

"Circumstantial at best, and I don't even have the evidence anymore."

"What scarf?"

I pulled out the drawing.

He frowned. "I don't understand."

I sighed. "A scarf with this pattern was found in the area where Smithy was murdered, but I've lost it."

"Or someone stole it," Angie added.

"Oh." He had the strangest look on his face.

"What's wrong? Have you seen one of your customer's wearing it?"

"No." He cleared his throat. "My scarf went missing from the pub about a week ago, and that pattern looks just like it."

Oh.

Chapter Thirty

Behind the pub, was a small closed-in garden with some tables and heating lamps. I'm not one for crowds or stuffy air and the pub had both. I was the only one out there, and I liked it that way.

Mara wasn't supposed to work, but the pub was overrun with customers. I'd offered to help, but she sent me outside and promised that as soon as the other servers arrived, she'd join me.

Craig waved with one hand and held a tray of pints with the other. "Mara sent this to you," he said. He set the giant glass on the wooden table. "She feels bad that she invited you on her night off and she's having to work."

"It's no big deal. I like sitting out here." I felt guilty for trying to escape back to my quiet church.

"Don't blame ya, it's right barmy in there. The band's about to begin, but uncle put up outside speakers, so you'll be able to hear them. Save me a dance for later, aye?"

He left before I could answer.

My ex-husband had loved to dance, so I had learned to as well, for him. It had been years since I'd danced because the memories were too painful.

But the stabbing pain in my chest when I thought about him was gone.

Scotland had done at least that for me.

Even with a killer threatening me, Sea Isle was better than Seattle and its memories. Before I left, I'd turned into a sorry workaholic. Going home to an empty house had been the worst part of my day.

"Deep thoughts?" Angie giggled as she sat down beside me. "What are you doing out here by yourself?"

"Too warm in the pub. You look amazing." She was dressed in a black bustier and leather pants and jacket, with thigh-high black boots. On anyone else, the ensemble might look ridiculous, but Angie carried it off. She'd gone to her granddad's to dress, since her luggage had been there.

"Thanks, sweets. You look beautiful."

I waved a hand. "You don't have to say that." But I did feel great in my new blouse from Lulu's, and dark jeans. I wore knee-high, low-heeled boots.

Most of the patrons in the pub had been fifteen to twenty years younger than me, but I no longer cared about age or fitting in.

"Do you need another pint? I'm going to run and get one for myself," Angie said.

A few more people had come outside and filled some of the other tables.

"I'm good," I said. "Though snacks are always appreciated," I joked.

"Done." She headed back inside, and a huge cheer sounded in the pub as a catchy rock tune blared through the outdoor speakers.

"I wouldn't have thought this was your scene." Ewan had snuck up on me while I'd been watching people at the other tables.

I prided myself on not screaming. The man had to have been a ninja in another life.

"For Christmas, I'm buying you a bell to wear."

His confusion turned to laughter.

"With everything going on, perhaps you should stay more aware of your surroundings."

I rolled my eyes. "Don't you have drunk people to take to jail or something?"

"It's early yet."

"Ewan, luv. I didn't know you'd be here." Angie stood up to give him a hug.

"How are the wedding plans? Do you need anything?"

She kissed his cheek.

"You've done enough." She turned to me. "The castle he's letting us use has this incredible gothic architecture that is just perfect. Wait. Did I already tell you this? We drank a lot of wine."

"Not about the gothic style."

She smiled. "I have a feeling you're being kind. I'm so excited about all of it, and at the same time I wish it was over. You said you were married before. What kind of wedding did you have? Or is that too painful—sorry."

I smiled. "There's not much to tell. We were busy with our careers, so we married at the courthouse, and then we honeymooned in the Seychelles.

"Oh, nice. I've seen pictures of that place."

The first ten years, we'd been busy building our careers and creating what I thought was our perfect life. We felt so blessed to be working at the same hospital and being the heads of our department.

Then the worst day of my life happened.

"What's wrong?" Angie asked. "I knew it. I brought up bad memories. I'm sorry."

Ewan was talking to a group of men sitting on the rock wall that separated the pub from the path leading to my home.

"What do you mean?" I cleared my throat, as my voice had become husky.

"You had the saddest look on your face. Tell me."

I shook my head. "Everything is fine."

She cocked her head. "I'm not as flaky as I appear. You can tell me. At this point, you know my life story. I'd like to hear some of yours."

I hated talking about the past, but this is what real friends did. They told each other about the skeletons, and then if they stayed friends, that made them true ones.

"Even with my best friends, I don't really hash over personal things," I said. "I've always been like that."

"Then they weren't that great of friends," Angie said. "If you truly want to bond with someone, you must know the worst thing that ever happened to them. Friends who don't pry into the depths aren't worth your time."

"Is that a Scottish thing?"

She laughed. "No. It's a friend thing. Do you want me to go first? I have more worst moments than one person should."

"What are you two talking about?" Mara said from across the table.

"Did you escape?" I asked.

She sipped her beer. "The rest of the servers came in when I offered triple pay and an equal share of tips."

Angie pointed to me. "She had a look on her face that made me think someone had murdered her puppy."

"Oh, did someone here say something?" Mara asked angrily. "Who was it? I'll give them a talking to and throw their arses out. Was it Ewan again?"

She was so serious, I couldn't stop myself from giggling.

"My mind drifted to the past, and it must have shown on my face because Angie noticed."

"I'd just convinced her to tell me everything, when you sat down."

I glanced around. "There are so many people. I'm not sure this is the right place for the conversation."

"No one is close enough to hear over the music," Mara said. "But let's run upstairs for a bit. I need to change my shirt anyway. The brothers who worked with Smithy brawled and spilled beer everywhere, including on me."

"I wonder what they were fighting about?" I asked. They were each other's alibis, which still didn't sit well with me. And no one had yet confirmed they had sailed on the day Smithy had died.

* * *

228

Angie and I followed Mara up the back stairs to her apartment. The walls of the pub vibrated from the loud music and thrummed through my ears.

But when she shut the door, it was decidedly quieter.

"How is that possible?" I stared at the door.

"Soundproofing on the floor, walls, and door," Mara said. "It was the first thing I did when my grandparents said I could redecorate."

"Smart," I said.

"It comes in handy when I need things quiet." Mara ran to her bedroom and quickly changed. Then she grabbed bottles of beer from her fridge and handed us each one.

"Thanks," I said.

"You're welcome. Tell us what upset you?" Angie asked.

"Nothing, really. I wasn't upset. People were dancing and it made me think about the past."

"The ex?" Mara asked.

I cleared my throat. "Technically, we never divorced."

The pair of them glanced at one another in surprise.

"You may have noticed I'm a very private person. Except for my mom, who has passed away, no one knows exactly what happened. I've had a lot of therapy to deal with what happened."

"If it's too painful, you don't have to tell us." Mara set her beer down on a wooden coaster shaped like an owl.

I grabbed one of her sofa pillows and squeezed it. "I don't suppose one of you could share the worst day of your life first?" My stomach churned even mentioning the past. I hadn't lied: I'd dealt with the emotions long ago, but it was still difficult to talk about.

"I have a few," Angie said. "The absolute worst was when my boyfriend at the time walked in on me drunk, shagging his best friend."

"Oh no," I said.

"I remember that," Mara said.

"Not one of my prouder moments. The good news is I'm marrying that best friend in a month and half. I've always wished I broke up with the ex first, but that's not the way it turned out.

"The worst part was they beat the crap out of each other that night, and it was all my fault. I've never forgiven myself for that. I'm a little wild, but I don't usually do that sort of thing."

"A little wild?" Mara smiled to take the edge off her words.

"Sod off." Angie said, and then she laughed.

There was no way I could judge her. I was far from perfect.

"How about you, Mara?" I asked.

"Which time? The one where I quit my job and went tits up as I tried to make a graceful exit down the stairs? I ended up in the hospital with a broken arm and a case of extreme loss of dignity," she said.

"Oh no!" I said.

"I too had a drunk shag or two," Mara said. "Unfortunately, the last one was with my female boss. For the record, I like men. But I was just out of college back then, and did I mention I was drunk? I got fired the next day by her boss. He'd seen us in her car. Sad part is he'd been hitting on me for months, and I think he was jealous.

"I have so many of these stories I could go on all night. It took me most of my twenties to get my act together. Okay, now it's your turn."

"My husband was a neurosurgeon, and we supported each other's careers. We had one of those relationships people admired," I said. "Or, at least, I thought we did. Around year seven or so, something felt off. I couldn't quite place it. We'd drifted apart. We weren't arguing, but we were silent whenever we had a meal together.

"I decided we needed to break the cycle. I planned a second honeymoon to the Seychelles. At the beginning of the trip, he seemed sad about something. I was worried something had happened at work, but he wouldn't talk about it."

"One night, we drank a bit too much and danced until they closed the bar. Dancing was his thing. Then, we, uh, reconnected in a way we hadn't in almost a year."

"What happened?" Mara leaned in.

"I got pregnant on the trip. We hadn't planned to have children. We were married to our careers, and I'd been told long ago I'd never be able to have kids. It was as if the universe had reached out and said, 'Here's a little miracle for you.'" I put the palm of my hand on my stomach.

"He didn't want the baby?" Angie's brows drew together in anger. "Arsehole."

"I don't know," I said.

"What?" they said together.

"He was at a conference in San Francisco the day I found out. I was so excited. I decided to fly down and tell him in person. I'd been praying he'd be open to the idea. But he wasn't alone."

"I want to kill him." Angie shook her head.

"You can't. He's dead."

"What the—" Mara stopped herself. "Sorry. Do go on."

"When I arrived at his suite, the door was open. A man sat in a chair by the window and sobbed.

"I asked him if he was okay and where Derek was. The man pointed to some double doors. I went in, and Derek was there on the bed. At first, I thought he was asleep. But when I called out, he didn't wake." Emotions clogged my throat.

"I'm so sorry we did this," Angie said. "I didn't mean to upset you." She scooted close and then wrapped her arms around me.

Mara jumped up and grabbed some tissues for me.

I blotted my face. "I wish that was the worst part."

"I checked for a pulse, but he was gone. At first, I thought maybe the other man had killed him. But there were no marks, no blood. When I ran back out to the living area, the man was gone. I called the police and was careful not to touch anything.

"But I had to pee bad, and that's when I found it—a suicide note and an empty bottle of Amytal. He couldn't decide between me and his male lover. That was what he'd been upset about on our trip. I had no idea he was having an affair—like, totally clueless—or that he was bisexual.

"A few days after the funeral, I lost the baby."

Angie hugged me tighter, and Mara squeezed her way in.

I sighed. The knot loosened in my chest, and I breathed deeply.

"Now, you guys can be like Smithy and blackmail me."

Mara pulled away. "What do you mean?"

I shrugged. "You guys, my mom, myself, and the other man are the only ones who know the truth. The hospital hushed everything up. They couldn't have their top neurosurgeon, a guy who had created world-renowned techniques, commit suicide. He was their cash cow, and no way would they allow his name to be sullied.

"They covered it all up. As far as anyone outside knew, he'd died of a heart attack. If I wanted to keep my job, I had to sign a non-disclosure agreement. I couldn't tell anyone except my therapist. And I told my mom before she died."

"That's terrible," Mara squawked. "No wonder you wanted to leave Seattle."

I nodded. "I couldn't get away from the memories there."

"Well, I am glad you made it to our small, but slightly crazy, town." Mara hugged me again.

"Me too." Angie said. "I think we need to go downstairs and dance. No men involved. Just us."

I blew my nose. I wasn't much in the mood for dancing, but I didn't want to disappoint them. Angie had been right; I felt even more bonded to them.

"Yes, let's shake off all this negative energy," Mara said.

I made a quick stop in Mara's bathroom to freshen my face.

Once I was ready, we went downstairs. My boots had smooth bottoms and I slipped on some liquid on the bottom step.

That's when someone grabbed me and yanked me into a dark room.

"Don't scream," the voice in the dark said.

Ugh.

Chapter
Thirty-One

The self-defense training I'd taken years ago kicked in. I stepped on his instep hard and then threw an elbow into his gut.

"Oof," he said, and let go of me.

I grabbed for the door. Once it was open, I swung around, ready to kick the guy's knees.

Ewan held up a hand. "Wait," he huffed.

Blood boiling on high, it was all I could do not to punch him. I don't consider myself a violent woman, but I could be where he was concerned.

"It's one thing to be a ninja, but you don't go around accosting women. How dare you attack me like that!" The music stopped, and the entire pub turned toward us.

"I didn't attack you," he said. "When you slipped, I grabbed for you, to keep you from falling, but I lost my balance and fell back into here."

Angie and Mara stood behind me.

"Ewan attacked you?" Angie said. "Dunderhead, what were you thinking?"

Thankfully, the music started back up.

"I didn't bloody attack her. I was helping," he said the words through gritted teeth. I believed him. And we'd already established I'm a klutz.

"Why did you say for me not to scream?" I asked belligerently.

"Because as soon as I fell back, I knew what you'd think."

He'd been right.

"I've been trying to find you for the last fifteen minutes."

I sighed. "What's wrong now?"

Angie held up a hand. "Amelia is off tonight. We're dancing."

"Margie and Lulu fought out back, and I think Margie's arm may be broken," Ewan said quickly.

Angie gasped. "Is Lulu okay?"

He shrugged. "She won't let anyone get close enough to check. They both threw some punches, and then there was some rolling around on the ground. First of many brawls tonight, I'm sure."

"Where are they?" I asked.

"Out back."

The only people outside were the two women, who were on opposite sides of the small courtyard, and some of Ewan's men. I recognized them from when they'd brought Smithy's body in.

"You canna hold me here." Lulu slurred the words. Her blonde hairpiece had half fallen off, and her mascara had run down her face.

Margie didn't look much better. Her blouse had been ripped at the shoulder, and her short hair stood up straight all over her head.

"Auntie," Angie cried out as she ran over. She pulled a tissue from her pocket and wiped the black smudges off the poor woman's face. "Are you okay?"

"Fine," her aunt sneered. "That cow called me a dobber. I'm not the one who had to borrow from the bank *again* to keep my store from going under."

Margie tried to push away from the table, but she winced. She pretty much fell back into the chair. When she turned white, I headed her way. At first glance, Lulu seemed to be doing better.

"I'm not the desperate slag who dated Smithy. She's probably your killer," Margie accused.

Mara snorted.

"You're not helping," I whispered as I examined Margie's arm and shoulder. The elbow had been dislocated, and possibly the shoulder, though it was hard to tell under her ruffled top.

"Let's get them to surgery, so I can take a better look. It's too dark for me to examine them out here."

After quite a bit of cajoling, the women were escorted to my offices by Ewan's men. I turned on the lights, and Mara headed for the coffee maker. It wasn't a bad idea, since both women had to have help standing up, and it had nothing to do with their fight.

"Put Margie in exam one," I said to Ewan and his men, "and Lulu in exam two."

"Why does that cow get to go first?" Lulu's words were barely discernable.

"There will be none of that in my office." I used my "I'm head of the ER and you'll do it because I say so" voice. "This is a place of healing, and you will act like the adults you are—not like brawling school children on the playground.

"Understood?" The word came out harshly, but someone had to take control.

The women nodded, although their eyes were focused on the floor.

"You can be kind of scary," Mara whispered.

I clapped my hands. "I don't have all night."

Everyone moved quickly after that.

Ewan started to follow me into Margie's exam room, but I held up a hand.

"She will have to strip, and I don't think she'll want you in there for that."

His eyes went wide, and he stepped back.

"Mara, I may need your help. Ewan standby. I can handle her elbow on my own, but I may need your help if the shoulder is involved." I slid the door closed.

Mara got Margie out of her frilly blouse while I cleaned up the cuts on her legs. Gravel was embedded in her wounds from when they'd rolled around on the ground.

Once they had the shirt off, I examined her arms and torso. "Your shoulder and elbow are displaced," I said. "Did you fall on that side?"

She nodded.

"Okay, I'll have to reset it. I'll be back in a minute with a pain-killer that will help."

"Please knock me out," Margie whined. She wasn't much better than Lulu in the slurring words department.

"How many drinks have you had tonight?"

"Shix," she slurred.

"Then, no. I'll give you a local that will help with the pain. Do not move while I'm gone. Mara, wrap her upper torso in one of the sheets from the cupboard under the sink," I said as I left.

On my way to get supplies and meds, I stopped in to see the extent of Lulu's injuries.

She sat stark naked on the table.

Angie had plopped down on the rolling stool, with her hands over her face.

"Are you okay?"

"Yes," they replied in unison.

I knelt. "What's wrong."

"Blood is not my friend, and there's a lot of it on the back of her head," Angie said worriedly. "She has some pretty deep cuts with gravel in them on her back and knees."

Angie heaved, but nothing came out. I handed her a plastic basin from one of the cabinets.

"Sorry," she said.

"You're not the one who owes everyone apologies."

Lulu, who had been giggling like a schoolgirl, stopped.

I did a quick examination of Lulu and then handed her a gown to put on. "Head wounds bleed a lot, but the cut is small and has already clotted. We'll need to clean these wounds on your back and stitch them up. Did you roll over glass?"

"The cow smashed a bottle into my back, just because I kicked her in her p—"

"Auntie! Stop!" Angie yelled. "I don't embarrass easily, but I'm ashamed of you. One of you could have been seriously injured. You're in your late sixties."

"Doesn't mean I can't take a—what were we talking about?" Lulu asked. "Why am I naked?"

The head wound may have been more severe than I'd thought. I had a long night ahead.

"I'll be back," I said.

"What can I do to help?" Ewan asked.

"Do you have medical training?"

"Aye, we all do." He waved a hand toward his men.

"Good. I'll need help with Margie. We're going to have to reset her dislocated shoulder and elbow."

"Ouch."

"Exactly," I said. "I'll need some of you to hold her down. But first, Ewan, I need your help gathering the supplies."

He didn't question me, just followed along.

*   *   *

Three hours later, some of Ewan's men had pulled up an SUV and carefully loaded the women into it. I'd given them aftercare instructions and told them to come in Monday for follow-up appointments. Angie went home with Lulu, and Mara promised to stay with Margie.

"That was great work, Doctor," Ewan said. "I don't think I've ever seen anyone so efficient."

"That's why you pay me the big bucks."

He laughed.

I caught the scent of something that smelled like hamburgers.

"Are you eating burgers? And why aren't you sharing?"

"Nah. Craig just stopped by with a bag of them for you. He said he's sorry you didn't get to dance."

"That was nice of him." I smiled. "I'm starving."

"Are you seeing him?" Ewan asked. His face was completely unreadable.

"Why? Do I need permission from the laird?"

"Of course, not." The words had an edge to them. "I wasn't aware you knew him that well."

"Can I have a hamburger before your inquisition? How many are there? If there are more than two, I'll share."

He smiled. "Kitchen or here?"

"Here." I sat down at the reception desk and motioned for him to pull up one of the chairs. There were burgers, chips—I'd discovered that's what the Scots called all types of fries—and fountain cokes from the pub.

I didn't normally drink sodas, but I had a headache coming on, and the caffeine would help.

"I don't know him very well, but Craig is officially my favorite human tonight." I took a big bite of the hamburger and moaned.

Ewan grunted, and then he did the same.

"Maybe it's because I forgot to eat tonight, but that's the best burger I've ever had," I told him.

"Mara's granddad must have been in the kitchen tonight."

"If Mr. Wilson made these, then *he* is officially my favorite human."

"Can I ask you something?" He stared across the desk at me.

"Do I have a choice?" I replied.

He chuckled. "You looked like you had been crying earlier. I wanted to make sure you were okay."

The chat I had with my new friends seemed like years ago.

"I'm fine. Amid all the fun tonight, we decided to talk about the worst day of our lives."

"Mine was when my cousin Timmy decided we should go cliff diving, and he jumped first. He never came back up." The stricken expression said it all.

"How old were you?"

"Eleven, I think."

"Oh, that's awful. You can't process something like that when you're so young. It's tough at any age."

"And you?"

I blinked. "I—uh."

He shrugged. "It's fine. I thought we were friends."

"Are we?" It was an honest question. "We seem to butt heads a great deal. And you're always coming in my home unannounced."

He at least looked chagrined.

"Do you want to know the truth about that?"

"Please." I put my second burger down.

"I've been hoping to catch the intruder," he said. "Until I found out about the letter, I wasn't sure it was the person who killed Smithy. I thought it might be kids trying to sneak in to get drugs."

He took another bite of his burger.

"It happened before when Doc was living here. I came and went as I pleased when he was living here. But I can see how that might be disconcerting for you."

I smiled. "I don't mind you checking on me. Just knock first."

"Noted." He made a flourish with his hand like he was writing something down.

We laughed.

Then I picked up my burger again.

"Did either woman press charges?" I asked.

He grunted. "They know better. There were far too many witnesses. They'll be lucky if Mr. Wilson doesn't press drunk and disorderly charges. He won't, but I made them think he might."

"Good."

He jerked back, as if surprised.

"What? Someone had to put the fear of God in them," I said.

"I never know what you're thinking," he said.

I shrugged. "They ruined a perfectly fun night," I said. "Or at least it had the promise to be fun."

"You missed your dance with Craig."

"No big."

He glanced down at his burger.

"Do you really want to know the worst day of my life?" I asked him.

"Only, if you want to tell me."

"It was the day my husband committed suicide, and I found out he'd been cheating on me."

"With another woman?"

"No," I said bluntly.

The confusion on his face quickly changed to incredulity. "Oh. I'm sorry you had to go through that."

"I'm sorry you had to watch your cousin die when you were a kid."

And just like that the mood took a downward turn.

"Be careful with Craig," he said.

I wasn't sure I'd heard him right. "What do you mean? Everyone says he's a nice guy."

He glanced away and then back at me. "He is, but no one really knows what happened with his wife. A few years after she left, he produced a divorce decree from some lawyer in Australia. My dad was constable at the time, and he was never sure about Craig. His story always seemed a bit shaky, but he had an alibi for that night."

"Huh. I've only chatted with him a few times," I said. "I'd questioned him about Smithy, that first full day I was here. And then he was there the night I went to ask questions at Harry's Pub. His team asked me to play trivia with them."

"Wait. You went to Harry's after I told you to stop investigating? Well, darn.

"Uh. Yes. But it was too crowded, and I ended up talking to Cole, Craig, and Jasper, who has become a good friend to me."

"Why did you question Craig about the brothers?"

"I thought I told you that part. They took the boat out the day of the murder. Craig's shop has a direct view of the ship, and I thought he might have seen them. Their alibis are each other, but if Smithy hadn't paid them—you know. I was just looking to find someone to back up their story."

"I see. The harbor master will have that information," he said.

"That is why you are the constable. I didn't even know there was a harbor master."

It was nearing two AM, and I yawned.

"You should get some rest," he said as he cleaned our trash off the desk.

I'd have to go after it with some of Abigail's cleaner in the morning, or she'd be upset with me for eating at her desk.

"Are you staying on the couch?"

"Yes," he said. His voice was low and melty. "If that is okay with you. Your watchdogs are busy with others tonight."

We held each other's gaze for a moment too long. Warmth spread through my body.

Oh. My.

I cleared my throat and turned away.

Probably menopause.

I'd seen the kind of women he dated. Okay, I'd googled him. The women were at least ten years younger than I was, many of them closer to twenty years.

Even without the money, he was a handsome man. Not that I cared about how much people made.

"Your blanket and pillow are in the ottoman."

"Thanks. Tomorrow, you explain the stack of letters on your kitchen table."

"I told you about them."

"*Some* of them," he growled.

Well. Darn.

Chapter
Thirty-Two

After an hour of trying to think up excuses for Ewan about the letters I hadn't mentioned to him, I passed out. I slept hard until the scent of coffee wafted into my dreams the next morning. I glanced at my phone to see what time it was.

After a quick shower to wake up my brain, I headed downstairs to face Ewan. But it wasn't him I found in the kitchen.

"Morning," Mara said.

"Hey, how is Margie doing?" I asked.

She handed me a cup of coffee.

"Embarrassed and in a lot of pain. She didn't want to take the medication you gave her. She's worried about addiction. Her dad had a problem with painkillers, she said."

"I'll talk to her about it tomorrow, but both drugs I gave her are non–habit forming. Have you heard from Angie?"

She smiled. "I think she's ready to kill Lulu. I don't know if she's having an adverse reaction to what you gave her, or if she's just being Lulu."

"What's going on?"

"She keeps trying to leave the house naked. Angie called her cousin to come stay with her. Angie will be here in a minute. I feel bad that you had to work all night."

I shrugged. "So did you."

"Not quite the same."

"It is. We both have jobs that sometimes take over our lives."

"Yes, but yours has life or death consequences."

I waved a hand at her. "If you're hungry, I have leftovers from our party," I said.

She lifted a bag. "I brought breakfast from the pub."

"Thank goodness." I helped her get everything on plates. By the time we'd set it out buffet style, Angie showed up.

She was still in her clothes from the night before, and her hair was in a mess on top of her head.

"Rough night?" Mara asked.

Angie grunted and then piled her plate with food. "She was fine for about two hours, and then she wanted pain meds. But you said she had to wait another three hours after you sewed her up.

"She argued with me for a solid hour and then passed out. I woke up to find her naked again, trying to get out of her front door. I'd bolted it with the keys and then put them in my pocket. Otherwise— I don't want to think about otherwise."

We laughed.

"Let me guess, she popped some of the pain meds earlier than she should have."

She nodded and then stuffed some scrambled eggs in her mouth. "Yes. After I got her back to bed, I counted them. She'd taken three instead of one. I almost called you, but she seemed okay. I love her, but she is out of control."

"Did either of you find out why they fought so hard? I can't imagine name-calling would create such a fuss."

Angie sighed. "It's like Lulu said. She thought Smithy was stepping out with Margie. Of course, Margie came back with something rude, and then Lulu called her a few choice names, and it just gets more embarrassing from there."

"Lulu really did care for Smithy."

Mara and Angie shrugged in unison.

"I don't know why," Angie said. "He was so—I don't want to speak ill of the dead."

"He was an arsehole," Mara chimed in, and then seemed to realize she'd said it out loud. "Sorry. One of Margie's friends ended up staying with her. I couldn't sleep last night so I spent most of it cleaning up the pub."

"I have to tell you something," Angie said. "But you have to swear you'll never breathe a word of it."

"We'll put it under doctor–patient confidentiality. Am I your doctor?" I asked.

"Yes," she and Mara said.

"And I swear not to breathe a word." Mara held up her hand in a weird salute.

"I found this in a drawer when I was looking for face wipes to take off the rest of Auntie's makeup."

She pulled a thick piece of paper out of her huge bag.

I stared at it in disbelief.

"Is that what I think it is?" Mara asked.

Angie let out a deep breath.

In the middle of the table was a marriage license for Smithy and Lulu. Of course, it used their real names, and it was signed.

Angie sniffed. "She got married and never told anyone. Look at the date. It's almost three years ago."

"But they had separate houses, and this doesn't make sense." Mara turned the paper so she could see it better.

"What did Lulu say about it?" I asked.

"Nothing. She was asleep when I found it. And she was in no shape for me to interrogate her this morning. I don't know what to think. I've never seen her violent like she was last night. What if she . . ." Angie rung her hands.

"I'm sure it isn't what you think," I said.

"I'm confused," Mara interjected. "What does Angie think?"

"That her aunt may have killed Smithy in a jealous rage."

*   *   *

An hour later, we sat around Lulu's breakfast table. She poured tea as if she hadn't been in a drunken brawl the night before or tried to run around town naked.

Without her makeup and wigs, she could have passed for my age. Even though I knew she was a good twenty years older.

She was dressed in jeans and a pink tie-dyed sweatshirt.

"Auntie, you look much better than when I left."

"Amazing what a shower can do for one's soul. Now, someone tell me what happened last night. I don't remember much."

"That's probably a good thing," Angie said.

Lulu frowned. "I won't apologize for my behavior. I am who I am, and I'll never change." The words came out in a wash of anger.

Angie sat back and crossed her arms. "No one would want you to change, but sometimes—"

"What?" Lulu asked angrily. Her teacup shook in her hand, and Mara took it from her, then put it on the saucer.

"You could have been seriously injured or Margie could have been. You nearly broke her arm." Angie pointed a finger at her.

"Margie?" Lulu closed her eyes. "Was that old cow there? I don't remember."

"You've got to be kidding me," Mara said. "Darn, I said that out loud didn't I? Now I'm going to keep my mouth firmly shut." She made the universal mouth-closed-with-a-zipper action and then threw away the key.

I pushed my napkin against my lips to hide my laughter.

"Forget about last night," Angie said. "Doctor Em has something important to ask you."

She nodded toward me.

"Uh, I think that question might be better coming from you."

"It's a professional question from an investigator." Angie pretended to be innocent.

"I see it as more of a family situation. Perhaps, Mara and I should give you time alone."

"No," Angie bellowed. "I mean, you need answers as much as I do." Then. "Please," she mouthed to me.

"What do you need to know? I'm an open book," Lulu said. She'd been glancing at us like we were speaking a different language she couldn't understand.

"You were married to Smithy," Mara blurted out. Then her eyes went wide. "I said that out loud too."

"Get out of my house." Lulu stood quickly and then stumbled back against the wall. "Out."

None of us moved.

"Settle down, or I'll call the constable," I said. The sweet lady I'd met at her store was gone. She threw daggers at me with her eyes.

"Please," I said calmly. I'd learned to keep my cool while dealing with all types of people in the ER. "Right now, you've moved to the top of the suspect list because you have more motive than most."

She closed her eyes. It was if she were trying to wish us away.

"Auntie, please. Let's clear this up," Angie said softly.

Lulu opened her eyes and then sat down in a huff on her chair.

"We are not here to judge," I said. "I'm only after the truth."

Lulu pursed her lips and then crossed her arms. Not the most open of body language signals.

"The marriage license is a fake," she said, "though I didn't find out until after he died."

My friends and I glanced at one another. "Tell us what happened."

"About three years ago, I met a nice gent in Edinburgh on one of those online sites. We had a good time together. The man and I became serious, and I'd told Smithy that I didn't want to see him anymore. He kept coming around, but I ignored him when he knocked on the door."

She took a sip of tea. "He followed me to Edinburgh one night and was waiting for me on the curb outside Charles's flat."

She sighed, then continued speaking.

"In his way, I think Smithy might have loved me. He was so jealous of Charles. I told him I was done with my wild ways, that I'm getting up there in age and wanted to settle down with a good man."

Lulu shook her head. "Smithy was so sweet and said he wanted to spend the rest of his life with me. He'd never acted like that before.

"A few weeks later, he arranged for us to be married in a small church in Edinburgh. It was just us and the minister. Neither of us was ready to tell our friends and family.

"I know what everyone thought about him, but I loved him. I still do, the rat bastard."

She sniffed, and her eyes watered. Mara handed her a tissue.

"I'm so sorry for your loss," I said. "You must be heartbroken."

"I was a fool," she said. "When he didn't want to tell people at first, I understood. We'd rushed into things, and like I said, I was in no hurry to announce it to the family." She glanced at Angie.

"I don't know about the rest of them, but all I've ever wanted for you is to be happy, Auntie."

Lulu patted Angie's hand. "You're a good girl. He lived here the first year or so except when he was out on the boat. But then the meanness in him took over. He drank all the time, and we nearly came to blows one night. I kicked him out."

"Did he hurt you?" Angie asked. She clasped her aunt's hands.

"He tried, but only once. I punched him so hard he fell to his knees right here in this kitchen. After that, he didn't come back for a long time.

"Then a few weeks ago, he came to the door with flowers. Said he wanted to earn my trust back. He coaxed me into going out to dinner with him, and for once it wasn't at the pub. We had a lovely time. He said he'd been drinking too much but he'd stopped. After apologizing for everything, he begged me to take him back."

She sighed again. "I told him I had to think about it. I thought that would send him on his way. But he came back every day and was so kind. I started to believe he'd really changed. But I still didn't trust him.

"I've lived long enough to be wary like that. It's why I followed him that night to the docks. Something wasn't quite right."

"How did you find out about the marriage license?" I asked.

She shook her head in disgust. "After he died, I checked with the lawyer. Smithy kept saying he was about to come into some big money. That he had several deals going, but he never discussed them with me.

"When he died, I worried I might be responsible for his estate. The lawyer did some digging and discovered it had all been a sham and I fell for it.

"But Smithy did leave me something." The words were bitter. "He'd used that document I'd signed to forge loan papers. I'll be paying off that fifty thousand until the day I die."

"Oh no, Auntie." Angie wrapped her arms around her aunt.

"I was a gullible, silly old woman. I deserve it."

"No, you don't," I said. "Your lawyer can prove those documents were forged." At least, I hoped so. "I asked this before, but did you know Smithy was blackmailing people in town?"

"No. Who did he blackmail? He was mean, but I never thought he'd stoop to something like that."

"We're still working it out," I said. "You cared about him, but from all accounts, he was not a good man, Lulu. He didn't just hurt you. He angered someone so much they murdered him."

"I'm such a fool," she cried out. Then the sobs started, and Angie held her tight.

"No, you were in love," Angie said. "Trust me, I've made a lot of mistakes, because the heart can be really stupid sometimes."

Lulu shuddered, and it felt like Mara and I were intruding.

"We'll leave you two alone," I said. After putting our teacups in the sink, we left quickly.

"Poor Lulu," Mara sniffed. "And this is why I will never marry."

"My heart hurts for her," I said, "and I know what you mean. After Derek died, I decided relationships were too stressful. And like you, and millions of other women who have been burned, I have severe trust issues. I'd been working on them with my therapist, but I'm not sure I'll ever be able to trust someone like I did my husband."

Mara put an arm around my shoulders. "Right there with you, sister. At least, we have each other."

I laughed. "Yes, we do. Get some rest. That's doctor's orders. I need to clear my head. I feel like the answer is staring right at me."

The pub door opened, and Craig and Jasper nearly bumped into her.

"Mornin'," they said in unison.

"What are you two up to?" Craig asked.

"I haven't slept in twenty-four hours, so I'm headed upstairs." Mara gave them a quick wave.

"Long story," I said when they gave me curious looks. "What are you doing?"

"I've convinced Jasper to join our team permanently for the Highland Games next year. We were about to head off to practice."

"Please explain what you've said to the American. What are the Highland Games?"

They laughed.

"It's a huge sporting event that focuses on strength, agility, and special talents," Jasper said. "All of Scotland participates, and it isn't like any sports program you've ever seen."

"Why don't you come to practice with us and get a real taste of Scotland?" Craig said.

I looked from one man to the other.

Poor Jasper looked so hopeful. I'd promised him I didn't consider him a suspect. I believed what he said about his scarf being stolen. He was also incredibly kind and had no motive to kill Smithy.

"I'd love to watch, but some other time. Like Mara, I'm exhausted. I worked all night."

Craig frowned. "Okay." He appeared genuinely disappointed.

How long had it been since a man had been interested in me? Maybe I'd misread the signals.

"How about dinner later?" he asked.

Or not. I meant what I'd said to Mara. I'd never be able to have a relationship with a man that was anything more than mutually agreed-upon fun. Craig was handsome and interested. Why not?

I smiled. "What time?"

We settled on a time, and they left.

Craig looked back and smiled.

I waved.

By the time I made it home, I was in full-on panic about what to wear.

As soon as I stepped inside the waiting area, I stopped. Strange noises came from the back of the house. Nerves churned in my stomach, and bile rose in my throat.

Something fell off one of the counters.

I grabbed the can of pepper spray from my bag and ran for the kitchen.

"Get out of my house," I yelled as I neared the doorway. I wasn't about to back down, but I desperately wanted to avoid any kind of confrontation that might get me killed.

There was another weird noise that sounded like a groan or a growl. It was tough to determine.

Was someone hurt?

After taking a deep breath, I ran into to the room with my pepper spray held high.

"Get. Out!" I bellowed.

Chapter
Thirty-Three

As I relayed to Craig at dinner what had happened in my kitchen, his body shook with laughter. We were having a perfectly lovely dinner at a steakhouse about a half hour out of Edinburgh.

I didn't blame him for laughing. Only in my life, it seemed, did weird things like this happen.

"What happened when you screamed?"

"They were smart and scampered off. There was a third squirrel on the counter that I hadn't seen, and it nearly flew out the back door."

"How did they get in?"

I shook my head. "As I said earlier, I hadn't slept much the night before. I probably didn't close the door all the way when I left. I'd never seen red squirrels like that, though."

"They are native, and we have more than our share here. They can be a nuisance this time of year as they gather things for the winter."

"Poor things probably thought they'd hit the motherlode. Most of the food from our party two nights ago was still out on the counter. I mean, the stuff that needed refrigeration was put away. But I didn't have a chance to clean up with everything going on this weekend."

"You said you were afraid it was another intruder. Has someone been bothering you?"

I glanced down at my half-eaten steak. "Can you keep a secret," I said softly.

He grinned. "I'm aces at it. Tell me what's been going on."

I may have just met this guy, but I was so at ease with him.

"Weird things have been happening around the house and someone broke in a couple of times."

He leaned back against his seat. "What? That must have been terrifying."

"At the beginning, yes. Now, I'm angrier more than anything. I know in my gut it was the killer."

"Of course, it's the killer. Lass, I'm so sorry you're going through all of that."

"I probably shouldn't be discussing any of this with you, but you're Mara's cousin. Has she filled you in on any of it?"

"Well . . . I was curious about Smithy. A long time ago, when my wife left, he was good to me. He convinced me to quit my job in Edinburgh and buy the bait shop. I love fishing, and it had always been a dream of mine to own something like that."

"I only knew him for a day, but he didn't seem the type to be encouraging," I said. Then I slapped my hand over my mouth. "Sorry."

Craig smiled again. "You're right. He and I had a falling out a few months ago. I can't even remember what happened exactly. He came in the shop in a drunken rage, yelling that I owed him for God knows what. The truth is, he'd lost quite a bit to me in cards. That day, it was as if he'd gone mad. I had to throw him out before he destroyed the shop. After that, we barely spoke."

"That sounds more like what other people have been saying."

He frowned. "He was a tough old goat, but if he liked you, he was different. He didn't care for most people."

"At least he was there for you when your wife left."

"True. We're divorced now. I'm the first to admit it took me a long time to move on. At first, we thought something might have happened to her. Then, I tried to figure out why she'd moved so far away."

"Did you ever find out? Or is that too personal?"

He chewed on a bite of steak.

"Never mind. It's too personal."

He shook his head. "Nah. Sorry. In the end, she had no answers—other than she hated this place and no longer loved me." He sighed.

I scrunched up my face. "And now I've ruined our happy dinner by asking rude questions."

"Not at all. I'm glad to have it in the open. The rumors in Sea Isle are rampant. I'd just as soon you knew the truth."

"Thanks for that. So, can I ask another question?"

He laughed. "Sure?"

"Are you ordering dessert?"

"Do you want dessert?"

"Always."

"Then, we'll have one of each."

I really liked this guy.

*   *   *

A few hours later, he drove me home and then walked me to the door.

After punching in the code, I opened it.

I'm a grown woman who was married for years, and I still wasn't sure about what to do when a man dropped me off at the door.

Before I could think too hard about it, I went up on my toes and then kissed his cheek. "Thank you for a lovely night," I said.

"I hope we can do it again sometime." He brushed a wisp of hair off my face. I'd worn it down, and the Scottish wind whipped it around my head.

"Me too."

"Do you need me to do a once-over of the house for you?"

I shook my head. "I'll be fine, but thank you. Mara will be coming up after her shift in a few minutes. She's been staying on my couch most nights."

"I don't know how great my cousin would be at fighting off an intruder."

I laughed. "I don't know either. She's sweet but feisty. And she was a rock the other night when she helped me in surgery. Nothing seemed to phase her."

"Good. Well, I'll be off. Is it okay if I text you to set another date?"

"I'd like that."

"Go in and lock the door behind you."

I did what he asked. Then I set the code on the alarm. Mara would text for me to let her in when she came up.

I'd had a successful outing with a man. I wasn't sure what to do with myself. After changing clothes, I decided to look at Monday's schedule.

The laptop came to life, and then all the lights went out.

"What the . . .?"

I used the flashlight on my phone to check the fuse box in the laundry room.

Everything looked as it should.

The house alarm beeped loudly, and I ran back to the front to reset the code. It flashed a warning about the power being out and that the backup battery was in place.

My phone rang, and I might have jumped.

"Is your power out?" Mara asked.

"Yes. Is yours?"

"Yes. We're trying to move all the food down to the cold storage below the pub. Are you going to be okay by yourself for a while?"

"Of course. Do you need help?"

"No. Whatever you do, don't go outside. They are calling it a freak weather event. We don't usually get snow so early, but we're about to get several centimeters."

Snow? In late August?

"Okay. Is there anything I should do to ready the house in some way?"

"You might text Abigail to see where your generators are. I wouldn't run them until the temperature drops another twenty degrees. Are you sure you're okay? No one saw this coming, and we weren't ready. But it's your first big storm."

"I'll be fine," I said. "You get back to work."

I texted Abigail about the generators. And she called me back.

"Do you want us to come down?" she asked.

"No. I'll be fine. I just can't remember where you said the generators are."

"They're in the main surgery room, behind the double doors on the right. The instructions are on top, but you just pull the cord and flip the switch."

Tommy said something in the background, but I couldn't understand him.

"Right. Tommy says don't forget to do those things at the same time. If you have any trouble, just text or call. We're happy to come down."

"No. You stay safe and warm."

"I'm sure you've seen it, but Tommy stacked extra wood for you out back. It's on the right side under the portico. You may want to grab some before the snow starts."

"Okay." Firewood. Check.

My nerves weren't rattled easily, but I thought I'd have more time to prepare for the Scottish winters everyone had told me about.

"Are you there?"

"Yes," I said. "Thank you, Abigail."

"Oh, and don't turn the generators on until the temperature drops."

I smiled. "Got it."

I set my phone down on the kitchen table. After putting on my coat, I opened the back door.

And ran into an intruder.

Chapter
Thirty-Four

I screamed—and then stumbled back into the laundry room. The figure lunged for me, and I punched at him wildly. He grabbed my arms and flipped me around so fast, I didn't realize what was happening until I was shoved against the washer. I couldn't move any part of my body to defend myself.

"Emilia. Stop. You're okay. It's just me."

"Ewan? Let go of me."

He did. I swung around. "You must stop scaring the hell out of me like that. What are you doing here?" I may have stomped into the kitchen like a small, angry child.

The man was on my last nerve.

"Two things."

I crossed my arms and leaned back on the kitchen counter. I'd cleaned up after the squirrels, so at least there wasn't food everywhere.

"First, I was about to knock on the door when you opened it. You scared me as much as I scared you."

"I doubt it." I was still trying to lower my heartbeat with deep breaths.

"Second, I came up from the pub. Mara was worried about you. None of us expected to get hit so soon."

I rolled my eyes. Maybe it was silly for an adult to do so, but eye-rolling came naturally when Ewan was around.

"I've already talked to her and Abigail. I'm fine."

"Right. Have you checked the pilot light? And why were you going outside? The winds are already dangerous."

I may have growled at this point. "I wanted to grab some firewood."

"I'll do that. You go check the pilot light on the gas."

I remembered Abigail saying something to Tommy about it, but I had no idea where it was. The heating system was new, Abigail had said, but other than knowing how to lower or raise the temperature with the app on my phone, I had no idea how it worked.

"Change of plans," I said. "I'll get the firewood. You check the pilot light."

His eyebrow went up. "You don't know where it is, do you?" The tone was a bit accusatory, and I was already annoyed.

"Just check it," I bit out. I shoved past him and headed out the back door.

That's where the air froze my lungs.

It had been cool and windy when Craig had dropped me off a half hour ago. The temperature had to have gone down more than forty degrees. I grabbed two cords of wood and balanced them on top of each other. They were heavy, but the more I carried at once, the fewer trips I'd have to make.

I placed them on the long folding table in the laundry room. My idea was to get as many inside as quickly as possible.

The table was full in a matter of minutes, and I stacked more underneath.

By the time Ewan returned, my arms were about to fall off.

As a doctor, I understood that was impossible, but if I were to survive winter here, I might need to work on my upper body strength.

"I'll grab a few more," he said.

At that point, I was too tired to argue. Even with an hour nap, this had been another long day. I tried to turn the kettle on and then felt like an idiot. There was no electricity, which was why I'd been using my flashlight the last half hour.

I stared at the Aga, trying to remember what Mara had said about it the other day.

I took out a pot and then filled it with water. One side was supposed to be hotter than the other. I took a guess, and set the pot down, and stared at the stove for a full two minutes.

Nothing happened.

Then I moved the pot over to the other side. In a few minutes, the water bubbled up.

While Ewan walked back and forth carrying logs to the storage area next to the fireplace, I brewed tea.

He already had a fire going, and it was nice to have some light in the room. When he'd finished sorting the wood, he sat down on the couch. Then he took the tea I offered.

"Thank you for helping me," I said stiffly.

"How was your date with Craig?"

I sputtered my tea. "How do you even know—never mind. It's none of your business."

He shrugged. "Only trying to make conversation."

"Don't you have damsels in distress to save or something? I don't want to keep you from your duties."

"Nae. I'm good. The only damsel who needed saving tonight was you."

I grumbled. "I was fine."

"Yes, of course. Except the pilot light is finicky, and it had gone out. You might have died, and then where would we be? No doctor to care for our ill."

Was he serious? "You could have called with that information. I'm far from helpless."

"You're right about that. But this being your first storm, we were worried you might not be prepared. *Farmers' Almanac* says it's going to be an especially harsh winter, but no one expected it to begin today."

"And you believe a book that predicts the future?"

"It's more right than wrong for the last hundred years. So, yes."

I just stared at him.

"Since you don't want to talk about your love life, let's talk about the case. What was all the commotion with Lulu? I heard Angie talking to Mara before she left town."

"Do you always eavesdrop?"

"Not eavesdropping if you're a part of the conversation. Angie and I were at the bar, talking about some of her wedding arrangements, when Mara came down and asked how Lulu was doing and if she was okay emotionally. They were speaking in code, like women do, but from the gist of it, I understand you found out about a connection to Smithy."

"Don't you have to get home and prepare for the storm?"

"Nae. I'm staying right here tonight." He patted the sofa.

I sighed. "I don't think we have to worry about intruders in this storm."

"I don't know—it's the perfect opportunity for him to attack. No one would see him, and the snow would cover any tracks. Might be hours or a day before someone discovered you dead."

A shiver slid down my spine, and my hands shook. Leave it to Ewan to make me think about the worst.

"Thanks for that."

He shrugged. He did that a lot. "What is it you Yanks say? I'm keeping it real."

"No one says that anymore."

"Tell me about Lulu."

I was stuck with him. "Fine. But she is no longer a suspect."

"I didn't know she was one."

I cleared my throat and then went on to tell him what she'd said. At the end of my story, he shook his head.

"That man was a scoundrel. Lulu's a bit wild, but she has a kind soul. She didn't deserve that."

"Well, that's one thing we agree on."

"I'll talk to my lawyer and see what he can do about that loan. She won't be liable. I'll make sure of it."

Annoying as he was, he did take care of the people in Sea Isle.

"So, who else is a suspect?"

"I have yet to find proof of the brothers' alibis. They said they waited and then went out. But there are no witnesses. I've asked around. And I don't trust those two."

"You have good instincts. They are no better than Smithy when it comes to conning people out of money. They used to run the drug trade here with their father."

"Drugs? Here?"

"You should learn more about the history of our town."

I didn't roll my eyes, and I considered that a sign of true maturity.

"I've learned a great deal, but why don't you enlighten me."

"There's a cove not far from the docks, where a good smuggling trade went on for many years. My father put a stop to it."

"Did he put the brothers in jail?"

"Aye, and their father. They didn't do much time, as they were underage, and their father died in there. But those are some rotten eggs. I'm fairly certain that's why Smithy took them on."

"What do you mean?"

"It's not only fish they catch. Occasionally, we raid the boat and find everything from cigarettes to women's perfume. Doesn't happen every trip, and we've had more misses than hits, but they were up to no good."

"If he wasn't paying them what he owed, that is still a good motive for murder. They aren't the nicest guys and seem the most likely suspects." I looked at him. "Did you talk to the harbor master? What did he say?"

"That he had no record of the ship leaving or coming back, but they aren't the best at keeping track of things. Who else do you have on your list?"

"Don't laugh," I said, but I was prepared for just that.

"If you say Margie, I won't be able to contain myself."

I frowned. How did he know?

"She and Lulu were fighting, and her dog was found on the scene."

"Nae. Fred loved Smithy. That dog is a terrible judge of character. He was always following him around. Fred is one of the few beings who could make that grump smile."

"How do you know Smith and Margie weren't having an affair?"

"Because Margie spends most nights at Sharon McGregor's house. Smithy is not her type. She and Sharon are discreet, but anyone paying attention would understand what's between them."

That was insightful and unexpected.

"What about Craig? Is that why you went on a date with him? Did you give him the third degree?"

"Craig and Smithy were not friends. He's not a suspect."

"He and Smithy were thick as thieves for years. It's only recently they had some kind of falling out. Smithy was scruffy and could hold his own in a fight. But Craig's a big guy. He fits your profile."

"You're messing with me, aren't you?"

He smiled. "A bit. But you have to keep an open mind when you're investigating. It's best never to assume anything. They did have a very vocal falling out at Harry's Pub one night. Might be worth asking about."

"Craig's been nothing but helpful, and we already talked about what happened."

"And what was that?" Ewan leaned back on the couch and put his feet on the ottoman.

"That Smithy came in one day and tried to destroy his shop. Craig was worried he'd gone crazy. Smithy kept yelling he owed him, but Craig says it was the other way around. That Smithy had lost a lot of money over cards."

"Aye. He speaks the truth."

"You're also a likely suspect."

Ewan coughed and then sat his tea down on the end table.

"What? I thought we had this conversation."

"Well, you were close enough to the bothy to hear me scream. You're a big, strong man as well."

"And my beef with Smithy would be?"

"He was a criminal. Maybe you caught him doing something bad and things went wrong."

He laughed so hard, I thought he might hyperventilate.

"It's not that funny. You always seem to show up here when there is an intruder."

He started laughing again.

"Do you think I really did it, Emilia?" He grinned.

The way he said my name made my toes curl. No. Ewan was not fodder for fantasy. He was an annoying, pigheaded man.

I sighed. "No. While I sometimes find your company disturbing, the rest of the town seems to think you walk on water."

"Disturbing. Can't say I've ever had a woman say that before."

"You probably weren't listening."

That set him off again. It was a full minute before he caught his breath.

Annoying jerk. But I smiled.

"There is one more thing," I said. "Once I can decipher it, I may have some more suspects."

He set his cup on the tray and then turned to face me.

"Are you saying you have evidence you haven't told me about?"

Once again, I'd stepped right into trouble.

"Technically, I'm not sure it's evidence. I found Smithy's black book. It's gray, but you know what I mean. I think the people he blackmailed might be in there."

"Bloody hell, that is evidence. Why didn't you tell me?"

"It's written in code, so I can't be sure what it is exactly. If you and your men were as thorough at Smithy's as you said, then it should have been found."

"Get it. Now. We could have bloody well figured this out weeks ago if you'd handed it over."

"I doubt it. Even if your men had found it, they'd think it was some navigational thing," I said.

"Why is that?"

"Part of it's written in Morse code."

"Part of it?" He faced the fire, and I had the good sense to stay silent.

"Dr. McRoy, may I please see the book you found at Smithy's?"

The words were sharp, but at least he'd asked nicely.

I grabbed my purse from the side table by the couch. I always kept the journal with me. Since the scarf had been stolen, I thought it best to keep it safe.

I handed him the journal.

He opened it and then squinted at the writing. Even with the fire, it was dark. He jumped up and moved closer to the light. Then he pulled a pair of black-framed glasses from his shirt pocket.

"It's Morse code," he said absently.

"Yes. Like I said. But it's gibberish if you don't know the other code he used. We haven't figured that out yet."

He glanced at me. "We?"

I'm smarter than this.

"My friends have been helping me research the code."

He closed his eyes and took a deep breath. "Who else knows about this?"

"Only us. Me, Mara, Abigail, and Angie. And maybe Tommy. He listens and absorbs way more than anyone gives him credit for. But none of them would say anything."

"I'm not so sure about that. People accidentally say things without realizing it. You should have come to me with this."

I might have trusted the wrong person with information that could get me killed.

Just as I was about to admit my mistake to Ewan, a loud boom shook the walls.

While I jumped, and knocked over the teapot, Ewan went running toward the lobby.

"Stay there," he said.

I never was good at taking orders.

Chapter
Thirty-Five

By the time I made it to the lobby, Ewan had grabbed someone by the collar and shoved him against the wall. He had his arm against the guy's windpipe. The lobby was so dark, and snow swirled in through the open door.

"Sir," the man squeaked. "Donnelly, sir."

Ewan didn't let him go.

"It's one of your men, Ewan. Donnelly."

"What are you doing here?" Ewan growled.

"If you took your arm off his throat, it might be easier for him to talk."

He stepped back, and the poor guy's feet hit the floor as he sagged against the wall. Ewan was big, but I might have underestimated how strong.

"I ask again. Why are you here?"

"Someone broke into the tea shop," the man whispered.

"There's a bloody storm—it can wait," Ewan grumbled.

"The owner is in my lorry," the guy said. "Got a pretty good bang on the head and doesn't seem to know his name. I was bringing him to the doc, sir."

"Ewan, help him bring Jasper into exam one."

Thankfully, Abigail had come down earlier in the day and sterilized everything.

The door slammed and Ewan and Donnelly had Jasper between them. His head hung down, but there was no sign of blood.

"He's unconscious," Ewan said.

They put him on the exam table.

"Jasper." I examined his head and found a huge hematoma. "Jasper, it's Emilia."

Nothing. I checked his eyes with my flashlight. His pupils were dilated, and his breathing was shallow.

"Grab the gurney from the OR. I need to get him in the MRI so I can see what's going on."

"I'll carry him," Ewan said. He picked up Jasper, who was nearly as tall as him, and raced toward the back.

I ran ahead and pushed the button to open the double doors leading to the rear of the facility.

Donnelly helped straighten Jasper out on the table.

"What do you need us to do?"

"Stand in the hall while I do this." I snapped my fingers. "Wait. Is there any safe way to get Abigail down here? I could use her help."

"My lorry has four-wheel drive. I'll go," Donnelly said. It was almost as if Ewan hadn't tried to strangle him a few minutes ago.

"I'll turn on the generator," Ewan said.

The room was dark. I should have thought of that.

After they left the room, I put on the apron that protected me from radiation and then started the machine.

It was an open MRI, and I kept a close watch on Jasper. I worried he might wake up and freak out. The storm banged on the house, and the stone walls seemed to shudder.

Images popped up on the monitor.

Poor Jasper. The swelling was worse than I'd imagined. Whoever had hit him, must have been intent on killing him.

The images stopped, and the table slid back out of the machine.

"Is it safe?"

"Yes." I pulled off the apron.

"What's wrong with him?"

"He needs surgery to help with the swelling, but I'm no neurologist, and that's who we need. We have to get him to the hospital."

Ewan shook his head. "The pass is already closed and there's no way to fly a helicopter with these winds."

When Abigail said we'd have to be ready for anything, she hadn't lied.

Think, Emilia. No way I'd let Jasper die.

Without the proper equipment, it was too dangerous to do the surgery blindly.

"I have an idea. Can you get him on one of the patient beds?" I pointed to the glass door behind me. "I need to run and get supplies."

I didn't wait for him to answer.

I'd become quite fond of Jasper, and I hurried to gather the meds I needed.

Ewan had him on the hospital bed.

"Help me get his sweater off," I said. There was blood all over it, and I had to run an IV.

Ewan lifted him so we could pull it off quickly.

I cleaned his arm and found a vein.

"What's happening?" Ewan asked as I hooked up the IV to the liquids.

"Osmotherapy," I said. "High-salt saline in the bags will help draw water from the brain. This"—I held up a syringe—"will help keep him in a drug-induced coma until the swelling goes down.

"It isn't the best solution but if we do nothing—he could end up with severe brain trauma or maybe even die."

Abigail slid into the room.

"What can I do?"

I smiled. "First, thanks for risking your life to get here."

"I should have come down before it got bad. People often get hurt when storms like this hit."

I explained what had happened.

"Run labs for me. Let's do a full panel and an ABG. I want to keep a constant eye on his carbon dioxide levels. Right now, I need them below normal. We want to slow down the flow of blood."

"Got it," Abigail said, and set about doing what I asked.

Ewan opened his mouth, but Donnelly rushed in.

"Have another one for you, Doc," he said, breathlessly. "Head wound in a car accident. She slid into a tree. Swears she's fine, but she's breathing funny."

"Ewan, do you think you can clean out the head wound for me?"

"Yes," he said without pause.

One after another, patients came in all night. We were so busy that Ewan went down to the pub to get Mara.

Between her and Abigail, we managed to stay on top of everything.

Around five in the morning, things had slowed down enough that I had time to sit down at my desk. Ewan had brought in extra generators so we could keep the machines going.

There were several sprains, a couple of broken bones, cracked ribs, but Jasper was the one I was most worried about.

His levels were fine, but another MRI confirmed my worst fears. The swelling hadn't gone down much. I hoped we could get him to the hospital in the next twelve hours, before irreparable damage had been done to his brain.

We may already be too late.

No. I wasn't going to think that way.

The storm continued to whip around the building. When I looked out the window, the only thing visible was a white swirling mass of snow. I'd never seen anything like it.

I shuffled some papers on my desk, and a note fell out.

I recognized the writing.

"You've got to be kidding me."

"What's wrong?" Ewan asked from the doorway.

I pointed to the letter. "I found another one. I don't have the energy to deal with it right now."

267

He pulled some gloves from his pocket. After examining it in the lamp light, he opened it.

His face turned dark, and his jaw tightened.

"It's bad, right?"

"This is an order," he said.

"I don't understand."

"You are not to be alone under any circumstances, do you understand? For your safety, I need you to promise me that you won't argue with me putting one of my guys on duty twenty-four/seven. We cannot afford to lose you. Tonight proved that. I'm not sure what we would have done without you."

"Show me the letter." A knot had formed in my throat, and the words came out in a whisper.

He shook his head. "Emilia, I'm sorry this is happening. I can promise you this town is normally quite safe and very quiet."

"Show me."

He opened the note and turned it toward me.

Doc is dead.

Chapter
Thirty-Six

I'm not sure when I fell asleep on the couch in front of the fire, but the storm had still been raging around the house.

Give me emergencies all day every day, but that letter from the killer had done me in. I'd dragged myself to the couch, and I didn't remember much after that.

I glanced at my phone, which was about to die, and it was nine AM on Monday. The wind still whipped around the stone building, but there was a glimmer of light through the stained glass.

"Jasper." I jumped up and ran straight into Ewan. There were dark circles under his eyes, and his hair was mussed. He probably hadn't slept at all.

"Abigail is with him. She ran another MRI a few minutes ago. I was coming to get you so you could see the images."

I covered my mouth as I yawned. "Thanks. Sorry I fell asleep."

"Don't be sorry. You saved lives last night. You needed a rest."

I followed him back to the surgery suite. Abigail was typing into the computer.

"How is he?"

She smiled. "Look."

The images were far different than they'd been a few hours ago. The swelling had gone down.

"That is significant. It should have taken days or weeks for it to go down that much."

"I know," she said. "The therapy worked."

"Good. Good. Let's keep him sedated and continue to watch those levels for a few hours. We can't let them get too low, or—"

"He might suffer permanent brain damage," Abigail said.

"Yes."

"Is he going to be okay?" Ewan asked.

"Too soon to tell, but that the swelling is going down is a good sign."

I turned back to Abigail. "Where is Tommy?"

"He's at Ewan's house," she said. "Ewan told us to take him there because he feels safe."

"Oh," I said. "That was good of you," I said to Ewan.

He shrugged. "I didn't want Abigail to worry, and we like having him at the house."

Sometimes it was easy to forget how kind he was.

"Is the storm any better?"

"The winds have died down some," he said, "but the roads are icy, and the snow is falling hard."

"So, no chance to airlift Jasper out?"

"Not yet," he said.

"Abigail, have you had any rest?" I asked.

She smiled sweetly. "I'm fine, Doctor."

"I told you to call me Em. We are friends."

"Yes, but still doesn't feel right, uh, Dr. Em."

I chuckled. "I can live with that. Do you mind if I clean up a bit and change clothes? Then I'll relieve you."

"Take your time," she said.

The hot water wasn't working, so I bathed at the sink. After some cold water to the face, and a change of clothes, I almost felt human.

My stomach grumbled.

Abigail yawned when I entered the surgical center.

"Hey, go lie down. That's an order."

"I'm okay, I promise."

270

"Right. That's why you look like you might pass out any moment. Jasper is our only patient for now. I'll be fine. My room is a little chilly, but it will be quieter than the couch. Go to bed. I'll keep an eye on things."

She opened her mouth and then shut it. "I ran another blood panel, and the computer will ding when it's ready. I took his blood pressure and temp. Everything is on his chart."

I shooshed her out the door. "I've done this before," I joked.

Ewan came in with a worried look.

"What's wrong?"

"An emergency," he said. "I need to go."

"Do you want me to come with you?"

"Nae. But I don't have a man to spare to make sure you're protected."

"Abigail is here, and I'll lock the door behind you. Go. I'll be fine. Let me know if you need me."

He nodded. "Make sure to set the code."

"I will. Go."

After he left, I set the code and then went to wait on Jasper's test results.

My stomach growled again.

Mara texted, *How's Jasper? Do you need me?*

I'd sent her down to the pub a few hours ago to sleep.

I typed back that he was holding steady. It really was too soon to give anyone false hope.

She promised to send some food up.

For that, I was grateful.

I checked on Jasper and then glanced at the computer. The test still had a few minutes to go. I ran to the kitchen and grabbed a small cake filled with jam. Abigail had brought them the night of the party. It had only been a few days since then, but it might as well have been a million years.

The greatest blessing was that at some point, Abigail must have made coffee. The warm pot was on the Aga. I poured a cup and drank it hot. Then I poured another cup.

There would be a lot of sitting and waiting, so I grabbed my bag and stuffed it with some of the code-breaking books.

The computer dinged, and I was relieved to see that Jasper really was holding steady. His numbers had improved over night.

I put the books on the tray table in Jasper's room, along with my coffee and makeshift breakfast.

I set a timer on my almost dead phone and then plugged it into the jack by the computer.

Determined to solve the puzzle, I skimmed the books again. That's when one of the pages caught my eyes.

Caesar's code was often used in combination with other puzzles. All you needed was a letter key to figure out how to shift the letters.

"After all of this, it can't be that easy."

Well, "easy" might have been an overstatement. Thankfully, we'd deciphered the dots and dashes. Even though the words didn't make sense, the letters were there. But what was the key?

I opened the journal and stared at the first page again.

There was a big initial "C," and then the rest of the page was in Morse code.

"Maybe 'C' is the key. It's worth a try."

Jasper didn't disagree, so I tried it.

Shel. Buried. Miller. Pond.

My eyes went wide, and my stomach swirled with anticipation. Had I cracked it?

Who was Shel? And why was he or she buried in or by a pond?

Wait, wasn't that where my ancestor had died? Was this a list of people Smithy had killed?

I'd seen a show where serial killers liked to keep souvenirs and track what they did with their victims, either through newspaper clippings or keeping journals.

Smithy might have had a partner who knew he did this. That person was probably our killer.

Right. And there's evidence of that where?

My mind was all over the place.

I took a deep breath.

The very last notation on the page was *5k/mt*.

"Oh. Maybe he'd discovered the truth and was blackmailing the person who did it, five thousand a month. That's a lot of money."

My phone dinged. I closed the books and got up to see who had texted.

Craig bringing food, Mara texted.

I smiled. The small cake I'd eaten hadn't done the job. I'd need brain power to finish deciphering the journal. Adrenaline pulsed through my body. The person threatening me might be on those pages.

Not long after the text, someone knocked on the door. I rushed to answer so they didn't wake up Abigail.

Craig's face smiled on the alarm's screen.

"Hey." He held up the bags. "I brought supplies."

"Do you want to come in?" I opened the door a little wider. The poor guy was covered in snow.

"I don't want to keep you from your patients."

"You aren't." He came in and I closed the door behind him.

"Do you want me to take these to the kitchen?"

"Nah, follow me. It's probably not the most sanitary, but I can't leave Jasper alone too long."

"How is he?"

I sighed. "We saw some improvements overnight, but he's not out of the woods." I pursed my mouth with worry. "I'm surprised you were able to get up the hill in this weather."

He chuckled. "I'm a Scotsman. A little weather doesn't bother me."

"I was led to believe it's treacherous out there. Ewan had to leave on an emergency. And I had patients all night."

"Bloody idgits should know better," he said. "Anyone who goes out in a blizzard deserves what they get."

"And yet, here you are delivering food." I said it as a joke, but he seemed perturbed about something.

"Aye. Sorry. People around here understand we don't go out unless absolutely necessary. We have a few tourists left, and my guess is they are who Ewan is tending to. I would still be at home, but Mara said they needed help. The pub is one of the few places with electrics, and half the town is there."

"Oh, I shouldn't keep you, then. You probably need to go back and help."

He shrugged. "They'll live."

He glanced into Jasper's room as I sat down at the desk outside the room.

He'd put several bags of food on the edge of the desk, and I opened them to see what Mara had sent.

"Poor bugger. He doesn't look good at all. Who the hell would break into his store and hit him with a mallet?"

I froze. Ewan's men had no idea what Jasper had been hit with when he was attacked. They hadn't found any kind of weapon.

How does Craig know?

I turned in the office chair to find him rifling through the books on the tray table. "What's all this?"

I gulped.

"Did you find Smithy's blackmail book?" He picked it up and stared at it.

Had I mentioned the book to him?

No. No.

I had to get him away from Jasper.

I texted Ewan: *Help!*

"Do you want some coffee?" I asked.

"I'm good," he said, and didn't take his eyes off the journal.

"Craig, how did you know Jasper had been hit with a mallet?"

"Mara said so, or maybe it was someone else at the pub." He went very still and then glanced at me.

I kept my face expressionless. I just had to keep him talking until help arrived.

"Were you able to figure this gibberish out?" He waved the book at me. His brows drew together.

I shook my head.

"I don't believe you," he said. "You wouldn't be looking at me like that if you hadn't found the truth."

"What truth? What did you do?"

I tried to stand up, but his hands were on my shoulders before I could move, and his knee shoved down across my legs. I was pinned in.

"Is anyone else here?"

Abigail.

I swallowed hard. "No. What's going on, Craig?"

"You're not dumb," he said. "You know."

"Are you the one who killed Smithy? I'm betting it was self-defense, right? There was a scuffle and he fell against the tree? I mean, you should have told the constable what happened, but I'm sure he'll understand."

"Right. Because Ewan has always been on my side. He and his pa have been trying to grass me up since Shelly died."

Shel. Buried.

Well. Hell.

Keep him talking. "Died? Oh. I thought she lived in Australia."

He grunted. "I think you know the truth. That's why you're scared."

I forced myself to breathe. "I'm scared because you're acting weird. Have you been drinking?"

"No, lass." His voice was menacing and hateful. "You and the boy wonder have to go. It's a shame. From what Mara said, you're an excellent physician. And young Jasper was a good add to the Highland team. But you both know too much now."

So, this is how I die.

"You killed your wife, didn't you?"

"Aye. She tried to leave me."

"And Smithy found out about it?"

"Helped me bury the body. We were friends back then, and I had a few things on him. We kept each other's secrets."

"But he started blackmailing you."

"Aye. The bloody bastard threatened to go to Ewan if I didn't pay up. I made the first payment, and then he wanted more."

"I'm sure everyone will understand why you were angry."

"None of them will ever find out. Once I finish you two off, I'll be headed to Australia to join my wife."

"But . . ."

"Yes. She's been sending me emails about how she wants to reconcile. It's been going on since Smithy died. Quite a coincidence, right? I'll be so sad over you, Doc, that I'll be running back to the woman who treated me so badly."

He'd planned this all along. This guy wasn't just psychotic, he was methodical.

And I'd thought he liked me.

Good to know my man radar was still crap.

"Why all the notes? Why didn't you just kill me?"

He sighed. "Mara liked you. Say whatever you want about me, but I have a soft spot for my cousin. She's a good lass. Was me who killed that bloody ex of hers. Beat the shite out of him and then tossed him off a cliff.

"She thought he'd run off with someone, but I made sure he'd never hurt her again."

There was no way I'd live through this. But I had to do something to save Jasper.

Before I could think about what a bad idea it was, I head-butted Craig's stomach hard enough that stars floated before my eyes. He fell away from me.

With my heart in my throat, I dashed for Jasper's room.

I slid the glass door closed and locked it.

Weapon.

The glass came shattering down on me. I ducked over Jasper to protect him and reached behind me to find anything I could to use as a weapon.

"This could have gone so much easier if you'd been a good little lass."

I glanced up to see a huge knife coming toward me. Throwing up one arm to protect myself, I used the other hand to stab him in the stomach with the hypodermic needle I had grabbed.

"What is that?" he shoved me down on the floor. Glass bit into my legs and hands as I caught myself.

I had no idea which medicine I'd grabbed.

"Poison," I said.

"Nice try." He hit me with the back of his hand, and my head swung hard against the floor.

My eyes blurred.

"I may die tonight." Blood spit out of my mouth as I tried to talk. "But so will you."

He stumbled toward me. "What did you give me?"

I was losing blood fast. He must have hit an artery with the knife.

I'm sorry, Jasper.

"Poison," I hissed out again.

The room became a tornado of lights and then something hard fell on top of me. Breathing was impossible. I shoved against it, but it was useless.

I tried to stay conscious, but the blackness in my peripheral vision closed in, and my heart slowed.

And then there was nothing.

Chapter
Thirty-Seven

A loud beeping woke me from a dream where I was running around the emergency room in Seattle. Someone had a knife and was trying to kill me. I kept yelling at everyone there, but no one noticed me.

Where am I?

My head hurt. I'd been looking after Jasper, and then . . . Craig.

"Jasper," I tried to say, but something was in my throat.

"Is she trying to talk?" Was that Angie?

Opening my eyes was impossible.

Just blink.

I did, but the light above was too bright.

"Cut the lights," someone said.

Was the power back up?

"Dr. McRoy, I'm Dr. Ingersoll. You're in Edinburgh at the hospital. We have you intubated. Can you blink for me if you understand?"

It took a few seconds, but I did it.

"Good. Let me get a kit, and I'll be right back."

"Oh. My. God." Angie said. "I'm so happy you're alive. You scared us to death."

I tried to focus on her, but my vision was blurry.

I had to find out what happened to Jasper. Had Craig killed him?

The more I tried to concentrate, the harder it became.

I slipped into the blackness again.

* * *

I don't know how long I was out, but when I came to, my throat and arm hurt like crazy.

"Ouch," I said. My throat was dry.

"She's awake. Go get the doctor." That was Ewan and he sounded worried.

I forced myself to blink, and this time my vision was a bit clearer. It helped that there wasn't much light in the room.

"Hey, Doc. You get an A-plus for drama. Glad you're back."

"Jasper." I tried to say his name again, but it sounded more like Jaws.

This is ridiculous.

I tried to use my arm to point toward the pitcher of water, but nothing would move.

The door opened, and the light from the hallway forced me to close my eyes again.

"I don't know if you remember," a man said. "I'm Dr. Ingersoll. You sustained major trauma, but you're healing more quickly than any of us expected. The best thing is to rest."

I was able to move my left hand, and I pointed to my throat.

"Right. That will be from the intubation. You can have ice chips and small sips of water."

Something was against my lips, and I opened my eyes to find Ewan trying to feed me ice chips with a plastic spoon.

Desperate, I opened my mouth.

The cold water dribbling down my throat brought a welcome relief.

"Only one person at a time in the room," the doctor said. "She needs to rest."

"I'm not leaving, and neither is her friend," Ewan said sternly.

The doctor's expression wasn't happy, but he nodded.

I would not have allowed that response for one of my patients, but maybe they did things differently here.

"Jasper," I said in a horse whisper.

"I don't understand," the doctor said.

"He's awake and doing well." Ewan's hand covered mine.

My shoulders sank back against the pillow.

"Oh, the man who came in with her."

Ewan nodded.

"Yes, you saved his life," the doctor said. "That was some quick thinking with the osmotherapy."

"Test," I whispered.

"He's testing well, and as far as we can tell, there are no ill effects. He's having some mobility issues, but overall, he's doing fine."

Mobility issues? Had I kept the carbon dioxide too low?

"Issue," I said.

"He's good, Em," Ewan said. "Slight problem with the fingers on his left hand. Doctors don't think it had anything to do with the brain swelling, and more how he cut off oxygen to his fingers when he fell on them."

I tried to think back. Had I even checked him out thoroughly? I'd been so worried about the brain injury, maybe I'd forgotten.

Jasper needed his hands to work. I prayed I hadn't deprived him of that.

"I can see those wheels turning," the doctor said. "I need you to relax and rest. That assistant of yours did a bang-up job of saving your life. Her work is better than most surgeons I know. I may steal her."

He laughed like it was the funniest joke ever.

I just stared at him.

"I'll be back to check on you at the end of rounds," he said. Then he was off.

"Assistant?"

"Abigail," Ewan said. "She found you first. Before we arrived, she had Craig in zip ties and stuffed in a locked closet. You were on the operating table, and she was sewing you up.

"I've never seen her like that. She barked orders like you do, and we all pitched in. When the storm died down enough that we could fly, she stayed with you until they wheeled you into the operating room.

"Tommy was asking for her, or she would still be here."

"How long?"

He looked confused. "How long? Oh. You've been out for two days. The doctors were worried when you didn't wake up, but you'd lost pints and pints of blood. He cut one of your arteries."

Abigail. I was so going to hug that woman when I saw her. I can't imagine what she must have thought when she walked in on that scene.

"Tell me," I said.

"I promise I'll share every detail of what we know, but the doctor says you need to rest, Em." He was so tender, and he squeezed my hand.

"Need to know."

"There's a video of the whole thing," he said. "Abigail had turned the camera's on so she could keep an eye on Jasper with her phone. Everything you went through was recorded. We know what that arsehole did, and his confession is recorded. You'll never have to worry about him again."

I sighed.

"And if you ever bloody do something like that again, I'll kill you myself." He squeezed my hand.

"What?"

"You could have run for your life, but you stayed and protected Jasper. You nearly died."

I tried to smile but my lips hurt. They were so dry.

"My job."

He chuckled. "We'll chat about that later. Now get some rest."

I had so many questions, but my eyes fluttered closed. As hard as I tried, there was no opening them again.

"How is she," someone whispered. The voice was too low for me to hear who it was.

"Good," Ewan said. His hand was still on mine.

I squeezed his fingers, and he did it right back.

I'm alive.

No one was more surprised than I was.

Chapter
Thirty-Eight

A few days later, I was released from the hospital. If the doctor hadn't done what I asked, I would have signed myself out. My room had been filled with flowers, but I gave them to the nurses to share with other patients.

Except for the bouquet Tommy had made me. That I'd asked Ewan to bring along.

As he landed the helicopter on the pad behind his house, there was no sign of the blizzard from a few days ago. The snow had melted, and it was a blindingly bright day.

When he opened the door to help me down, it was crisp outside.

"Did summer decide to come back?"

"Aye. Beautiful weather for your homecoming," he said.

Home?

I'd been through so much, and I wasn't sure I'd ever be free of the anxiety already pushing against my chest.

I learned the details from Ewan about how Craig had been watching me for weeks. He'd killed his wife and Smithy, and nearly murdered Jasper and me. Would I ever be able to walk into my home and not feel this overwhelming anxiety that threatened to choke me?

Even in the hospital, I'd thought about catching a flight to anywhere out of Scotland.

But the stubborn side of me urged me to go home. I couldn't keep running from life. I'd convinced myself to give Sea Isle a few more weeks while I healed.

After loading me into his Land Rover, Ewan went back for my suitcase and flowers.

The man hadn't left my side. He'd been sweet and considerate. He'd questioned the doctors and listened to the aftercare instructions like he was committing them to memory.

When he settled in the driver's seat, he stopped himself from pushing the engine button.

"You can stay at my house, if you'd rather."

I forced a smile.

"No, I'm ready."

That was a lie.

But the faster I did this, the sooner I'd know if it was time to leave Sea Isle.

I'd made such amazing friends, but a man had tried to kill me. It wasn't like it had been the first time. I'd had drug addicts take a swing or stab me with a scalpel. An elderly woman had tried to impale me with her IV pole because she thought I was a demon.

But no one had come close to succeeding—until Craig.

"I'll take you home, but if you change your mind, it's okay."

"Ewan?"

"Yes, lass?"

"Thank you."

He smiled. "Think nothing of it."

As he drove down the mountain, the sea came into view, with the shops lined up like pastel soldiers.

"It's so beautiful here."

"Aye," Ethan said. "It'll do."

I smiled. That was just his way.

Angie kept rolling her eyes and smiling, but she, too, was at the hospital constantly. She'd been in tears when we left, and promised to visit on the weekend.

Since my mom had died, there hadn't been anyone who cared about me like these people did.

As we neared the church, the street was lined with people.

"What's all this?"

"No idea."

"Did you tell them I needed some recovery time?"

"Aye." He parked the car. "Hold here just a minute."

He went over to the first person in line. It was Millie. I recognized her from the time she'd shut the door in my face. Ewan's back was to me, and I had no idea what was going on.

Millie tried to peek around him and into the car.

He came back and opened the passenger door.

"They've brought gifts to welcome you home," he said. "I'll tell them to bugger off to the pub. I'm sorry. I gave them all strict instructions to leave you alone."

I smiled. "They seem to listen to you about as well as I do."

"True," he said, and then he smiled. "What do you want to do?

"Let them stay, though I don't need gifts."

He made a strange face.

"What?"

"It'll be right rude to refuse them. The whole town is embarrassed by what happened. Everyone wants to make it right with you. I mean if that's what you want."

I had no idea what I wanted.

The door opened and Abigail came running out. She shoved Ewan out of the way, and gently wrapped her arms around my waist.

Then she sobbed, and so did I.

"Thank you," I said. Her head was still on my good shoulder.

"For what?" She asked as if she had no idea.

"For saving my life. I wouldn't be here if it weren't for you."

She sniffed and backed up. "I'm just glad to see ya. I don't seem to be the only one."

I laughed.

She and Ewan helped me to the sofa. By the time I sat, I might as well have run a marathon. I leaned my head back against the cushions and took a deep breath.

"You need to rest. I'll help you up to your room," Ewan said.

"I'm good. I don't want to be rude, but maybe I could see everyone another day."

"Don't you worry. I'll handle this." Then Abigail ran off.

Tommy came into the room and put a beautiful bouquet of flowers on the mantel.

"They are gorgeous," I said softly.

He didn't look at me, but he nodded.

"I brought home the ones you sent to the hospital. They made me so happy."

He nodded again.

"No more peonies. Roses and your laces." The delicate flowers had been artfully arranged.

I smiled. "Yes. They are perfect. I love them. Thank you, Tommy."

He nodded twice and went to the kitchen.

My eyes watered a bit. How could I even think about leaving Tommy and Abigail? They were my family. At least, I thought of them that way.

Just then Mara bustled in, her arms loaded with packages.

"I'm a terrible person," she said as she put them down by the fireplace.

"No," I said.

"My cousin nearly killed you, and I encouraged you to date him. The Wilson family is properly mortified."

"It's okay," I said. "I told you that at the hospital. You aren't responsible for his actions."

She sniffled. "Just the same, I'm so, so sorry this happened. I understand if you'll never be able to forgive me or my family, but please know how much we love and adore you. I'd do anything to take it all back."

Then she sobbed. Seemed to be a lot of that happening.

"What are you doing in here?" Ewan's voice boomed and we jumped. "I don't want you upsetting her."

"I need her," I said. "She's my best friend, and I need her."

Mara stared at me and then sobbed again.

"Stop it. I already cried with Abigail. My head hurts. I need coffee and food. Make it happen."

She half cried and then laughed. After giving me a weird salute, she took some of the packages by the fireplace and ran to the kitchen.

Ewan sat down on the couch.

"You don't need so many people around. The doctors said that for the next week you were to stay in bed. It was one of the conditions for letting you out of the hospital early."

"Don't worry, Dr. Ewan. I'm not moving off this couch. What's happening with the gang outside?"

"They've put their gifts in the reception area. Abigail is supervising."

There was some commotion and a very loud man demanded someone see his wife.

Ewan took off in a run.

It wasn't easy, but I used my good arm to push myself off the couch and slowly made my way to the waiting room.

When I arrived, there were several people in the lobby, and everyone was yelling.

"You'll have to go to Edinburgh," Abigail said sternly.

"There isn't time," a woman said. "It feels like the baby is about to fall out."

"What's going on?" I used my head-of-Emergency voice and the seas parted. A pin could have dropped, except a woman moaned.

"See, they are only a minute apart." The woman lifted her head, and it was Caitlin.

"A minute. There's no time. Get her into surgery," I barked. "Ewan help Mike."

The two men carried her to the surgery, with Abigail and I following closely behind.

"You can't deliver, you only have one arm," Abigail said.

"I'm not going to do the heavy lifting—you are."

"But it's a baby," she said.

I glanced over at her.

"Much easier than clamping off an atrial flow and sewing it up with some of the finest stitches anyone has ever seen. Did anyone tell you the surgeons there took pictures? They were amazed by your work."

"Really?"

I nodded.

"Delivering a baby is cake compared to that. I'll walk you through it all."

"What if—" she stopped. "If there are complications?"

"Abigail, you've got this. I promise. There isn't time to worry. If the contractions are a minute apart, we need to deliver the baby."

Three hours later, Mike held his son in his arms. He stared down with such love and adoration, I couldn't imagine how I'd ever considered him a suspect.

"He's perfect," Caitlin said. "Does he have everything?"

I smiled as Mike checked his fingers and toes.

"Yes," he said, relieved.

Abigail had been a trouper and was nearly finished with the rest of the delivery.

"We'll keep you overnight," I said. It was all I could do not to yawn.

"Is something wrong?" Caitlin asked. Tears formed in her eyes.

"Not at all," I said. "Your body's been through a lot. It's only a precaution to make sure we give you both a good head start."

Mike put his son on his wife's chest. "Oh, precious babe. I can't believe you are here."

The baby snuggled into her chest, and my eyes might have been a bit watery. Or maybe I was just tired.

"Abigail, you okay?"

"Almost done," she said in her singsong voice. I sat on a stool directly behind her. The doctors had been right about her stitches. She should have been a plastic surgeon.

"Get them set up in a room and find some diapers."

"Go rest," she said. Her voice was filled with confidence. She'd changed so much.

I shuffled down the long hallway, praying my legs would get me to the couch. Wobbly didn't begin to describe how I felt.

When I walked into the waiting room, it was dead silent, but there were even more people than had been here before.

Ewan jumped up and put his arm around my waist. I didn't even pretend to be strong. I leaned into him.

"It's a boy," I said. "Mom and son are doing very well."

"Oh, can we see him?" It was a young girl I didn't recognize.

"Not for a bit," I said. "We must keep him safe from germs for a while. I love that you're all here, but I'm very tired."

"Of course," Millie stood. "We'll be on our way. Thank you, Doctor. And when you're feeling better, you just give me a call. I'll help you find those records you need. The mayor has my number."

"Thank you."

Ewan ushered me into the living area. "Bedroom or couch?"

"Couch is closer."

"I can carry you up if that will help."

"No. This is good for now." I shivered. "I wouldn't mind a fire and a blanket."

He did what I asked.

"Thank you, Em. For all you've done."

"Why do people keep saying that?"

"After everything you went through, you delivered a healthy baby."

I snorted. "Technically, Abigail did all the work."

"You know what I mean," he said. "You're special, Em. I don't think you know how incredible you are."

"Stop being nice," I said.

"You don't have to worry."

"About?"

"Leaving. After everything we put you through, there's no way I can hold you to your contract."

I opened my eyes.

His face was unreadable.

"I can't leave, Ewan." I smiled.

"Are you sure? We'd understand—if—I worry you need to do what's best for you. The doctors said the kind of trauma you experienced can have lasting effects."

"They are right."

His brows drew together. "Being away from this place might be best for you."

"Are you trying to make me quit?"

"God no," he said. He sat down beside me. "I can be an arsehole, but I very much want you to do what is in your best interest. If we must, we'll find another doctor."

"How long did that take you the last time?"

He blew out a breath. "This place will be full of bad memories, and your health is important to me. I mean, the town."

"You sound like Dr. Ingersoll."

He shrugged. "He beat the mental trauma into my brain."

I smiled. "Ewan, I'm good. I wasn't sure when we arrived today, but helping Abigail deliver that baby—it reminded me why I came here in the first place. One of the ways to heal from that sort of trauma is to make better memories. And I already have done that thanks to Caitlin and Mike's little guy."

I smiled up at his inscrutable Scottish face. A very handsome one, at that.

"I've made some of the best friends of my life in Sea Isle, including you. Even though you are stubborn, bossy, annoying, and drive me nuts sometimes."

"Your drugs must have kicked in."

We laughed.

"Ouch. Don't make me laugh."

"So, you're not going back to Seattle?"

"There's nothing left for me there."

"I'm glad you're here, Em." He squeezed my good hand.

"Me too." I meant it. No place was perfect, but I'd found my family on this colorful coast, and I had no plans to leave. "One thing."

"What's that?"

"Any chance you might hire a real coroner?"

"Can't." He smiled.

"Why?"

"We already have the best one in Scotland. What would we do with another one?"

I did a fake sigh, and he laughed.

"I never did get my coffee and treats."

"I'll make that happen."

I'd never admit to Ewan, but I'd enjoyed solving the mystery—I mean, except for dating a psychopath and almost dying.

But I'd meant what I'd said. I loved my new home and the people here.

I was in Sea Isle to stay.

Acknowledgments

A big shout out to my agent Jill Marsal for putting up with my crazy. Tara Gavin you are a wonder of an editor and such an amazing soul. I've never had such a positive editorial process. Thank you. You helped me to love what I do again.

And to the rest of the Crooked Lane team, if no one has said it today, you are awesome. You've walked me through everything with such grace and taught me a great deal. I appreciate you all.

To my friend Lizzie Bailey, I couldn't do this without you. There are not words to express how much I appreciate you picking me up off the floor when the sad stuff happens and celebrating the good times.

Dear Readers, thank you, for taking a chance on me. I consider you family, now. That's right. You're stuck with me.